I0748216

CHARLIE AND THE SPITFIRE

K. J. Millard

© K. J. Millard
Published in 2025 by The Bruges Group

Illustrations by Sarabpreet Chopra

ISBN: 978-1-917743-04-4

The Bruges Group Publications Office
246 Linen Hall, 162-168 Regent Street, London W1B 5TB
www.brugesgroup.com

Bruges Group publications are not intended to represent a corporate view of European
and international developments. Contributions are chosen on the basis of their
intellectual rigour, and their ability to open up new avenues for debate.

Scan me for Bruges Group

Twitter ✖ @brugesgroup, LinkedIn in @brugesgroup
GETTR ⓕ @brugesgroup, Telegram ⊘ t.me/brugesgroup, Facebook ⓕ @brugesgroup
Instagram ⓞ @brugesgroup, YouTube ▶ @brugesgroup

To Her Late Majesty Queen Elizabeth II

(1926 to 2022)

I dedicate this book.

"I cannot lead you into battle. I do not give you laws or administer justice, but I can do something else – I can give you my heart and my devotion to these old islands and to all the peoples of our brotherhood of nations."

Her Majesty Queen Elizabeth II's first televised Christmas broadcast to the nation 1957.

'I see this aged Kingdom not dispirited, not weak, but well remembering that she has seen dark days before. Indeed, with a kind of instinct that she sees a little better in a cloudy day and that, in storm of battle and calamity she has a secret vigour and a pulse like a cannon.'

Ralph Waldo Emerson's tribute to Britain.

1

'There is something more, something greater in this war than a [battle] between opposing armies; something more eternal than a grapple in the skies between the Spitfires of Britain and the Heinkels of Nazi Germany; something more desperate than a death struggle between the U-boats and the Destroyers. There is a conflict between the forces of good and the forces of evil and what has to be determined is which shall possess the soul of countries and of men.'

Hore-Belisha (War Secretary 1937-1940) Broadcast October 1939.

Jam-Jar as a young man.

The author, at age 10, with Jam-Jar.

Contents

Prologue
2nd July 1940 – Brighton - Royal Albion Hotel - 8pm

"I used to watch fleas performing in a circus over there when I was a boy." [2] The elderly man spoke thoughtfully, old memories swirling in his old eyes, that Father Christmas-like, twinkled merrily. "It always fascinated me how it was done – how the fleas could be harnessed to do their handler's bidding - performing circus tricks, pulling little wheeled contraptions, walking on high wires." He cast his gaze across the road from the hotel dining room to a kiosk on the pier, where soldiers were preparing a machine gun post. The Palace Pier stretched majestically out into a silver sea, which glittered and sparkled in the evening sun.

"Rather like the Naaarzis, you know!" he suddenly said, exaggerating the word with a seriousness, that failed to conceal the defiant, boy-like mirth, which still bubbled underneath. He fixed his eyes on the quizzical face of his dinner guest, who was seated opposite him at the table - a man in his fifties, wearing the combat uniform of an ordinary soldier, but clearly of a much higher rank, as his shoulder pips revealed – a General, looking every inch the hardened professional he was. His features were as thin and pointed, as his jovial companions were rounded.

"I don't trust politicians!" the guest thought to himself. "They got us into this mess in the first place." A sudden shot of anger flooded his veins, surprising him with its intensity. "This one's different though – he tried to warn the others, but they wouldn't listen and now it's happened!"

"Now, Montgomery. What will you take to drink?" his companion asked.

"I'll just have water, Sir," he replied.

"Water! Come, come man. You must drink something!" said the older man, clearly shocked at this admission.

"No thank-you, Sir. I do not drink, or smoke and I am one hundred percent fit."

The older man scoffed at this, retorting immediately, "I both drink and smoke and I am two hundred percent fit!" he said, drawing deeply on the cigar that was clamped, firmly between the fingers of his right hand.

1

Unsure how to respond to this remark, the guest changed the subject.

"You went to school here, Sir, didn't you?" he replied.

"Hove, actually," his companion answered with a chuckle that shook his belly. "I used to come here to the pier and watch the flea circus in the very kiosk where those soldiers are positioning that gun. It is strange how calm and serene the sea appears when on the other side of the channel there is a very great evil amassing, an evil that is threatening everything that we hold dear – our freedoms, our culture, democracy itself. Those Naarzis must not be allowed to succeed. How they managed to ensnare a whole nation to do their bidding, to perform like those circus fleas, to fill the soul of a whole nation with a terrible infection, a belief in a cruel and perverted science – the rot must be stopped, the infection cut out before it spreads." He spoke emphatically, strength and determination pouring from him like a smouldering volcano. He suddenly looked directly at his stunned companion, locking eyes with him, as if trying to gauge the strength of the man before him. His voice deepened menacingly, his lip curling in anger.

"Hitler has his eye fixed on us – even now he is planning his invasion; our shores are already threatened. Scotland has suffered a cruel blow – Wick in Caithness bombed only yesterday - fifteen people killed – this is just a foretaste of the days that are to come." He spoke in measured tones, as if bearing the weight of the knowledge of long years on his shoulders. His words hung in the air like smoke, as he drew on his cigar again. His dinner guest listened, rapt, in awe.

He continued. "My ancestor, the 1st Duke of Marlborough, saved this country from domination by another European superpower – then it was the French – Louis XIV. This time it is Germany and France are our friends. It is curious, maybe it was in large part due to the very great influence of my ancestor, but since my childhood I have had this strong, nagging feeling that I was meant to do something, something important, something that would save Britain from a foreign invasion.[3] This is what I am meant to do. I feel it. This land has long remained free and I intend to see that it continues to be so."

His dinner guest felt the words filling his mind like a spell. He drew breath, stealing himself to speak.

"The problem is, Sir, people do not realise just how much danger we are in now that France has fallen. They see the evacuation of Dunkirk as a great victory."

"Victory it most assuredly was not," the older man agreed, "but, nevertheless, it was a great success." He fixed his now steely eyes on his General, chin pulled in close to his chest. "Yes, we lost much of our equipment, but we brought home our boys to fight another day!"

Montgomery felt his withering gaze. The other dinner companions shifted uncomfortably in their seats, but Montgomery was not deterred.

"Sir, it seems curious to me that my division is immobile. It is the only fully equipped division in England, the only division fit to fight any enemy, anywhere and here we are in a static role, digging in along the south coast."

"And you have carried out your orders most efficiently and satisfactorily." The older gentleman had softened his tone. He cast an approving glance along the length of the shore; the long line of defences along the beaches and the cliffs could clearly be seen.

Montgomery took a deep breath, pleased to hear the compliment, but batting it aside, as he pushed home his point.

"Release me from this static role, Sir! May I suggest, Sir, that some other troops should take on my task."

The older man was warming to the conversation. He could feel the energy, drive and determination in this younger man, which accorded with his own.

"Tell me, Montgomery. What do you need?"

"Buses!"

"Buses!" the older man saw the humour in this request but felt the seriousness of the moment.

"Yes, Sir! Buses! There are thousands of buses in England. Let me have some of those buses so we can be held in mobile reserve, ready at a moment's notice for a counter-attack. If I have the buses, then my division can rehearse and prepare for this role."

The two men locked eyes – each feeling the strength of the other.

"Very well! I think that is an excellent idea. The War Office will be told to let you have your buses." The older man looked approvingly at his General. Drawing deeply on his cigar, he glanced out of the window.

"I think I can expect great things from you," he said. "This war needs men like you."

General Montgomery smiled.

"This country needs a man like you, Sir!"

It was the older man's turn to smile, now.

"Please, call me Winston."

Chapter 1 – The Present Day

It was a glorious spring morning, and the woods were bathed in a soft green light, which filtered through the Silver Birch trees. Their young leaves, freshly unfurled that morning and still wet with dew, stretched their silvery fronds to the sky and fluttered in the warm sun like bunting, while all around, soft clouds of Blackthorn and white May blossom foamed on bushes like bubbles on a milkshake. The whole world sparkled with newness.

The last of the sleeping trees had finally awoken. Their dark branches shimmered expectantly, as fat, sticky, green buds burst like balloons at a party, eager to see the sun.

The season of frothy pinks and snowy whites was just beginning. Delicate blossom floated in the clear, blue sky, like confetti at a wedding - a spring snowfall, which perfumed the morning air, while sugary, pink Cherry blossom still clung to old, gnarled branches like sweet cotton-candy on a stick and a deliciously warm, rich fragrance floated dreamily on the gentle breeze.

Tall, waxy flowers decorated the branches of Horse Chestnut trees, like Christmas candles, floating as if by magic, as the heavy boughs swayed gracefully, while the zesty green of Lime and Beech trees punctuated the darker green of the woods with a zingy freshness, like sour apple sweets.

The trees were alive with the chattering of small birds, flittering and busying themselves about their new nests and below, in the Hazel thickets, cloudy drifts of white Cow Parsley hovered above the grasses like a mist, blurring the edges of pathway and lane alike, with a billowy softness.

Only that morning, it seemed, the first of the Bluebells had appeared. Gentle and shy, they had emerged against the silvery paper backdrop of Birch bark, their delicate scent mingling with the smell of rising sap and damp earth and the winter leaf fall, which still littered the dark ground. They flowed through the glinting shade of wooded hillsides in cascades of blue, eddying in deep pools in the shadowy depths of the woods and tumbled in streams of purple down to the edge of the lake, where swans glided lazily, dipping their beaks into the sparkling water, which dripped from their bills like jewels, shining in the morning sun.

And flowing with the bluebells amongst the trees, a distant sound of joyous laughter could be heard, playfully dancing in the green air; a tinkling sound of merriment, which floated down the hillside and into the wide expanse of a lovely park, which stretched out beside the cool, clear waters of the glistening lake and the mauve hills in the distance on the other side of town.

By the water's edge, beneath a beautiful Willow tree, not far from the spreading branches of a huge, old Oak, three small figures could be seen, running and laughing together, a mother, a father and a small boy, named Charles. They were playing football in the park and the sun shone warmly on their backs. Suddenly, there was a wonderful sound in the air, a rich purring, which filled their ears. Looking up, they saw, in the distance, coming from over the hills, a vaguely familiar shape moving through the sky. The atmosphere throbbed with energy. Charles felt the hair stand up on the back of his neck, as the thrilling noise grew louder and closer.

"Oh look, Charles!" shouted his mother, excitedly. "It's a Spitfire!" and sure enough, flying rapidly towards them, from over the North Downs, was a beautiful SPITFIRE, its camouflage colours becoming more distinct by the second. The low hum of its engine intensified, propelling it through the morning light.

"Oh wow," shouted Charles. He had been learning about the Second World War at school and his parents often talked, enthusiastically about the Spitfire, but he had never actually seen one before.

"Wave, Charles," called his father over his shoulder.

"That's come from Biggin Hill," said his mother, beaming and already, joyfully flinging her arms above her head to wave.

Charles felt a thrill of excitement and did the same, jumping excitedly, in the hope that the plane would see them.

AND IT DID!

It seemed to fly straight towards them, as if coming to say, "Hello!"

"Listen to that amazing engine," shouted his father. "That's a Merlin engine, made by Rolls-Royce and it's fast."

"How fast?" Charles called, excitedly.

"400 miles per hour – that was the top speed of the Mark 9!" bellowed his father.

"A lot faster than I can drive on the motorway," shouted his laughing mother, as she shielded her eyes from the morning sun, "and the Mark 18 flew at over 430 miles per hour and could go as high as 43,000 feet. That's higher than most planes fly when they take us on our holidays!" she hollered.

"Wow!" exclaimed Charles, as he stared in excitement, at the fast-approaching plane.

The Spitfire powered through the sky, the note of its engines dropping a little, as it drew nearer and suddenly, there it was, flying right above their heads, the deep purr of the engine pulsing through Charles' body, as if a large cat was sitting on his chest. Eyes wide with wonder, he marvelled at the shape of the plane, how the nose looked like a face - a friendly face. It seemed alive.

Time slowed.

As if in a dream, Charles gazed, watching the Spitfire bank and turn, revealing the pilot in the cockpit, who looked down at them and raised one hand in acknowledgement. Charles held his breath, his waving hand poised in mid-air. The seconds ticked by...

...then, the pilot fixed his gaze on the distant hills and just as suddenly as it had appeared, the Spitfire flew away into the morning light, rolling from side to side a little, as if waggling its wings in salute, waving a friendly 'goodbye'. The sun glinted on its back, as it disappeared, west, along the line of the hills.

Charles felt something shift in his mind, as the realisation dawned on him that he had seen something very special...

Time returned to normal.

"Oh! That was amazing," said Charles' mother. "I'm so glad you saw that!"

Charles' ears were still ringing and little thrills of excitement were running up and down his tingling spine.

Buzzing with happiness, the three of them walked home through the woods. The fresh, spring air felt cool among the trees, rich with new life. A gentle breeze ruffled the leaves and showers of blossom floated past them, dreamily. It was strangely quiet, which was unusual, as there were always people walking their dogs at this time of the morning. They were alone together in the softness of the woods.

Walking on, they chatted happily about all they had just seen, when Charles paused for a moment.

"Why did the war happen?" he asked, thoughtfully.

"Well," answered his father, taking a deep breath, "after Germany lost the First World War, they were forced to disarm, under the terms of the Treaty of Versailles, so they couldn't be a threat again. The Germans had been a major industrial world power, but now they felt humiliated.

"But, when the Wall Street Crash happened in America in 1929 and the banks ran out of money, lots of people lost everything. There was a terrible economic recession, which affected countries all over the world, including Germany. It was called The Great Depression. Lots of people were out-of-work and many lost their homes and starved."

Charles thought of the photographs of The Great Depression that his teacher had shown to the class – dark, dirty streets, boarded up shops, grey-faced people in old, worn clothes, huddling together for warmth around makeshift fires, hopeless and miserable and then it was as if the photograph came alive in his mind. He heard a rasping, angry, urgent voice drawing the attention of those miserable crowds, who, pulling themselves out of their torpor, were looking up, expectantly, listening to a voice that was filled with hatred and menace, as the people smiled and cheered – their faces lit up with a kind of frenzy, a madness, which seemed to grip their souls.

Charles had heard that voice before on old films. It sent a shiver down his spine, as his father spoke,

"In Germany, out of this misery, one man started to gain power. He was really good at making speeches, you see and people listened to him. He encouraged the Germans to believe they could become a great nation again. The problem was, he also made them believe they were a 'superior race'!" said Dad, with a sarcastic tone in his voice.

"What does that mean?" asked Charles.

"Well," replied his father, "this man made the German people believe they were better than any other nation on Earth and had a right to rule. He made them believe it was the only way to regain their pride and that other countries, like Poland and people of different faiths, such as those of the Jewish faith, were inferior and lesser beings. In his warped and twisted mind, he believed they could be treated like slaves and have all their rights as human beings taken from them. Slowly, this twisted logic poisoned the minds of the German people, so much so that in 1933, they actually voted him into power."

"And can you guess who that man was?" asked Charles' mother.

Charles was sure he knew the answer, "Adolf Hitler!" he said, sadly.

"Yes, it was, sweetheart," his mother replied, "and in March 1935, Hitler ordered Germany to rearm."

"Why?" Charles asked.

"Because, he wanted to be ruler of an empire, a bit like the Roman Empire," answered his mother. "A deal had been made by the German military with the Soviet Union to allow Germany secretly, to build tanks and to train officers in Soviet territory, so nobody in the West would see what they were up to. The German army and air force started to grow in size, even though the terms of the Treaty of Versailles had forbidden it.

"Hitler then ordered new fighter planes to be developed, like the Messerschmitt and Heinkel and lots of young men learnt to fly, training to become pilots in Hitler's new air-force, the Luftwaffe. Hitler even appointed a famous fighter pilot ace of the First World War, called Hermann Goering, to be its Commander-in-Chief. He became one of the most powerful figures in the Nazi party."

"But, sadly," said Dad, "very few politicians or journalists in Britain seemed to be worried about this. In fact, they seemed to believe Hitler was doing a good job for his country, getting Germany out of the economic depression. Stupidly, they didn't think Hitler or Germany were a threat to Britain at all, or to the world, for that matter!"

"That was a bit silly of them!" exclaimed Charles.

Charles' father paused for a moment. The woods were hushed, as if listening to their conversation, pressing close, leaning in to hear. Charles felt safe, almost cosy, surrounded by these great, old trees.

"Where is everybody?" he wondered.

"Is it me, or are the woods really quiet?" exclaimed his father, echoing Charles' thoughts. "Where is everyone? It's as if the trees are listening to us?" and all three of them peered round, eyes wide with pretend fear.

A sudden gust of wind moved through the quiet woods, waking the trees from their slumber; their branches swayed and their leaves rustled gently, whispering to each other in a soothing, almost hypnotic sound.

"Susurration – that whispering of the leaves," Charles' mother said sleepily, speaking as if on the edge of dream. "Beautiful, isn't it? It could almost be the sound of flowing water. Listen! The trees are talking. They're talking to each other!"

In stunned silence, the three of them stood and listened to the quiet murmurings of the woods. The language of the trees, of Oak, of Ash and Yew, filled the air, as their graceful branches swayed in unison and a chorus of soft whispers drifted amongst the green shadows, floating on the pink blossom, which swirled like breath around them.

Charles was sure he could hear a voice calling softly on the breeze - an urgent voice, carried on the air from far away and long ago,

"*...the old grim choice...*", the sound was indistinct at first, as if coming from the speaker of an old, crackly radio, "*...whether we shall submit to the will of a stronger nation or whether we shall prepare to defend our rights, our liberties and indeed our lives...*".

The voice grew clearer and stronger with every word that moved through the woods.

"What's happening?" exclaimed Charles, not knowing whether to be excited or scared.

When his mother spoke, her voice was deep and resonant. "I know who that is!" she said, awestruck. "It's Winston Churchill!"

Unsure if they were dreaming, they stood listening - Charles' mother holding him tightly.

The voice was strong and determined, sometimes clear, as it mingled with the blossom, which swirled around them, sometimes almost lost in the sound of rushing leaves; sometimes near as the trees stilled and held their breath in hushed awe and sometimes almost blown away on the breeze.

And this is what they heard, "*There is a nation which with all its strength and virtues is in the grip of a group of ruthless men preaching a gospel of intolerance and racial pride, unrestrained by law, by Parliament or by public opinion.*"

"What's going on," said Charles' father, amazed. "That's Churchill's radio broadcast to the nation in November 1934, but how are we hearing it now?"

Another strong breeze rustled the leaves. The air seemed to clear and the whisperings faded with the voice, like a radio being turned down, only to return on the wind, reanimating the woods, as the leaves whispered to each other once again,

...and with that, everything changed. The atmosphere became more oppressive. The sky darkened and a cloud passed in front of the sun, as the three of them listened to the grave tones of Churchill's voice, calling to them from the past:

"Who is in charge of the clattering train?
The axels creak, and the couplings strain,
And the pace is hot, and the points are near,
And Sleep has deadened the driver's ear:
And signals flash through the night in vain,
For Death is in charge of the clattering train." [4]

Charles shivered.

Suddenly, the voice was close at hand, speaking urgently in their ears. Wide eyed, Charles and his mother looked around, only to find Dad reciting the words himself.

"Oh, it's you!" they both exclaimed, chuckling, as they rolled their eyes and laughed with relief, but Charles was sure he could still hear the warning echoing in the trees.

"Of course, it's me," smirked his father, cheekily, "but you know, Churchill often recited that poem to friends and colleagues, trying to warn them of the approaching danger. War was coming and Europe was sleep-walking into a disaster!"

Then as quickly as the wind had arrived, it flowed away, disappearing through the trees, Churchill's voice fading with the dying breeze, which curled on up through the wooded hillside, as if Churchill himself was walking just ahead of them, calling over his shoulder. The faintest smell of cigar smoke hung in the air, before it too, faded with the sounds, but not before Charles heard these last words,

"Free Parliaments and Democracy have been trampled down in most of the great countries of Europe. They have reverted to despotism and dictatorships; and all the apparatus of science and Civilization can be perverted to the propaganda of tyranny."

He didn't quite understand the last statement, but he was sure it meant something bad, something that meant disaster for the world.

"Churchill said those words in 1935," exclaimed Dad.

"And nobody was listening," Mum sighed, deep in thought.

The whisperings faded into the woods, floating away with the blossom.

The note of doom rolled aside like a passing storm. The atmosphere lifted and the sky brightened. Charles blinked, as if waking from a long sleep. Even the trees seemed to relax, exhaling, uncurling themselves from their tight huddle and standing tall again.

The birds began to sing and the bees hummed softly. Little flies, caught in the sun's rays, like dots of light, hovered in the air. Everything was peaceful as they headed home, strolling on in thoughtful silence.

"So, what happened after 1935, after Hitler ordered Germany to rearm?" Charles asked, afraid to disturb the peacefulness of the woods, but curious to know the answer.

"Well," replied Dad, "in March, 1936, Hitler ordered his troops, called the Stormtroopers, to occupy the Rhineland, which was an area of Western Germany that NO army was meant to enter. Two years later, he absorbed Austria into his new empire, then a part of Czechoslovakia, called the Sudetenland, then the whole of Czechoslovakia and then, on the 1st September 1939, he invaded Poland, which is why Britain and France finally declared war on Germany on 3rd September."

"But why hadn't they declared war already?" Charles asked, confused.

"The British government was too weak," answered his mother. "It kept making half-hearted threats, but never carrying them out and Hitler began to think that they'd never declare war. He thought he could get away with anything."

"You see," said his father, "after the slaughter of the First World War, the British government was afraid of another war, but the crazy thing is, France had the largest army in Europe and Great Britain had the largest navy in Europe. That should have been enough to put Hitler off, but when he invaded Poland, Britain and France weren't actually ready to go to Poland's aid. It was weeks before France mobilised their artillery and British planes couldn't even reach Poland without refuelling and by then Russia had also invaded Poland. So, awfully, Poland was lost."

"Those poor people," said Charles, sympathetically.

"I know! It was very sad," his mother replied. "Instead, Britain sent the British Expeditionary Force, the BEF, to France to help the French defend their borders against the advancing Germans."

Suddenly, the trees seemed to shiver in a breeze, even though the day was growing warm. Their branches swayed, the glimmering light nosing its way through the spreading leaves, which seemed to reach up like imploring hands - children's hands! Charles blinked away the image, deep dread turning somersaults in his stomach.

"The Battle of France didn't get going until May 1940," his mother continued, looking around warily. "Before then, people in Britain called the war 'the Phoney War', because the British government didn't seem to be taking any decisive action, but then in 1940, events sped up. Germany invaded Norway and Denmark, then the Netherlands, Belgium and France, one after the other, in what was called the Blitzkrieg, or 'Lightning War'."

"It took everyone by surprise," said Dad, "and the situation suddenly changed really quickly. It was 1940 - the year Britain proved it had spirit!"

He counted off the famous events in order on his fingers. "There was the invasion of Norway, the Battle of France, the evacuation of Dunkirk, the Battle of Britain and the Blitz," he said.

"And all of that happened in just one year?" exclaimed Charles.

"That's right," he replied, "not to mention the Battle of the Atlantic, which had begun earlier in 1939. German battleships and submarines called U-boats constantly tried to destroy ships that were taking vital supplies of food and equipment to Britain."

Then Charles' mother spoke, "but, you know, sweetheart, one thing stood between us and the Nazis: a technical marvel on wings called, the SPITFIRE," she said, smiling. "And it was designed by a very clever designer, called R.J. Mitchell.

The Germans had fast fighter planes too, like the Messerschmitt Bf 109, but none of them were a match for the little Spitfire, with its tight turning circle, which meant that it could twist and turn out of trouble and evade enemy fire quickly," and she demonstrated this to Charles by pretending to be a 'Messerschmitt' flying at him.

He pretended to be the 'Spitfire' turning quickly out of the way, whilst his mother's 'Messerschmitt' carried on 'flying' in a straight line past him. All three of them laughed and the sound echoed through the trees.

"The Spitfire also had a rounded bubble shaped hood covering the cockpit," she continued, "which meant that the pilots had a 360-degree field of vision and could look all around them to see if enemy planes were coming. The Me 109s had far less visibility."

"I wish I could fly a real Spitfire," Charles exclaimed.

"So, do I," replied his mother, laughing.

Then Dad spoke, "It was the Spitfire and the Hawker Hurricane, another amazing plane, that saved us. The Hurricanes would attack the slower German bombers, and the faster Spitfires would attack the much quicker escorting German fighters. Without them and the bravery of the young men who flew them, we wouldn't have won the Battle of Britain."

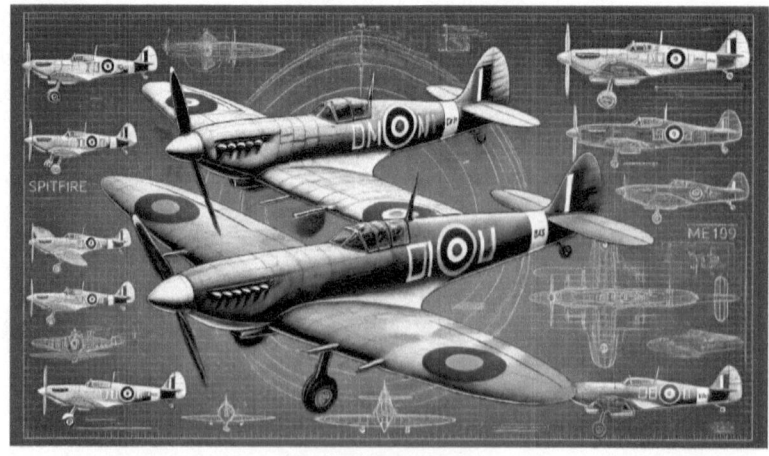

"The Spitfire and the Hurricane were both powered by Merlin engines," said his mother, "really fast, high-tech engines made by a famous British car-making company called Rolls-Royce. It was called a Merlin after a small bird of prey, which quickly attacks its intended victim, before it has time to react," and she playfully pretended to grab at Charles, her fingers hooked like bird's claws.

"Good name!" exclaimed Charles.

"Yes, it was," his mother agreed. "Every pilot, who flew a Spitfire said how easy it was to fly. They all said it was like putting on clothes. You just wore it. They loved its speed, too. It was so fast. You see, the propeller turned relatively slowly, even when flying at high speed, which meant that the plane didn't shake or judder. Flying a Spitfire felt like you were just casually cruising along, when in reality, you were going really quickly! The Spitfire was that smooth to fly."

"What do you mean by 'smooth'?" asked Charles.

"Do you remember when it snowed last winter and we went sledging," Mum asked.

Charles thought of the previous winter when he and his mother had gone sledging in the park with friends after school. By the end of the week, the snow was so smooth and icy that he had almost flown down the hill. He remembered how he had become so good and knew his sledge so well, that he could just do the slightest movement to flick the sledge past people without running into them. It was almost like the sledge knew his mind... He remembered the sound of the crunching ice, sliding beneath him, the roar of the rushing wind in his cold ears and the 'whoops' of joy at the end of another successful decent.

"So, the Spitfire was like my sledge," said Charles. "It was quick because there wasn't any bumpiness or friction."

"That's right, sweetheart," replied his mother. "Every pilot believed their Spitfire had a life of its own. The test pilot, Jeffrey Quill, said when he tried to land his Spitfire for the first time, 'the aeroplane showed no desire to touch down'," his mother quoted from memory. "It didn't want to land. He could feel that the Spitfire really 'enjoyed flying'."

"Like it was alive," said Charles.

"It was alive!" said his mother, eyes widening in emphasis. Charles felt the hair stand up on the back of his neck, as he thought of the Spitfire that had flown over their heads and imagined it now, sitting quietly somewhere, on an airfield runway, waiting...

His mother's voice broke into his reverie... "The Spitfire's first test flight was on 5th March 1936 and not a moment too soon, because, just two days later Hitler invaded the Rhineland, you know, the bit of land we talked about, that no army was meant to occupy and from that moment, many in Britain could see there would be another war."

"Gosh!" exclaimed Charles. "The Spitfire was born just in time."

"That's true," his mother replied, "because the prototype of the new Messerschmitt was made that same year!"

"But, thanks to a man called Hugh Dowding," said Dad, "who was Air Chief Marshall during the Battle of Britain, the RAF adopted the Spitfire. Like Goering, he'd been a very successful fighter pilot in the First World War and had a major influence on the designs of the aircraft, which were later used in the Battle of Britain, like insisting the windscreen shields were bullet-proof to protect the pilots. Do you know," said Dad, "the Spitfire was the only plane to be in continuous production throughout the war. It was still being used by the RAF in 1954 and in service in many other countries up until the 1960's. That's how good and ahead of its time Mitchell's design was!"

"But of course," said his mother, smiling gently at Charles, "the Spitfire and the Hurricane will forever be associated with

Britain's determination not to be beaten by a force far greater than its own. This one little country had the guts and the strength of will to stand its ground, alone against the might of the German Luftwaffe."

Charles thought for a moment and then asked, "You mean if Germany had beaten Britain, the war would have been over?"

"More or less," his father replied. "We had help though. All the countries of what is now called the Commonwealth joined immediately, including Canada, New Zealand, Australia and South Africa, who all declared war on Nazi Germany themselves when Britain did and in India, two hundred thousand men volunteered, actually *volunteered* to join up and help us in the fight against Nazism. By the end of the war, over two and a half million volunteer soldiers from India had fought on three continents, Europe, Africa and Asia – the largest volunteer army in history - isn't that wonderful!" his father exclaimed.

"Troops were quickly sent to support our troops, but none of these countries could have fought the war without Britain," said Mum. "They were just too far away to fight Germany without having Britain as a refuelling point. If Britain had been invaded, that really would have been it. There were no free countries left in Europe, you see – no one to fight back, except us."

Charles closed his eyes, and imagined a map of Europe, at what seemed like dusk. A darkness was moving from the East, swallowing one country after another, like lights being turned off in the rooms of a house - the darkness descending, spreading across the map of Europe, until only Britain was left alight, shining like a beacon of hope for those desperate to make it to her shores.

Charles suddenly opened his eyes again, shocked at the intensity of his feelings.

"That's why Britain had to fight for the cause of freedom," said his mother. "That's why Britain couldn't give in. Britain gave hope to people, people who had managed to escape Nazi occupied Europe, hope that Britain could fight and would fight, hope that Britain would defend the cause of freedom. People flocked to Britain to find safety and many of them joined the British armed forces, too, because they were so desperate for a chance to fight Hitler."

In his mind he saw an image of a powerful consciousness throwing all its dark magic at the forces of good and a goodness determined to shield itself from that wave of evil, with an equally powerful will to survive, a light which deflected the darkness and shattered it to a thousand pieces of broken glass. He seemed to hear the sounds of battle - the thunder of war from long ago and a country's struggle to protect its freedom. Now he understood why young men, not long out of school, had been so willing to fight.

Charles was filled with pride. The birds sang in the trees overhead, the air was soft and clear, the land was at peace and now, he knew why.

Chapter 2 - The Battle of Britain and The Blitz

The morning was promising to turn into an unexpectedly warm day, as sometimes happens in Spring, when everything feels right with the world. The woods were still unusually quiet, and Charles was beginning wonder if he had strayed into a Fairy Story and was, by now, fully expecting, that any minute, he might see knights in shining armour and ladies with long flowing hair and rich robes, wafting along the top of the hill, until his father broke the silence.

"Did you know that Churchill sometimes used to visit friends here and stayed at what is now your school, Charles? He actually wrote some of his speeches right here in this town!"

"Really? So, Churchill actually stayed at my school?"

"Yes," replied his father, "before the war, but it wasn't a school then."

"Wow!" Charles exclaimed. It amazed him, how such an important person like Churchill could ever have visited such a small town.

"Don't be fooled by this town's size," said his mother, with a smile. There was a wistful, far-away look in her eyes, as she spoke.

"This town has long been an important defensive position against possible invasion and strangely, it has strong links with the sea. It was home to two famous admirals. One beat off the Spanish Armada, in 1588. He was called Charles as well - Charles, Lord Howard of Effingham. He was the son of Anne Boleyn's uncle, so he was her cousin and a long time ago your school was his house where he lived."

"I know that name," said Charles. "Wasn't Anne Boleyn Henry VIII's second wife?"

"She was," said his mother.

"So, her cousin lived here, at my school?" Charles was amazed.

"That's right, sweetheart. Your school was a private house then. Lord Howard of Effingham defended us from King Philip of Spain, who wanted to rule over this country himself and replace Queen Elizabeth I. He sent over his fleet of ships, the Spanish Armada, to try to invade us, rather like Hitler tried to do in 1940. Like Hitler, the Armada was defeated and the Spanish Empire failed in its invasion attempt and it was largely due to Lord Howard and his daring, second-in-command, Sir Francis Drake."

"There was another Admiral, who lived in the same house much later," said Dad, "in the first half of the twentieth century. His name was Admiral Beatty and he commanded the Royal Naval Battle Cruiser Fleet in the First World War. He was very brave and equally daring and became First Sea Lord of the Admiralty in 1919, as Churchill did twenty years later."

Then Charles' mother spoke, sensing his thoughts. "You see, there's a powerful energy here, which connects us with the sea. It's in the chalk downs," she said, inclining her head to the hills on the other side of town, "and it's in the land. The chalk links us with the coast and the White Cliffs of Dover. It links us with the past and with the strength of this country that produced the likes of R.J. Mitchell and won the Battle of Britain."

Then Dad spoke, "The Battle of Britain lasted from the 10th July to 15th September, 1940. Hitler's army was preparing to invade Britain in what Hitler called, 'Operation Sealion'. We were next in line after France, but Hitler quickly found that it wasn't as easy to reach us as he'd expected."

"Why?" said Charles.

"The sea, Charles, the sea protected us," said his mother, wistfully, "It's a natural barrier, like a moat"

"Anyway," Dad said, emphatically, "if the Germans had tried to invade this country, our Royal Navy would have had something to say about it!"

"So, the Battle of Britain raged above people's heads," said his mother. "The fighting became so intense that the pilots had no time to rest. They were flying up to eight missions a day, only landing to refuel and then up they would go again, so desperate was the situation and so desperate were those boys to save this country and their families. During the worst days of fighting from mid-August 1940 to early September, the Germans were averaging one thousand attacks a day and we were losing more planes than could be replaced...".

The three of them were now in a clearing at the top of the hill. The whole park and the town beyond stretched out below. It seemed so safe and serene and looking up, he found it hard to imagine that the bright blue skies above his own home had once been criss-crossed with fighter planes and gunfire.

"So, if I'd been alive back then, in 1940," said Charles, "I would have seen Spitfires and Hurricanes fighting enemy planes in the sky right here?"

"Yes, Charles," answered his mother, "and sadly, you would have seen planes being shot down and crash landing."

The events of this war, which to Charles had just been history, had suddenly become very real.

He glanced again at the sky and then at his mother and father, who were standing either side of him. They, too, were gazing upwards and for a moment, he could have sworn that he saw his mother in a smart 1940's jacket and skirt and a matching hat of deepest burgundy, her long hair pinned up at the front - she looked so different; his father in a smart suit and trilby hat and Charles himself in a little tank top and shorts and all of them carrying their gas-masks in bags on their shoulders.

He was stunned. It all felt so real. He blinked the image away, as the scene returned to normal. His mother looked at him gently. The blueness of her eyes seemed to reflect the intensity of the Bluebells surrounding them.

"On August 15th," she said, "there were more than 1,790 raids – Britain couldn't cope with the onslaught for long. Airfields, factories and radar stations were being destroyed and soon Britain would have to surrender. Then Hugh Dowding was heard to say that what Britain needed right at that moment was a miracle - and that miracle came," said his mother, emotion deep in her voice. "It came on the 7th September 1940 when the Germans turned their attention to London. Nearly one thousand German aircraft attacked London in a massive daylight bombing raid."

"How was that a miracle?" Charles asked. "Lots of people in London must have been hurt. It must have been horrible!"

"Yes, it was, sweetheart, a terrible shock," his mother replied, sadly, "but, it was also Hitler's big mistake. He ordered London to be bombed, instead of the air-fields."

"Why was it a mistake?" Charles asked.

"Because while the German Luftwaffe was bombing the cities," his mother replied, "the plane factories and the airfields were spared. The bombing of London actually gave the factories, radar stations and airfields time to repair and get up and running again, because if the Luftwaffe had continued to bomb them, they wouldn't have recovered, but now they had time to build more Spitfires and Hurricanes, to replace those which had been lost."

Charles tried to imagine what it must have felt like to be in the midst of that first air-raid on London with one thousand bombers heading his way...

He could still hear his mother's voice beside him, but he was aware that they were no longer standing among the bright, spring woods near home. Was it just his imagination, or were the three of them now standing on the banks of the River Thames in London? They seemed to be looking east, down at the long, dark, snaking line of the river.

Charles was scared. The river's tide had turned and the murky waters flowed towards them, bringing the sharp salty smell of the sea to his nose and an ominous noise to his ears - a low, angry, rolling drone, which hummed threateningly. Charles gripped his mother's hand, as she anxiously looked at his father.

Suddenly, coming from around the bend of the river they saw it; a black cloud in the sky, moving at speed, following the line of the Thames, as if following a road. Charles' eyes widened in fear as the cloud revealed itself to be planes - hundreds of German planes - bombers!

"It's ok," said Charles' father, trying not to sound alarmed, "They're going to break up in a minute and fan off to bomb different airfields," but he didn't sound convinced.

"But I thought you said on the 7ᵗʰ of September they didn't do that?" exclaimed Charles.

"Yes," said his mother quietly, staring fixedly at the planes, fear etched on her face. "They bombed London!"

And sure enough, the planes just kept coming.

"This is the East End," Dad exclaimed, fearfully glancing at the tall buildings nearby. "We're in the Dock Yards! This can't be real! What's happening?"

Desperately, Charles glanced up at the wall of one grimy building, "East India Dockyard", he read on a sign.

"It's all jam-making factories, paint works and timber yards round here," Charles' father exclaimed. "All extremely flammable!"

Charles' mother and father stared, their eyes wide with fear and looked at their son. Terror gripped them. Frantically, they scanned the buildings for somewhere to take shelter. Running in blind panic, they held his hands tightly, as if they would never let him go. The planes seemed to be chasing them!

Just ahead, there appeared a long, low building, with arched doorways, right on the banks of the river. One of the enormous doors was open a little. Shoving it hard with their shoulders, it opened, reluctantly, with an eerie creak, disturbing the dust concealed within, which seemed to awaken like a ghost.

"Quick, in here!" Dad shouted, as they ran through the door into the cold darkness. Instantly, Charles' throat was choked with dust. It settled on their clothes, as all three of them leant hard on the heavy door, which closed slowly, too slowly, slowly blocking the light...

As the last sliver of day squeezed around the warehouse door, Charles glanced at the river. The reflections of the German planes danced manically on the surface of the water, almost taunting them like bullies in a playground, whilst the three of them waited for the bombs to fall...

...when suddenly, from out of nowhere it seemed, Spitfires and Hurricanes poured in from either side, intercepting the bombers and attacking them from all directions, like sheep dogs chasing off wolves, but there weren't enough of them! He watched as they buzzed in and out, weaving this way and that, in a desperate attempt to protect London, but the bombs still fell.

He buried his face in his mother's side and waited for the bombing to stop...

Suddenly, all was quiet and peaceful again. He lifted his head. They were back on the soft hillside of home, with the sun shining on their faces.

Unsure what he had just experienced, Charles glanced at his parents for any sign they had seen the same vision. It had seemed so real, but they appeared quite calm and relaxed – not looking at all like they had just narrowly escaped with their lives!

"It must have been my imagination!" thought Charles, relieved. "I hope that doesn't happen again!" and he shivered.

Mum and Dad looked at him, concerned.

"Are you alright, sweetheart?"

"Yes, I'm fine," he said, thankful that the awful scene had passed and they were all safe.

His mother put her arm around his shoulders and held him close. He felt her love wrap around him like a warm blanket, as she rested her chin on the top of his head and felt the softness of his hair against her cheek, as she spoke,

"Hitler hoped that bombing our great capital city, would frighten people so much, they would lose faith in Churchill and turn against him and his government, but just the opposite happened – it made people angry and even more determined to fight on. On 11th September in a famous speech, broadcast on the radio, Churchill said the bombing raid had '...kindled a fire in the British hearts...'. He said that Hitler didn't understand 'the spirit of the British nation, or the tough fibre of Londoners' and he said that Hitler had lit '...a fire which will burn with a steady and consuming flame until the last vestiges of Nazi tyranny have been burnt out of Europe...'. Charles was sure he could hear Churchill's voice in the trees again, echoing through his mother's words.

The leaves whispered and the blossom floated on the breeze. Almost in a dream, he heard a voice, 'Every man and woman will therefore prepare himself to do his duty, whatever it may be, *with special pride and care…'*[5] but it wasn't his mother's voice he was hearing – it was the voice of Churchill…

…and then Dad spoke, as if from far away. "In September 1940, the Luftwaffe pilots were told that the RAF was down to its last fifty aircraft. They'd been given false information by Admiral Canaris, who was the head of the Abwehr, which was Hitler's own military intelligence service and they were shocked when they realised that the RAF had more planes than they'd been led to believe. Thanks to Canaris, they'd flown into a trap. It was the 15th of September and our boys were waiting for them. Churchill was at the RAF underground headquarters at Uxbridge, watching the action unfold. The radar had detected swarms of German aircraft approaching rapidly…"

Suddenly, Charles felt dark walls close around him and a large table stretch out before him, covered with a map of the South of England. The table was surrounded by smart women in uniform, who were pushing with long sticks, what looked like little counters, like pieces on a board game. Above, illuminating the whole table, was a circle of green shaded lights, which floated like stars in a constellation and on the wall was a board, rather like a railway station time board, with names of different RAF air-fields – the names hovered before him, names which seemed to evoke deep feelings in Charles – Tangmere, North Weald, Hornchurch, Kenley, Biggin Hill, Debden, Northolt… The names seemed to float around Charles' head, as he turned to look behind him at the gallery, which overlooked the Operations Room and there, observing it all, he felt, rather than saw, the massive presence of Churchill, whose question boomed in the air,

'What other reserves have we?'

The room crackled with anticipation. Looking at those green shaded lights again, hovering above the map, Charles knew what the answer would be, as Air Vice-Marshall Keith Park answered with heavy heart,

'There are none…'.

Everyone present gazed at the table, willing those RAF pilots to win, understanding all too well there were no more planes left in reserve on the ground to help them. Every single one was in the skies above England, taking its part in a final decisive battle. This was the moment when all would be lost or won.

"Go on boys," Charles heard himself say, "Go on!"

GO ON BOYS. GO ON!

The green lamps began to spin and swirl above his head, weaving and diving in and out of swarms of German aircraft, as RAF pilots desperately fought, each instinctively knowing that this was the day when the fate of Britain would be decided. Everything depended on them. The battle was nearing its climax - the German pilots exulting in their victory, when suddenly, almost at the last moment, more Spitfires appeared, diving headlong into the great swirling mass of death and confusion, as fear and triumph, heroism and pain fought for control in the mind of every man. The moment of fate was at hand and with one, final, decisive push, the Luftwaffe pilots seemed to lose heart, as victory slipped from their grasp. Charles felt their resolve fail and turning tail, they departed the skies, heading back across the sea, as he again, heard his father's voice, saying,

"And the Luftwaffe suffered such huge losses, it never really regained its full fighting strength again."

Charles' breath came quick, as if he had run a race. His felt his mind squeeze, as if through a small hole, the intense pressure dazing him with its intensity. He closed his eyes, wondering to where he was being drawn. He felt a strong pull, as if on his heart and sensed the area around him opening out. A cool breeze played around his face and he could hear birds calling to each other in the trees close by, but an all-too familiar and ominous noise was approaching from the near distance.

He opened one eye and then the other, knowing instantly where he was, the surprise momentarily causing him to forget the sense of dread that was even now filling his stomach.

BUCKINGHAM PALACE!

"Why am I here?" thought Charles.

"What am I meant to see?"

A discarded newspaper blew towards him along the ground, as if propelled by some unseen force. It wrapped itself around his ankles, as if demanding to be read. Quickly, Charles glanced down. The date on the newspaper leapt out at him – 15th September 1940.

"It's the same day! I thought it was all over!" said Charles to himself, as his eyes slowly tore themselves away from the paper, forcing him to bear witness.

Looking down the great, long road of The Mall, he saw it coming! From the direction of Trafalgar Square, flying over Nelson's column and now only a little way above Admiralty Arch, almost skimming the tops of the trees, he saw a lone German bomber, a Dornier, heading straight for Buckingham Palace.

Horrified onlookers stared open mouthed, paralysed with fear.

"No! No! No!" Charles heard the words scream in his head, as the realisation of what was happening burst in his mind, like an explosion.

"The King! He mustn't die!"

Charles started to run towards the gates of the palace, as if trying to warn someone of what he could see bearing down on them, trying to warn the guards, frantically waving at them through the bars of the high fence, trying, but failing to draw their attention, but it was hopeless. No one could see him.

Panic stricken, he looked back at the fast-approaching plane, tearing at his hair, desperately searching his brain for an idea of some way to stop this awful scene from playing out, but powerless to do so, when, just as the guards noticed the impending doom, taking positions to fire, a lone Hurricane fighter plane appeared in the distance, heading straight for the Dornier, clearly intent on preventing it from reaching its target.

"Yes! Yes! Go on! Get him. Get him!" Charles screamed out loud, not caring if he could be heard.

He stared intently at the racing Hurricane, imagining the pilot fixing his gaze on the enemy before him, who was still aiming straight for the palace.

Nothing else mattered. Charles willed him on. "Go on! Go on! You can do it!"[6]

The tension was mounting.

In that instant Charles could see with his own eyes, the German pilot's thumb hovering over the button, ready to release his deadly cargo – the bomb sitting there in the hold – waiting.

"Come on! Come on!"

Charles heard the words swirling around in the crackling air, unsure if they were his or the Hurricane pilot's, who, in that instant, depressed his finger on the machine gun trigger.

Da, da, da, da, da! A short volley of bullets rattled off – then STOPPED!

OUT OF AMMO!

The Dornier was still heading straight for Buckingham Palace.

"I'll ram him! I'll ram the blighter!"

Charles heard the Hurricane pilot – heard his words – felt his bravery, his anger, his resolve – saw him aim for the tail fin – saw the shadow of the Dornier darkening his cockpit, the Hurricane hastening to do his pilot's bidding.

Closer, closer – the planes almost touching. Closer.

Then the sudden jagged crash, as the Hurricane's wing sliced through the Dornier tail-fin, as easily as a hot knife through butter, in an explosive burst of shattered pieces.

"Yes! Yes!" shouted Charles, or was it the pilot he heard?

It was like watching a comic strip come to life...

"Take that, you darstardly Dornier!"

"If it hadn't been for you, you pesky Hurricane, I could have done it! I'll get you next time..." the words trailed away, as the Dornier veered off course and almost gracefully plummeted towards the ground, the words floating away in the air.

"We'll never let you win!" the Hurricane screamed, as it too plummeted towards the ground at 500mph.

"Save yourself! Bail out!" said the little Hurricane to its pilot.

"But you'll die!" shouted the pilot back to his trusted friend.

"It doesn't matter!" was the reply. "We did what we had to do! Bail out now! Go, before it's too late!"

The pilot took one last look at the palace safe below; quickly, lightly, rested his palm on the control panel for a split second, as if stroking the head of a beloved dog.

"Goodbye!" he said, released the catch and was gone.

All was silent, the cleansing wind a shock after the noise of the cockpit. The pilot fixed his gaze on the spiralling Hurricane, determined to watch to the last, as his trusted companion disappeared from view. He felt, rather than saw when the end came. He closed his eyes in love and gratitude and Charles did the same.

His breath came quick, as if he had run a race. His mother looked at him again, concerned.

"Are you ok, sweetheart?" she asked.

"I'm alright, Mum!" he replied, but he could tell by the loving look on her face that she had sensed something, too. She put her arm around him and kissed the top of his head.

"Fifty-six German aircraft were shot down that day," she said, "double the British losses.[7] The RAF had seen them off," she said, with pride, "and on the 17th September, Hitler called off 'Operation Sealion', because winter was setting in. He never attempted to invade Britain again. He'd lost the Battle of Britain and all the German forces that were massing along the coast of France, ready to invade us were redeployed elsewhere. The RAF and our Spitfires and Hurricanes had dealt a decisive blow and Hitler never really recovered. He blamed Hermann Goering, the Head of the Luftwaffe, for the failure, but really, it was down to Admiral Canaris and the false information he had given, that had caused the Luftwaffe to fly into a trap."

"Phew!" exclaimed Charles. "We were lucky! What happened to Admiral Canaris?"

Charles' mother replied, "Right up until 1944, Admiral Canaris secretly worked with the Allies against Hitler and was involved in a plot to kill him, but sadly he was eventually found out and sentenced to death by the Nazis, just days before the downfall of the Nazis and their Third Reich. Canaris was a very brave man."

"But," said Charles' father, "although Hitler called off Operation Sealion, the Blitz continued for another fifty-seven nights and then on and off throughout the war. Later, other cities and industrial targets were hit, too," Dad said, "including Coventry, Plymouth, Portsmouth and Liverpool. Although the Blitz itself ended in May 1941, the bombing didn't really stop."

Charles imagined the devastation and thought again of all those wartime films he knew his mother and father loved so much.

"Did you know," said Dad, "that my mum, your grandmother, Mary, saw Liverpool being bombed when she was a little girl?"

"Why was she there?" asked Charles.

"She and her mother had been living in Canada with family, but when the war broke out, her mother apparently said, 'My country needs me!' although your grandmother wondered exactly what it *was* that they could do to help their country!"

"But weren't they safer in Canada?" asked Charles.

"They would have been, sweetheart," his father replied, "but they did come back, on a ship named 'The Duchess of Atholl' and during the voyage, they passed another ship, called the SS City of Benares, going in the other direction to Canada, carrying ninety evacuee children, which was tragically, torpedoed by a German submarine and sank. Many of the children lost their lives. As it was sinking, it sent out a distress call to the Duchess of Atholl, which was passing, but it couldn't stop to help, as it was being chased by a U-boat as well. It sent a message back saying, "U-boat on our tail. Running for our lives."

"That's awful," said Charles, at which point his mother spoke,

"The weird thing is, my grandmother, Gloria, was meant to have been on that ship which sank, with her brother and two sisters."

Charles was shocked. "Really! What happened?" he asked, alarmed.

"They were going to be evacuated to Canada. Their father had put them on the ship, but as he waved to them from the dock, he suddenly had a bad feeling that something was wrong. He just couldn't do it. He couldn't let them go. He went back on the ship before it departed and took them off."

"Wow!" exclaimed Charles. "They could have died! You wouldn't have been born," he said, looking at his mother, "and I wouldn't have been born either!"

"Life is full of strange twists and turns, sweetheart!" said his mother.

Charles was stunned by the thought, that in just one night, both sides of his family could have been obliterated.

Then Dad continued, "My mum's ship arrived at Liverpool docks on the night of 5th September 1940, just in time to see Liverpool being bombed by the Luftwaffe. The captain ordered that they wait out at sea until after the raid had finished."

With a sudden shock of realisation, Charles found himself there, standing on the deck. The ship was in darkness to avoid being seen by the enemy bombers that were flying above them through the night, heading straight for Liverpool! The relentless droning of their engines hummed ominously, throbbing in Charles' ears and making his headache. He heard the awful whistle, as the bombs tumbled from the planes towards the innocent houses and docks below. He pitied those poor people cowering in shelters beneath, praying to be spared the danger, which rained down like death...

The night-sky glowed a fierce orange and the whole of the city was ablaze. He could feel the scorching heat on his face, as Liverpool burned, the light of the flames dancing in his eyes. He looked down at the water, which shone an angry, livid red and was surprised to see hundreds of little boats, bobbing on the gentle swell, full of people, who had put out to sea to get away from the raid. They all looked on, sharing the terror, with those left on land.

He turned and saw other passengers standing beside him on the deck, watching in horror, powerless to help those poor souls trapped in the city. There was a young girl, a little older than him, standing close by, looking on in stunned silence and Charles instantly felt that she must be his future grandmother, Mary! Everything in him wanted to speak to her, but he knew she would be too dazed and scared to feel his presence.

A man's voice broke the shocked silence - a member of the crew, who exclaimed,

"Remember this. You'll never see the likes of it again!"

"I 'ope!" replied another, ironically.

Charles blinked, wide-eyed. The scene had vanished, as suddenly as it had begun.

"When the raid finished," said Dad, "the ship finally docked on the morning of the 6th September and my mum'ss passport, which I still have, is actually stamped with that date. Can you imagine the devastation they must have seen! Streets bombed, ambulances rushing through the city, the cathedral damaged, people searching rubble for survivors! Terrible!"

Charles thought of the destruction that must have greeted them - ordinary streets bombed beyond all recognition. He could only imagine how shocked she must have been and he pitied her.

"She'd come from a lovely life in Canada," said his father, sympathetically, living on the Prairies, with her great-uncle's family - happy days at school with her friends, skating on the ice in winter – to be ripped from that and going back to a war-torn country, which she didn't know and where she didn't know anyone. She never got over it. She always said her childhood days in Canada were the happiest days of her life."

Charles thought of the bewilderment his grandmother must have felt when she returned on that fateful night.

"It wasn't over though," said his father. "The Luftwaffe came back that day, in a rare daylight raid. Mary and her mother didn't stay in Liverpool though. Can you guess where they went to live, Charles?"

"Surely, not London!" exclaimed Charles.

"Yes, sweetheart, London! Talk about 'out of the frying pan and into the fire!'" said Dad.

"She must have been so afraid," Charles remarked, "knowing no-one, with only her mother to keep her safe. It must have been terrible! Where was her father?" asked Charles, suddenly concerned.

"Her father had died of tuberculosis in the twenties, when Mary was just a young child; you see, tuberculosis was a terrible disease then, with no cure and it killed so many people, because living conditions were so different then, so when Mary and her mother arrived in Liverpool on that frightening night, they really were all alone.

"And then, later, when your grandmother was just fourteen" his father continued, "she did fire-watch duty in London, putting out incendiary bombs, which were designed to burst into flames as soon as they hit the ground?"

"How did she do that?" asked Charles alarmed, "and at fourteen!"

"Shocking to think of it now, isn't it?" said Dad. "All she had was a bucket of sand and a bucket of water with a pump!"

He could hardly imagine how his grandmother must have felt, only a few years older than him, on her own on a burning roof...

He tried to picture the scene – a lone little girl, hearing the sound of enemy planes flying overhead in the darkness, as a shower of fire poured from the night sky...

"She must have been very brave," said Charles.

He thought of his grandmother, whom he had only seen in photos and wished that he had had the chance to meet her. A sudden thought struck him,

"Did bombs fall here as well?" he asked, looking back at his father, although he already knew what the answer must be.

"Yes, Charles," said his father, ruefully. "Quite a lot of bombs fell round here. You see, the Germans knew that South East High Command's headquarters was based here in the tunnels, which had been built into the hills above the town. They tried to bomb it several times!

"One bomb fell near there - a direct hit on a house, just as the owner was arriving home. Sadly, the man's house was destroyed, but luckily, he survived and found himself with the front door key still in his hand, door intact, but no house left! The door had protected him from the bomb blast!" [8]

"Oh dear - a little funny, as long as the man was ok!" exclaimed Charles and he imagined the scene, like a cartoon, with the cartoon character standing blackened, but unhurt, steam rising from his sticking-up hair, hand still clasping the key in the lock and a smouldering door still in its frame, but nothing left of the house at all!

"And the famous World War II British Army general, Field Marshal Bernard Montgomery, General Montgomery, was based here too for a while, at South East High Command," said Dad. "Everyone knew him as Monty, though. He was most famous for his epic battles against the equally brilliant German General, Field Marshal Erwin Rommel. During the war, these men pitted their wits and their armies against each other in the Africa campaign, but especially at El Alamein; you'll learn about this later. Monty also commanded in every theatre of war, especially the D-Day landings and the campaign in Normandy."

"Wow," exclaimed Charles, "and he actually lived here in our town?"

"That's right," said Charles' father, "for a short while. Monty, as everyone called him, used to take his officers for a drink, although he didn't drink himself, to a pub in town, which was later called the 'Desert Rat', until some bright spark decided to change its name! He was a stickler for fitness, too. Every morning, he used to take his staff on long runs up and down the hill. The famous United States military leader, General Eisenhower used to visit regularly and stay here, too!"

Charles was impressed.

"You see, Charles, this town has always provided a strong defensive position because of its hills, even as far back as the Norman Conquest in 1066, the last time this country was ever invaded. That's when the castle in town was built, by one of William the Conqueror's followers."

"The last time!" Charles said, surprised.

"That's right! Since then, for over a thousand years, this country has protected itself from invasion and there were several attempts over the years, mind you. Ironically, the caves under the castle were used as air-raid shelters during the Second World War, protecting people from another potential invader!"

Charles had been there and remembered it clearly. He thought of the rows of bunk beds that he had seen down in those cold, dark caves and imagined how it must have felt when the power went off, the only light coming from a few flickering candles in tin holders, as the bombs fell unceasingly...

At school, a few days later, Charles and his classmates were taken on a tour of the old air-raid shelter in their school basement. They all huddled in the cramped cellar together and took it in turns to try on an Air-Raid Warden's helmet. It felt strange and heavy and rather uncomfortable on Charles' head and in the damp confines of the dusty cellar, they listened to a recording of an air-raid – the eerie wail of sirens going off, the frightening whistles and cracks of bombs raining down overhead and the scream of planes desperately attacking and firing at the enemy all around them. Charles was vividly beginning to feel the reality of this war, as if the pages of a history book had started to come alive.

When he arrived home from school, later that day, he told his mother about it and how he had felt. His mother listened.

"But remember," she said. "The Spitfire and the Hurricane really did live up to their names. They gave as good as they got. Often horribly outnumbered, those boys in those planes, many of them only just out of school, kept on going and going and never giving up, flying mission after mission, with very little rest, just to keep this country safe from a terrible evil."

Charles thought about it. He was surprised to hear how the Spitfire pilots were just boys.

"How young were they?" he asked.

"As young as eighteen."

The thought shocked Charles.

"And the pilots came from many different countries too," continued his mother. "Many were volunteers from the British Empire and many were refugees and exiles from Nazi occupied Europe, all coming here to help fight Hitler.

"35,000 Polish airmen, soldiers and sailors and even more French, made their way to Britain to join the fight. There were also Belgian, Dutch, Norwegian and Czech airmen, men from Barbados and Jamaica and men from the Australian, New Zealand and Canadian Air forces in the RAF, too. All fought fiercely and bravely alongside our British lads. Do you know, there were even American pilots, who fought in the Battle of Britain?"

"Americans," exclaimed Charles, "but I thought they didn't join the war till much later."

"That's right," replied his mother, "not until December 1941, but the one thing that united all these American lads, was the fact that they were desperate to fly the famous Spitfire - young men like Billy Fisk, previously a gold medallist in the Winter Olympics and Vernon Keough, a professional skydiver and stunt pilot back in America before the war and others too, who all actually risked imprisonment and loss of their American citizenship for breaking American neutrality law, just to be a part of the fight against Nazism.

"They mostly pretended to be Canadian, and some risked their lives just getting here! They came over on supply ships from America. You see, even though America hadn't joined the war at this point, they were sending supplies of food and equipment to help us to defend ourselves, on the Atlantic Convoys and it was on those ships that the men came over, ships that were regularly being bombed and sunk by German submarines, called U-boats, which used to hunt in packs and pick off ships that were straggling behind. When news of these men's brave sacrifices reached America, public opinion there started to change from being against joining the war."

"Sacrifices?"

"Yes," said Charles' mother, sadly, "like all too many of those brave lads in the RAF, some of them didn't make it; some of them died, or were badly injured doing what they saw as their duty. They paid the ultimate price and it made people in America start to think, to the point where the law was changed so that anyone going to Britain to join up no longer risked losing their citizenship, or being put in prison when they returned home."

At that moment, Charles' father walked in and joined in the conversation.

"It took a long time for America to realise that this war was going to affect them. If Germany had beaten Britain, Germany would have controlled a large part of the world. The selfless actions of those men made the American people think."

"And another young person, who made the people of America think was our own Queen Elizabeth II," said Charles' mother. "In October 1940, the Queen, when she was just a child and just a princess then, made her first ever radio broadcast, to the children of the Commonwealth and to all the children evacuated from Britain to Canada, Australia, New Zealand, South Africa and the United States of America. When people in America heard this broadcast, our future Queen of England, sending a message to those children, it also helped change public opinion in America."

Then Charles' mother found a recording of the young Princess' speech and Charles heard the voice of a future queen.

"And when peace comes, remember it will be for us, the children of today, to make the world of tomorrow a better and happier place.

My sister is by my side, and we are both going to say goodnight to you.

Come on, Margaret."

Then Charles heard the much younger voice of the Princess' sister, Margaret, speaking,

"Goodnight, children."

And then both spoke together,

"Goodnight, and good luck to you all." [9]

"You see, even the smallest act of kindness or bravery can make a difference," said his mother.

Chapter 3 - The RAF

"One plane can make a difference too," said Dad. "If it hadn't been for the RAF, the Royal Air Force, we wouldn't have won the Battle of Britain and it was only because of sheer luck and determination that it was formed at all! It had only been in existence for twenty years, when the Second World War began. It was formed on 1st April 1918, just towards the end of the First World War."

"The First World War!" exclaimed Charles. "It's frightening to think of all this war."

"Yes," Dad replied, sadly, "1914-1918 - another war when the world seemed to go mad for a little while; another war we fought against Germany. You'll learn about it soon, but it's too much information for now," smiled his father, gently ruffling Charles' hair.

"Anyway, during the First World War, the Germans had a plane called a 'Fokker', which for a while, was the faster and better plane and difficult to beat, but then a new British plane was invented, called the SE 5 and it was a bit like the Spitfire of its day and in 1917 it helped the allies regain control of the skies."

"What does that mean, Dad?"

"Well, it helped us to win the war in the sky, let's put it that way and that was because of its speed. It could go at 140mph, must faster than the Fokker and it could turn more easily and more quickly, but to begin with, the only weapons the fighter pilots had were their pistols, which they used to fire at the enemy!"

"Pistols!" exclaimed Charles. "Doesn't that mean they had to fly really close to each other?"

"That's right," said Dad. "Later they were given machine guns, but that's how basic everything was. The Wright brothers of America had only invented and flown the first successful airplane in 1903 and by the time of the First World War they were still just made of wood and a sort of fabric to hold it all together. The cockpit, where the pilot sat, was open too, so it was really cold up in the sky in those planes."

"They don't sound very safe," said Charles.

"They weren't really," said Dad. "You know those old planes we sometimes see, flying over our house that come from the old aerodrome near us?"

"Oh, yes. Those biplanes, with two wings on each side?" asked Charles.

"That's it," said Dad, "those are the ones."

Charles tried to imagine what it was like to fly in one of those little planes – the roaring sound of the engine, the constant thrumming of the propellers, the rushing wind in his face. The noise must have been deafening, but exciting too, he thought.

"Well," continued his father, "that's what the first planes in the RAF looked like and my grandfather, my mum Mary's father,"

"The one who died of tuberculosis?" asked Charles.

"That's right!" replied Dad, "He was called Frank too - I was named after him; well, he was a pilot in one of those planes, during the First World War in the Royal Naval Air Service!"

"Really!" exclaimed Charles. "Wow!"

"He was underage when he joined up, only seventeen and when his father found out, he forced him to go back and tell them his real age, but by the time they got to the recruiting office, your great-grandfather Frank had convinced his dad to let him go! The other lads used to call him, 'Cherub', because he looked so young."

"Cherub - a baby angel," Charles laughed.

"One day, during the war, your great-grandfather Frank, was in a dogfight..."

"Dogfight?" asked Charles.

"Yes – not a fight with dogs," said Dad, smiling, "that's just what they used to call the fights. These battles were fought in the sky against enemy planes at close range. They'd fly really close to each other and fire their weapons. They'd try to surprise and out-manoeuvre each other, which just meant that they would each try to fly above the enemy and come at them from out of the sun, so that the enemy couldn't see them, bit like a game of 'Potatoes', you know, 'One potato, two potato, three potato, four'," and his dad mimed the game with his hands, putting one hand on top of the other.

"Oh! I see!" said Charles.

"So, Frank was in this dog-fight with a German fighter pilot and they went so high that his eye froze with the cold! Remember, they were in open cockpits."

"Yuk!" exclaimed Charles.

"Don't worry, Charles," said his father, smiling, "It defrosted!" and he chuckled.

Dad went to the bookshelf and pulled out a photo album full of old, black and white photos, pictures of families and children, frozen in time from another age and from long ago and there amongst them, was Frank, Charles' great-grandfather, but in this picture, just a young, gentle, serious-looking boy, holding a pair of gloves in his hand, looking away into the distance, as if thinking of his next flying mission.

"They bred them tough in those days," Dad said.

Charles thought of this man, his great-grandfather, as the boy he was in the First World War, looking so young and as Charles looked at the photo album, he imagined it as a comic book, with all the pictures coming to life, like a cartoon, moving across the pages, which slowly filled with the bright colours of a cartoon world and Charles was surprised to see Frank, the young boy in the picture in the pilot's uniform, actually turn his head and look at him! He waved and smiled and Charles waved back.

Frank's smile was warm and friendly, cheeky, almost mischievous and there was a twinkle in his eye, as if seeing the fun in everything.

"No wonder you were able to talk your father round," said Charles to the cartoon Frank.

"Come on, Charlie," Frank called, "Let's have some fun! Let's go hunt the Red Baron, the greatest German pilot there ever was."[10]

And either Charles jumped into the cartoon, or the cartoon came up to meet him, he wasn't sure, but the room quickly filled with those cartoon colours, like a bath filling up around him...

...and he landed in a seat, a leather seat, with seat straps, a seat that started to move and trundle just above the ground at great speed and as it moved, the plane grew around him – a First World War bi-plane! Charles reached forward for the control stick, as it appeared in his hands. Looking up, he saw propeller blades flash before his eyes over the front of the engine; his pilot's hat flapped against his ears; goggles fixed themselves onto his face, encircling his vision and intensifying everything. A sort of serious excitement settled on his shoulders. He felt older, in control and free.

The plane took off, Charles feeling the sudden dip and leap in his stomach, as if going over a hump-back bridge, or a ride at a fun-fair.

He soared up into the sky and levelling out, looked over his shoulder for his great-grandfather Frank's plane, which was close by, so close, in fact, they could almost have shaken hands. Frank was waving to him and grinning from ear to ear and Charles knew he was feeling exactly the same joy and freedom that he was.

Through the skies they soared, the wind in their faces, the smell of the hot engine, almost burning their nostrils. All around the cartoon colours flashed, burning vivid memories into Charles' mind. When Frank turned his plane, so did Charles, both wheeling higher and higher like eagles. It felt effortless, as the stinging wind rushed past his cold ears, but Charles didn't care. It made him feel more alive.

And then suddenly, just ahead of them, a little red dot broke from the cover of a cloud. "It must be the Red Baron," thought Charles. He signalled to his great-grandfather Frank, who'd seen it too.

Off they went, in hot pursuit. The Red Baron seemed to be teasing them, daring them to give chase, as he dived into another cloud and disappeared.

In his head, Charles could hear music, like the soundtrack to a film; it was fun, upbeat, exciting music, music that wanted to dive and soar with them, a deep pounding drumbeat and guitar, which fuelled Charles' adrenaline even more.

He looked over to Frank in his plane, who signalled to Charles to follow him. They climbed up, circling higher and higher above the clouds, their backs to the sun, which beamed down on them, as they waited for the Red Baron to break cover.

The music seemed to stop for breath too; the drumbeat was still there, but it was quieter, almost like a heartbeat, pulsing in his throbbing ears. Circling and looking, head turning and turning, scanning and searching, waiting for the chase to begin, Charles glanced over his shoulder to his great-grandfather, who was giving him a Thumbs-up.

Suddenly, a blinding flash of instinct made him fling his head round and, in that moment, the Red Baron was upon him, bearing down like a huge bird of prey. Charles flicked his control stick and his plane dived out of the way just in time, as Frank's plane shot in from the right and chased the Red Baron away.

The music started thumping again and Charles gave chase to help his great-grandfather. His heart was pounding, his mouth was dry. He looked down at his machine gun and he knew what he had to do.

The Red Baron flew expertly, sudden climbs and sudden dives, wheeling this way and that, out-manoeuvring them both every time, bearing down on them in sudden bursts of fire, which made them turn and scatter like birds; then the final deciding blow, as his great-grandfather rattled off a volley of machine-gun fire, that arched across the sky and seemed to flick the Red Baron away, his great-grandfather giving chase, as Charles called to him and called to him, falling, falling, falling, spinning and spinning in a dizzying fall.

The cartoon colours faded, as the action above in the skies grew smaller and smaller and farther away. The last he saw was the Red Baron saluting his great-grandfather, who saluted back, before both pilots turned for home.

The music faded with the colours, the room swam up to meet him and he was standing beside his father once more, looking at some black and white photographs, while in his mind, his great-grandfather flew past his vision across the faded photos of the album, the coloured exhaust fumes of his plane, printing red dots, which did loop-the-loops behind him. His great-grandfather waved and Charles smiled.

"Cheerio, Charlie," he heard him call in the distance. "I'll be seeing you!"

Charles' father looked at him, gently, aware that he had been far, far away.

"And then," he went on, as if he had been talking to his son all this time, "only twenty years later, in the Second World War, it was the Royal Air Force and the new Spitfires and Hurricanes that, again, saved this country from certain defeat; the RAF had become that important to the defence of our country."

Charles felt dazed, as if waking from a dream, as his mother joined in,

"Do you know," she said, "the Royal Air Force is the world's first and oldest independent air force; independent of the Royal Army, or the Royal Navy and it was because of two people, who both fought to keep the RAF independent. One person, was Hugh Trenchard, Marshal of the Royal Air Force, who was the man in charge and his nickname was 'Boom', because he had such a loud voice!"

"Boom," Charles mimicked and they all laughed.

"Yes, Charles and can you guess who else saved the RAF?"

"Not Churchill!" Charles exclaimed.

"Indeed, it was – Churchill, the man himself and luckily for us," Dad said, "Hugh Trenchard rose to become Chief of the Air Staff under Winston Churchill. You see, one person can make a difference, or in this case, two people, but there were many more like them."

"People can do amazing things, under the most difficult conditions," said his mother "In the Second World War, there were even women pilots, who flew in the Air Transport Auxiliary Service, delivering the planes to wherever they were needed, amazing women, like Mary Ellis, Joy Lofthouse and Diana Barnato Walker, who completed her first solo flight after just six hours of lessons! She learnt to fly at the famous motor racing circuit at Brooklands in Surrey." [11]

"Brooklands!" exclaimed Charles. "The museum?"

"That's the one!" replied his mother, "You remember we had a ride in a beautiful old car on what's left of the racing circuit there."

Charles remembered how fast they had sped around the steeply sloping track and the big grin on his mother's face. He was certain if she had had the chance, she would have driven that car herself.

He smiled at the memory.

"Someone else who made a difference, was a famous RAF pilot called Douglas Bader," said Dad. "He'd lost both his legs in a flying accident before the war."

"No legs!" exclaimed Charles. "How did he fly?"

"He had prosthetic legs. Nothing's impossible, when you put your mind to it," smiled Dad. "When the Second World War started, he tried to enlist, but the RAF wouldn't take him, but he persisted and eventually, they allowed him to join up. He fought in the Battle of France and in the skies above Dunkirk and then in the Battle of Britain. He was promoted to become Group Captain and Wing Commander, inspiring the young pilots with his own bravery and daring."

Charles' father opened the pages of a book and showed him a picture of Bader, who looked tough and strong.

"But then, unfortunately," his father said, "he was captured by the Germans, after having to bail out from his plane. One of his prosthetic legs became stuck and he had to bail out without it. When he was captured, the Germans notified the British that they had the famous Bader as their captive and that he needed a new leg.

45

They offered an RAF bomber safe passage, promising not to attack it, whilst it delivered the leg by parachute and that's what happened. Hermann Goring, Hitler's right-hand man, gave the go ahead for it. The parachute drop was called the 'Leg Operation'!"

"The Leg Operation!" Charles chuckled. He had a picture in his mind of Bader's prosthetic leg floating slowly down from the sky, suspended from a parachute.

Later that evening, Charles was unusually sleepy and his mother tucked him into bed early.

"I wish I could fly in a Spitfire," he said, yawning an enormous yawn and stretching out comfortably under his duvet.

"Maybe, one day, sweetheart," said his mother, as he snuggled down into his pillow, "and I'd like to fly in it too, with you!" she smiled and kissed him.

His eyes were already closing and as he drifted off to sleep, he dimly saw his model Spitfire gently moving in the glow of his night-light, which changed colour, softly casting floating shadows onto the ceiling, as his eyelids grew heavier and heavier...

Chapter 4 – The Shadow Grows

Suddenly, Charles was aware of a bright light and warm sun on his face. It seemed like he had only been asleep for a short while. He could hear the shrill cry of seagulls and the sound of the sea lapping a pebbly beach.

He opened his eyes, confused, because only a minute ago he had been nicely tucked up in his warm, cosy bed and now, before him, he saw the most wonderful sight; the sea stretching before him, sparkling in the sunlight, as little, glinting waves broke lazily on the shoreline.

"Hello, Charles!" said a kind voice.

Charles looked round in wonder. He realised that he was standing on a pavement behind an ornate iron fence with peeling, green paint and a wooden hand-rail. It all seemed somehow familiar. Charles blinked again and noticed, clasping the railing, the biggest pair of hands he had ever seen. They were strong looking hands with long, tapering, graceful fingers. Amazed, he glanced up at a brown wool, cardiganed arm and finally at the kind face of a man with the gentlest of smiles. The man seemed to beam with pride, as he looked at Charles. Little wrinkles played around his eyes and mouth with a smile that Charles had seen so many times before. It was his mother's smile and his grandma's, all rolled into one; a smile that simply meant, love, and Charles knew it.

"I'm your Great-Grandfather Bob, Charles, your mother's grandfather, but your mother never called me, Grandad. For some reason, she used to call me, 'Jam-Jar'! When she was a little girl, her friends at school thought I must be a tiny man, who actually *lived* in a jam-jar. She told me to pick her up from school one day, dressed in my best suit. When I turned up, all these little children came running out to see this tiny man in his jam-jar and were most disappointed when they saw me!" and he chuckled at the memory.

"Jam-Jar," said Charles in wonder. "I know that name! Mum talks about you a lot. There's a photo of you as a young man dressed in a Royal Navy uniform, on our book shelf at home."

The thought of home gave Charles a little shock. If he wasn't at home now, then where was he?

"Wait a minute!" he said. "I know this place. I've been here many times. This is Brighton beach!"

He turned to see the Palace Pier stretching majestically out into the sea. "There's the pier," exclaimed Charles. "I've been there with my mum and dad."

"That's right," said his great-grandfather. "The Palace Pier, although some bright spark decided to change its name and if you look over there, that's the West Pier, but in your time it's nothing more than a few rusting poles, sticking out of the shingle."

"That's right," said Charles, who was getting very excited now, "but my mum can remember walking on the West Pier when she was a little girl," and sure enough, looking even more like a palace than the Palace Pier, the West Pier stood proudly in the water, with its domed roofs and gilded iron-work. It looked exotic and beautiful, as if it could withstand anything, even the passage of time…

But suddenly, Charles realised that something wasn't right here. Brighton looked different and sure enough, when he gazed over the railings, the beach, which should have been full of people relaxing in the sun, was deserted. There were no laughing children playing in the sea, only lonely waves, which curled along the shore-line and a beach covered in long coils of razor-sharp barbed wire.

"They look an awful lot like vicious snakes waiting to pounce," Charles thought.

"That's to protect this island from our enemy," said Jam-Jar, seeing his gaze.

"The Nazis?" asked Charles, worriedly.

"Yes. A vicious enemy," said his great-grandfather, "who wishes to destroy everything, including our freedom and what we stand for!"

Charles cast his eyes to the sparkling water, so peaceful now and calm in the morning sun. Bubbles of salty sea foam fizzed and popped in the sand, as the waves retreated to the deeper safety of the all-embracing surf, leaving a chatter of bright pebbles running after them. A lone seagull called and for a moment Charles felt sad, until the sounds of the road behind him caught his attention.

He turned and saw people walking along the promenade, going about their normal daily business, seemingly unconcerned by the menace, which lurked unseen beyond the waves.

"Don't worry," said Jam-Jar, inclining his head toward the sea. "They don't win," and his eyes twinkled. Charles looked at his great-grandfather and his great-grandfather looked at him and the smile they shared was golden in the sun.

"You look so much like your mother," said Jam-Jar, "but your eyes, they're a different colour."

"My mother says they're the colour of the sea on a winter's day," replied Charles.

"Grey with a little green – a bit like my eyes," observed Jam-Jar thoughtfully, "Tawny in some lights," and he smiled again at his great-grandson, a warm smile that filled Charles with confidence that this was going to be a really big adventure.

He was still trying to take it all in – the people in their different clothes, the old cars that he knew his mother liked so much, the sounds, which were different somehow, calmer and less busy, when suddenly he heard a low, monotonous hum, approaching from across the waves. The hair on the back of his neck stood on end. It sounded like an angry wasp.

Everyone looked up and out to sea at a tiny, black dot in the sky, which was rapidly growing from a pin-prick into a shape they all recognised - a plane.

Somebody said, "It's alright. It's one of our boys. No mistake," and people visibly relaxed a little, as they stood and watched, hands on hips, or shielding eyes, as they looked at the fast-approaching plane silhouetted against the bright morning sun, when suddenly, it turned at an angle and flew along the length of the beach. Only then could they clearly see that it was a grey plane, a Messerschmitt, with its frightening symbol of hatred, a Swastika, emblazoned on the tail fin.

It flew close enough for Charles to see the pilot in the cockpit when, quite shockingly, it suddenly opened fire on the shoreline. Little puffs of air seemed to send mini explosions of sand and shingle up the beach, as the strafing fire drew closer and closer to the promenade, where people were standing, almost too stunned to move.

As if a spell had been broken, everyone ran and dived for cover, including Charles and Jam-Jar.

"Don't be scared," said Jam-Jar, as they hid behind a bench. "We're only shadows here. No one can see us. We can't be hurt. You're safe with me."

"Why are we hiding then?"

"I don't know," replied Jam-Jar and they both laughed.

As quickly as it had begun, the attack was over and the Messerschmitt flew away across the sea. People started to emerge, unhurt, from their hiding places, dusted themselves down and laughed at their folly.

"Cor, I'll be blowed. Chancin' 'es luck, that one, wa'n't 'ee?" one man said, whose glasses were still all askew. "Nearly blew me 'ead off!"

"'avin' one last pop at us, before 'ee went 'ome for tea, I'll be bound," said a woman.

"Serves us right for standin' and gawping at it like a load of daft ha'perths!" said another.

"One of our boys, my foot!" said the man, who had spoken originally. "I dun 'arf feel a right fool now! Well, at least none of us got 'urt."

Seeing the funny side, everyone laughed and then went on their way. A few said, "Ta da duck," good-naturedly to each other and then life went back to normal.

"Amazing lot, aren't we!" said his great-grandfather, pride deep in his voice. "Although, when France was invaded, we thought it was all over for us!"

"What do you mean, Grandad?"

"I'll show you, sweetheart. Come and look at this."

"Over there," said his great-grandfather, pointing towards the sea, "across the English Channel, is France. It's so close, you can actually see it from some parts of the English coast and on the 10th May, France was invaded by the Germans."

Charles followed his great-grandfather's gaze out over the waves to where the horizon met the sky. There was a slight sea fret forming out in the channel and beyond the hazy deeps, Charles imagined the coast of France burdened by the weight of a huge darkness that hung over the land. He saw it massing slowly, but surely, forming and coalescing like a great swarm of vicious wasps, all as one mind, smothering its victims and obliterating all with its evil. It made Charles shudder to think of all those innocent people there, watching their skies turn dark with a thick cloud of oppression, which at this very moment was gathering strength, ready to turn its hateful gaze on him and fling all its vile aggression at this little sparkling island home set in a silver sea.

Chapter 5 - The Triumph of Evil

The sun shone warmly on Charles' face, the sea sparkled brightly, but the Palace Pier he knew so well was silent. It seemed strange to Charles how quiet it was, a place he had only ever seen thronging with people eating ice-creams and doughnuts, whilst being dive-bombed by hungry sea-gulls. Now the threat from the skies was very different.

"Before I show you what happened in May," said Jam-Jar, "I need to show you what it was we had to fear, what came before that.

"You see, before the Second World War, a lot of people here just didn't realise how popular Hitler had become in Germany, or how nasty he really was. His followers, called the Brown Shirts, had been going around and frightening and intimidating an awful lot of people, many of whom were Jewish."

"Why would he want to hurt Jewish people?"

"I know, Charles – it makes no sense at all, but there were a lot of people in Germany, who felt the same way, who didn't like the Jewish people just because they were different. Many of these hateful people were genuinely nasty, but others were just ordinary men, women and children, who had somehow allowed this twisted notion about Jewish people to fester and grow in their minds, too, unchecked by any reasonable thought. It just became fashionable to think this way about Jewish people. People, who had been neighbours all their lives, whose children had grown up together, suddenly turned on their friends, because they were Jewish. It was completely illogical and the ones who didn't feel this way about their neighbours, were too afraid to help."

"I don't understand, Jam-Jar!"

"'All that is necessary for the triumph of evil is that good men do nothing.' A famous man called Edmund Burke said that a very long time ago and it still holds true today."

"What does it mean, Jam-Jar?"

"It means that if good people don't stand up to evil, then evil has won."

Charles looked thoughtfully out to sea, thinking about the evil festering across the waves and thought of those poor, frightened people.

Then, Charles asked a question, fearful of the answer, but guessing what it might be. "Did they hate Jewish children, too?"

At that, Jam-Jar turned his head and looking out to sea, closed his eyes. Then heaving a great, shuddering sigh, he gently looked at Charles.

"Yes," he said, simply.

That one word fell on Charles like a hammer blow. He felt sick with shock. His great-grandfather rested a hand on Charles' shoulder. The hand was strong, but gentle.

"There were some good people, though, who did help, even if all they could do was something small, but at least they tried. Any act of kindness and goodness is worth doing, no matter how small, because it always has an effect and kindness was much in need in those times."

A lone seagull was bobbing on the waves. His companions had flown away. The sun had disappeared behind a cloud, one single cloud in that beautiful clear sky, but enough to cast a shadow on the scene. Jam-Jar looked back at Charles.

"It was well known that Hitler had ordered the killing of anyone who didn't support him in June 1934 in what was called, 'The Night of the Long Knives'."

"The Night of the Long Knives! That's a strange name!" exclaimed Charles.

"I know," replied his great-grandfather. "It sounds funny, but it was no joke for the people Hitler had bumped off; some were people who had actually supported him in the past, but who had fallen out of favour with him. Later, in The Night of Glass, or Kristallnacht, in November 1938, Hitler ordered all Jewish synagogues, shops and businesses to be attacked. There was broken glass everywhere, hence the name."

"Why did Hitler order this?" exclaimed Charles, shocked.

"Because the man was evil," said Jam-Jar, simply, "and, somehow, he infected too many other people with his hateful doctrine." The sadness in his voice trailed away, as Charles imagined streets littered with glass, shop fronts burning, more glass breaking, crunching glass being broken under-foot, broken glass sparkling in the sunlight, reflecting in the glistening tears of children, as their parents looked on helplessly at the destruction of their homes and livelihoods. Charles blinked away the scene, but the image lingered on.

"Did anyone help the Jewish people?" asked Charles.

"Some brave people sheltered Jewish families and helped them to escape, often at the risk of their own personal safety, like the people who helped Anne Frank's family in the Netherlands."

"Oh yes! We've learnt about her in school, but she didn't survive!" said Charles, sadly.

"No, she didn't. Unfortunately, like too many people, her family underestimated the speed of Hitler's power grab and by the time they realised the danger they were in, it was too late to leave the country. The boarders were closed to them, which is why they had to go into hiding. Eventually, though, someone betrayed them and they were all taken prisoner and perished. Only Anne Frank's father survived."

Suddenly, Charles heard screams and scuffles and realised that he was in a tall apartment block...

...Two families, their children held close, are standing quietly, staring in fear at a door. They know it looks like an innocent bookshelf from the other side. They stand there, fearing their secret refuge has been discovered, hoping that what they can hear is not Nazi soldiers, but sensing the worst. Those scuffles and shouts on the other side of that door, are becoming too loud, too close to be safe. Slowly, the apprehension turns to a sickening dread, the awful realisation dawns on them - they have been found. Books are heard being ripped from the shelves, merciless hands searching all over for the secret handle, thumpings and scrapes tear the door away, the door seemingly reluctant to reveal the frightened family behind, suddenly faced with their worst terror made all too real, with nowhere to run and nowhere to hide. Shaking children's hands try to tie tiny shoes, grown too small after months in hiding; parents' hands cover theirs reassuringly, as tears fall, knowing no reassurance will ever be found again, whilst behind them the shouts of angry German soldiers order them to leave...

Charles was stunned by this awful image and involuntarily, he reached for his great-grandfather's warm, strong hand, which instinctively tightened around his.

"Anne Frank's father survived," said his great-grandfather, gently, "and after the Nazis had been defeated, he went back to the apartment where his family had sheltered and he found his daughter's diary. He had it published, to act as a reminder of a time when evil was allowed to take hold and to act as a warning of what we must do to stop it from ever happening again. Others did get out, though, Charles and made it to places like Britain. Thousands of children were saved in this way."

"Did the children's parents come with them?"

"Not all the time," Jam-Jar replied. "There were strict controls in many countries, including Britain and America on the numbers of refugees they would accept, but in 1938, the British government agreed to relax those rules and in the nine months before the Second World War started, the United Kingdom rescued ten thousand mostly Jewish children from Germany, Austria, Czechoslovakia, Poland and the city of Danzig and placed them in foster homes around the United Kingdom. British peopled actually volunteered to help in the rescue effort, risking their own lives in the process and the government sent them over to arrange for the children to be evacuated through the Children's Transport program called 'Kindertransport'. Most of the children were transported by train to the Netherlands first and then by ship to Britain, because, amazingly, the Nazis had agreed to this evacuation, but said that the evacuations mustn't block German ports."

"They'd agreed to it?" Charles exclaimed.

"Yes, sweetheart. I'd like to think that it was out of a sense of humanity, but I don't think it was. It just made them look less bad, but then they made it difficult for passports to be granted for the children anyway.

"A huge fundraising effort was organised in Britain and the British people raised half a million pounds in six months, a huge sum in those days, which paid for the children to be brought to this country and placed with families here, but sadly, many of these children never saw their own families again and when their countries were eventually invaded by the Germans, no more children could be rescued. Many who had made it as far as the Netherlands, still didn't make it out in time and were swept up in the Holocaust, never to be seen again. The last ship to leave the Netherlands was four days after the Nazis had invaded the country. As the last ship full of children left the Dutch port for Britain, on 14th May 1940, Dutch cities were being bombed and the Dutch army surrendered to Germany."

"That's awful," said Charles, sadly. "Those children must have been so scared."

He imagined standing on the deck of a ship, watching a city in flames, disappearing beyond the horizon and thought about how those children must have felt knowing their parents were left behind amidst the danger and destruction of the approaching evil.

"Yes, sweetheart. They must have been very scared," Jam-Jar replied quietly, and he looked at his great-grandson with his kind, gentle eyes. "Children evacuated from Europe to Britain. Children evacuated from Britain to Canada. So many children separated from their families. So much pain, so much loss," and suddenly he wrapped his strong arms around Charles and held him tightly. Charles felt safe and knew in his heart, that this big, strong man would do anything to protect him.

"There was one British man, called Nicholas Winton, who saved nearly seven hundred children in Czechoslovakia from certain death at the hands of the Nazis. His motto was, 'If something isn't blatantly impossible, then there must be a way of doing it.' He decided to try to organise the evacuation of as many children as possible. He saw for himself, what conditions were like for these people and many years later he said,

'I began to realise what suffering there is when armies start to march.'

In his mind, Charles saw a street, with high buildings and long queues of people lining the road, their desperate faces, etched with worry. He was shocked at the intensity of the feeling. He saw those frightened parents, clutching small babies in their arms and holding tightly the small hands of their little children, who were clinging to them for safety; fathers and mothers arguing with officials to at least allow their children to leave the country; some lucky few, their faces lighting up with relief and joy when the whole family was granted a visa, but all too many, the fear turning to dread, as the official shook his head, the stamp plunging down onto the paper, their fate sealed and all the while the distant sound of marching boots and rolling tanks seemed to be carried on the wind, a premonition of the evil to come.

"How did Nicholas Winton manage to help?" asked Charles.

His great-grandfather replied, "He worked very hard raising money and getting visas for the children and arranging families to foster them here. He arranged all the transport himself and managed to save nearly seven hundred children."

Charles saw a crowded station platform, with families thronging by a train about to leave; some rushing almost too late for it, caught up in the mass of frightened people; children hugging parents; fear floating in the air; a sense of danger and urgency; hurried kisses and last hugs; children prized from their parents' arms; those last, few, precious moments ending with the train labouring out of the station; parents, lost to sight, disappearing in the smoke, stalked by an unseen menace; their calls lingering as the darkness descends.

"There were meant to be many more." Jam-Jar's words echoed as if down a long tunnel, as he looked at his great-grandson. His mild, gentle eyes had the look of a parent. "There was one more train load of children, which was planned to leave Czechoslovakia on

1st September 1939, but on that day, Hitler invaded Poland and all boarders controlled by Germany were closed and those children never got out. Just one day too late! The memory of those children he never saved, haunted Nicholas Winton all his life."

"That's so sad!" Charles paused. "But he did save so many. He did save them!"

"Yes, sweetheart. He was a very good man."

Charles watched the rolling waves, as he listened intently to his great-grandfather's voice. The seagulls circled overhead, some had joined their lone companion in the sea and were bobbing on the water, looking for fish. The grand old buildings lining the road gleamed in the morning sun, people passed by on the promenade and the bustling road bustled on.

"A perfectly ordinary scene," thought Charles. "How could any of this turn to evil?"

Suddenly, his great-grandfather's voice broke through his reverie. He seemed to be reciting a poem.

'First, they came for the socialists, and
I did not speak out—
Because I was not a socialist.
Then they came for the trade unionists, and
I did not speak out—
Because I was not a trade unionist.
Then they came for the Jews, and
I did not speak out—
Because I was not a Jew.
Then they came for me—and there was no one left to speak for me.'

"That poem is by a German priest called, Martin Niemoller. Even he was fooled by Hitler to begin with, but he soon saw Hitler for who he really was and he started to speak out against him, along with a group of other German clergymen, opposed to Hitler, but it was too late and he was imprisoned in a concentration camp.

"But didn't anyone try to stop Hitler?" Charles asked.

"Yes, there was a group of young German University students, who called themselves The White Rose, who wrote and distributed leaflets which criticised Hitler, but two of its members, Sophia Scholl and her brother, Hans were arrested and sadly, executed in 1943. Not long after their deaths, though, one of their leaflets was smuggled out of Germany to Britain and millions of copies were dropped by the RAF over Germany as propaganda and then the following year, there was a plot by German army officers, led by an Officer called Claus von Stauffenberg, to try to assassinate Hitler and remove the Nazi party from power, but their attempt failed. However, it demonstrated to the Allies that there were people in Germany, who wanted to be helped to set themselves free from that evil man."

Then Charles thought for a minute. "Isn't that what Churchill used to call Hitler – 'that man'."

"You're right," Jam-Jar replied. "He hated Hitler and all he stood for and by calling him, 'that man', it made him sound less powerful and just an object of scorn." Charles imagined Churchill curling his lip in disgust as he said it.

Jam-Jar continued, "Lots of people used the same expression in the late 1930's, when they saw Hitler on newsreels or in the newspapers. They were getting so tired of seeing him, they'd just tut and say, 'It's that man again' and luckily for us, we had Churchill on our side. He was very good at speeches and persuasion and he needed to be, because at the time, our then Prime Minister, Neville Chamberlain just wanted to appease Hitler."

"Appease! What does that mean?"

"Appeasement, Charles is when you try to be nice to a bully and give him a little of what he wants from you, say, some of your sweets, for example, but that's not enough for him. He wants all your sweets and because you didn't say 'no' to begin with, he thinks he can just take them all and you won't stop him."

In his mind, Charles saw, as if in a cartoon, two little boys on a school playground, one dressed in an oversized Nazi uniform and the other, smaller one, dressed in a suit, several sizes too big for him. The bigger boy in the Nazi uniform, is surrounded by other big boys in oversized brown shirts that look ridiculously baggy. They are sneering at the little boy in the suit, who is about to give some of his sweets to the horrible boy, but he knows that the horrible boy will be back for the rest later, because he handed over his sweets so quickly the first time. He knows that he is just buying himself some time, before the horrible boy takes the rest....

Charles now understood what appeasement was and he could see that it could never have worked.

"You see, Charles, in Czechoslovakia, where Nicholas Winton saved all those children, there was a large area of land called the Sudetenland, which was on the borders of Germany. A lot of Germans lived there and before the war began, they started to demand that the Sudetenland become part of Germany, even though a lot of Czechoslovakians lived there too and they, naturally, didn't want to become part of Germany. Hitler had already helped himself to Austria for the same reason, because there were a lot of Germans living there.

"But Hitler threatened war and our Prime Minister, Neville Chamberlain and the leaders of France, went to Munich to meet Hitler. They all agreed that Britain wouldn't declare war on Germany if it took the Sudetenland, as long as Germany didn't try to invade the rest of Czechoslovakia. Winston Churchill was furious about this agreement, but he had no power to stop it because he wasn't Prime Minister at that point, you see. So, Germany annexed or took the Sudetenland and made it part of Germany and this is why so many families were trying to flee the country and why Nicholas Winton stepped in to help.

"But, as you can imagine, that wasn't enough for Hitler. He wanted more. Not content with just having the Sudetenland, he broke his promise and invaded Czechoslovakia itself, and he didn't stop there. Next, he invaded Poland."

"This was when Britain and France *finally* declared war on Germany on the 3rd September, 1939. Immediately after the announcement, air-raid sirens went off around the country. That put the 'wind up' people, I can tell you, but then, for nearly eight months, nothing happened and little was done to stop Hitler." Charles' great-grandfather shrugged in frustration. "Everyone started calling it the 'Phoney War', but there were those in government, people like Churchill, who were itching to get started and take this bully on, but Prime Minister, Neville Chamberlain was having none of it," Jam-Jar said, crossly. His eyes looked angry under his knit eye-brows; jaw clenched tight.

"When Hitler invaded Denmark and Norway in April 1940, French and British forces fought hard to help the Norwegian forces defend their homeland from German invasion, but once France itself was invaded, France had to withdraw to protect its own borders and the British eventually withdrew too, much to Churchill's disgust. It took sixty-two days for the Germans to beat Norway. That's the longest any country, apart from the Soviet Union, held out against the Germans before being invaded. A brave lot, the Norwegians and it was Norway's King, King Haakon VII, who refused to let his country just surrender to the German's; instead, he urged his people to see themselves as a country under occupation, not willing hosts of German forces. He knew how important it was for his people to keep their pride and honour, even under German occupation.

"King Haakon and his son wanted to stay, but the people pleaded with him to leave with his family, so that he wouldn't become a puppet king with Hitler pulling his strings. The retreating British Royal Navy evacuated the King and his family, and they came to Britain for safety along with the exiled Norwegian government. The Norwegians never forgot the help we gave to their country and their King and that's why they send us a Christmas Tree every year, the big one you see in Trafalgar Square. It's to say, 'Thank-you'."

Charles thought of the beautiful tree he had seen every Christmas in Trafalgar Square, glittering with lights, tall and strong, grown in a snow-filled, Norwegian forest, sent every year, uniting two nations in gratitude and respect.

Jam-Jar continued, "However, the brave example which King Haakon set was completely at odds with the actions of our Prime Minister, Neville Chamberlain, who was starting to lose the support of his own party members!" his great-grandfather continued. "He didn't seem strong enough. People were beginning to think that he didn't have his finger on the pulse, that he wasn't really taking charge of the situation. He wasn't even really making any effective decisions about how to increase food production in this country." Charles' great-grandfather was sounding more annoyed.

"What happened in Norway was a great disaster for the Allies. The Germans took the Norwegian ports far too easily and very little was done to stop them. Once the Germans had taken the ports, Norway was theirs, but Chamberlain called it a success for us, because we hadn't lost too many troops, but the free world lost Norway to the Germans!" said Jam-Jar in exasperation. "The war might have been much shorter if Chamberlain and his cabinet had shown more decisive action. The problem was, WE HAD A GOVERNMENT OF APPEASERS TRYING TO FIGHT A WAR. Their hearts weren't in it. Prime Minister Chamberlain and his foreign secretary, Halifax, didn't actually believe we could win."

As his great-grandfather continued to speak, Charles was becoming aware of a tension in his skull, like a dull headache before a thunderstorm. He was starting to feel the same frustration that his great-grandfather felt, that the whole country must have felt as they waited for the action, which never seemed to come.

Charles looked around him. Everything appeared the same; the people strolling by, enjoying the warm sun, the sea, so blue and serene, seagulls above circling in the summer sky, their calls mingling with the sounds of the waves breaking on the shoreline, but the atmosphere was getting heavier, more oppressive, a pressure was building, like an over-inflated balloon, which at any moment might go 'pop' and Charles looked out across to the horizon, to where he had earlier seen the sea-fret forming. It looked different. The haze had spread. It was larger, darker somehow and it seemed to be rolling across the water towards him. His heart skipped a beat. The pulse in his skull was growing louder, like a ticking clock. Rumbles of thunder could be heard in the distance, bubbling up from across the English Channel. The sound changed. It developed a beat, a march, the sound of boots marching along dusty roads, tanks rolling in with the storm-clouds. The ticking clock grew louder and more insistent and from somewhere nearby, as if inside his own skull, he heard a bell tolling, tolling the hour unceasingly, tolling the hour of reckoning. There was no escape. Charles knew the hour had come.

Suddenly, a crack of thunder exploded overhead. The deafening sound rang in his ears, as if he'd just put his head inside an enormous bell. For a split second there was whiteout – the blinding light stunning him in its intensity, then instantly the scene before him flashed to black and white, drained of colour, as if in an old photograph, the frozen image of all those people, seared into the retina at the back of his eyes. His mind screamed in fear, but no sound escaped his mouth.

All around him, the air fizzed with electricity, as the image before him split apart and cracked into a thousand pieces…only to be replaced by rows and rows of leather benches, all facing each other. The violent rumble of tanks, the marching beat of boots, the insistent ticking of the clock and the tolling of the bell all merged into one terrifying ringing in his ears, which, like the passing summer storm, ebbed away as quickly as it had come, fading as his breathing calmed and heart-beat slowed a little.

And then, beside him, he heard the soothing voice of his great-grandfather.

"The Palace of Westminster, the home of Parliament, where our British Government sits," he heard him say, quietly, beside him.

Charles blinked and looked around him. Sure enough, they were in the Houses of Parliament, in the gallery of the House of Commons, looking down at all the commotion below.

Noises and shouts swirled all around him, the words of these braying people, barking at each other, like so many farm animals, seemed to float in the air around his head, like captions in a comic. The room was thick with tension and paper fluttered in the air as angry MP's shook their order papers at each other, but one voice rose above them all…

"…it seems to me that the whole of recent events – not only in Norway, but the whole conduct of the war up to date – calls for searching inquiry…"

"Eh up!" said Jam-Jar, "That's Leo Amery, Conservative MP. He made this speech on the 7th May, 1940. He's had more than enough of Chamberlain and his cabinet," and Charles looked on, as the words seemed to float past him... His head was still throbbing, and the ticking beat of his heart was still loud in his ears, as Leo Amery spoke again,

"*Wars are won, not by explanation after the event but by foresight, by clear decision and by swift action...We cannot go on as we are. There must be a change...*"

"You see, Amery, like many in Parliament," said Jam-Jar, "thought Chamberlain had been fine as a peacetime Prime Minister, but he was no good in wartime. He thought Chamberlain was too cautious, that he lacked FIGHTING SPIRIT!" exclaimed Jam-Jar. Amery's words continued to float past Charles, swirling in his mind, as the threatening sound of marching boots receded slowly.

"*Vision, daring, swiftness and consistency of decision are the very essence of victory...Somehow or other we must get into the Government men who can match our enemies in fighting spirit, in daring, in resolution and in thirst for victory...We are fighting to-day for our life, for our liberty, for our all; we cannot go on being led as we are...*"

The clamour of cheering and 'Hear, hears', filled the room.

"Order, order, order," the Speaker's words rang out. "The Honourable Member for Hackney, South."

"Ah. Mr Herbert Morrison! Now it's May 8th," said Jam-Jar. "Morrison was a member of the Labour party. He had no faith in Chamberlain at all."

Morrisons words echoed around the chamber, "*Of all the dangers to be found in Government in time of war, perhaps there are two that are most important – one is bad ministers and the other is tired ministers.*"

"Ooo," Jam-Jar chuckled. "I bet Chamberlain doesn't like that, at all."

Charles' heart was still pounding in his chest.

Morrison continued, "*I have the genuine apprehension that if these men remain in office, we run the grave risk of losing this war.*"

"Ooo, ouch!" Jam-Jar laughed.

Charles' heartbeat rapidly, knocking against his chest, as if trying to escape, but it wasn't only his own heart he could hear. There was another beat sounding in the air. He turned his head this way and that trying to locate it, as Morrison's words filled the room,

"We are fighting for our lives. Humanity is struggling for its freedom."

...and still that heartbeat pounded all around him. The very atmosphere in the room pulsed and throbbed, expanding and contracting in time with the rhythm of Charles' own heart.

"We have assets in this war, the qualities of our people. We have for the winning of this war, British ability, British spirit and British determination. The qualities of our people are great, the abilities of our people are considerable, the spirit of our people is high."

His voice swirled in Charles' mind.

"But if that ability, spirit and determination are to be used, they must be led by Ministers who will command the respect of the population and whose lead the population will be happy and proud to follow."

Charles breathed deeply. His chest swelled and now he was sure that the heartbeat he could hear was not just his own. He looked around him, at his great-grandfather standing so tall and strong beside him and with a shock, he realised from where that heartbeat came. It came from the very walls of the room, a beat which answered his own. The building was alive, breathing deeply, in and out, in and out. Charles could feel an immense strength and energy, a powerful presence, vibrant and alive all around him.

"Yes, Charles," spoke his great-grandfather, suddenly. "This building *is* alive, alive with history; nearly a thousand years of history summed up in this idea of Parliament, of Democracy. This is what we're fighting for." He gestured to the room, "We are fighting for the preservation of democracy *itself*! We are fighting the great fight for the preservation of good, in the face of overwhelming evil."

"Order, order, order," the Speaker's words filled the room again and rose up to the ceilinged heights of the vaulted hall...

...and Jam-Jar's words mingled with them. Charles watched them go, floating by like clouds after a storm, as the rows of benches for a moment floated on the rolling waves before disappearing. Blinking away the vision, he saw the beach once more before him.

"At the moment," said Jam-Jar, watching with Charles, as the words disappeared into the brightening sky, "Hitler is getting very sure of himself. Like all bullies, he really doesn't think that anyone will stand up to him. Right now, he thinks that everyone is too scared of him and his army."

"Well, by the sounds of things, Jam-Jar," said Charles, looking out at the sea, "he's got that wrong!"

"You're right there, my boy!"

The tolling bell had ceased, the clouds had rolled away, the thunder had retreated back across the waves, but still it rumbled angrily in the distance...

...and from all around him, Charles could hear the quiet ticking of a clock, like a pulse, that same heartbeat, again, which mingled with his own, but now it was taken up by a beat of another kind – a drumbeat, slow and quiet, but strong and deep. It resonated in Charles' ears. It seemed to come from beneath his feet, from beneath the pavement, from beneath the road, from beneath the buildings, from beneath the town and pulsing from the hills and fields, which folded themselves around the streets, a pulse from the earth itself, the heartbeat of the land. The land was waking. Charles knew it had heard the call.

A shiver of anticipation shuddered in his chest. He faced the sea, the land behind him strong and reassuring. He felt rooted to the earth, as he imagined tanks spreading out over the countries of Europe like a swarm of ants turning everything black and obliterating everything in its path, but the strength of the earth beneath his feet gave him courage. The drum beats became louder and more intense.

"All was not lost," said Jam-Jar reassuringly. "Almost at the last minute, when it was almost too late, Britain's Prime Minister, Neville Chamberlain was forced to resign by his own Conservative party, because they could see that it was time for action and who do you think was made the new Prime Minister?"

Charles didn't need long to think. He heard those drumbeats, louder now and more insistent and he imagined that little boy in the suit again, facing the big bully...

...when suddenly, in walks another boy in a suit, a suit that actually fits this new boy quite well, and he stands beside the smaller boy and he tells him to put his sweets back in his pocket.

The horrible boy is sizing up this new arrival and he can tell that he's tougher, that he's made of sterner stuff. He's just trying to work out how much of a fight he's got on his hands with this new boy, when in walks some more, quite big lads. They stand beside this new boy and his little companion in the oversized suit.

...and the little Hitler looks at the not so little Churchill and at his friends standing beside him and the little Hitler realises that he's not going to win this war so easily...

"Winston Churchill!" exclaimed Charles. "Winston Churchill was made Prime Minister!"

The drumbeats sounded loud and sure.

"That's right, Charles," said his great-grandfather, speaking up over the noise of that beating drum. "He was made Prime Minister on 10th May 1940. He was sixty-five years old and people thought that he was too old and past it. They had no idea of what this man was capable. He'd always been underestimated, but this was his time, now, at this point in history; he saw this moment as his destiny, something for which he had been preparing his whole life and by some twist of fate, on the very same day that Hitler's army invaded the Netherlands, Belgium and France – three countries in just one day, Churchill was made Prime-Minister and now we, finally, had the right man for the job."

The drum still sounded all around them, as if rallying troops to war.

"Churchill didn't panic. He could have given in there and then, but he didn't. He appointed Ernest Bevin to recruit more workers for the factories and to increase coal production and he appointed Lord Beaverbrook to be minister of Aircraft Production to build more aircraft including fighter planes."

"Fighter planes!"

"That's right. SPITFIRES!" they both chimed together to the sound of one almighty drum-roll.

Chapter 6 - The Battle of France and Dunkirk

The drumbeats faded with the thunder, rolling away across the town into the encircling hills, where they continued to rumble threateningly, as if waiting.

Charles' head was still aching a little, as he tried hard to concentrate.

"So," he said, trying to get everything clear in his mind, "it's May 10th 1940 and Hitler, who has already invaded most of the countries of Europe, has now invaded France and on the same day, when it's almost too late, Churchill's been made Prime Minister?"

"That's right, sweetheart, and the amazing thing is that the new government is a coalition government that includes members of all the parties, Conservative, Labour and Liberal, who for once, have all put aside their differences to fight this common enemy; all the best people fighting this war together, regardless of their political affiliation.

"Churchill still has a struggle on his hands, though, from one of his own cabinet members, Lord Halifax, who believes that our war against Germany is over and that we cannot possibly win."

"Wait, let me get this straight," said Charles. "Lord Halifax is on Churchill's team, even though he doesn't believe in fighting Hitler. Why is he there then?"

"Halifax is Chamberlain's friend and Churchill knows he has to have Halifax in his cabinet, because Halifax had lots of friends in government, who could make things very difficult for Churchill and maybe could even force him to resign, so it's safer to have him on the team, than making trouble for him from the outside. As the old saying goes," said Jam-Jar, "'Keep your friends close, but your enemies closer'."

"But, why is Halifax like this?" asked Charles.

"Well, Lord Halifax, like his friend Chamberlain, genuinely believes that a war can be avoided by letting Hitler take whatever he wants, as long as he doesn't invade Britain. They both think that appeasement is the best approach, even though they know that Hitler can't be trusted. Halifax still wants to negotiate a peace with Hitler and he's putting a lot of pressure on Churchill to do this."

"So, at this point," said Charles, "even though Churchill is in power, he could lose his job, because Halifax thinks that what he's doing is wrong!"

"Exactly! Right now," said Jam-Jar, looking out to sea, "Our troops, the British Expeditionary Force, the BEF, which is most of the British army, is out there in France, trying to help the French defend themselves from German invasion and back home, Churchill is having to argue with Lord Halifax as to why it would be a good idea *not* to surrender, but to keep fighting. The odds are stacked against us. Defeat seems inevitable, but in France, the Prime Minister there, a man called Reynaud, also wants to fight on and resist the German invasion, along with his General, Charles de Gaulle,"

"Charles!" exclaimed Charles.

"Yes, a good strong name, Charles," said his great-grandfather, smiling at him.

"Unfortunately, though, there's also too many people in Reynaud's cabinet, who want to give in to Hitler's demands, particularly a man called, Petain," said Jam-Jar, grimacing, "who, like Halifax, is putting Reynaud under enormous pressure to surrender. Churchill and de Gaulle are doing everything they can to support Reynaud, but it's looking more hopeless and time is running out," he said, ominously.

"Why is time running out?" Charles asked, as a new sound filled the air, a ticking clock, keeping time with the distant, tense rolling of the drum.

"German troops have invaded France via a route that nobody expected and it's caught everyone off guard, literally."

"How have they got into France, Jam-Jar?"

"The German Army's Panzer tanks have surprised everyone by entering France via Belgium, through the forest of the Ardennes, which everyone thought was impossible with such a large army. They've cut off the British and French First Army from the rest of the allies. Right now, it seems like the game's up. The BEF is trapped at Dunkirk and it looks like they'll have to surrender, or be completely destroyed and Lord Halifax is really starting to apply the pressure on Churchill."

Suddenly, Charles was aware of being in a small, windowless room, crammed full of furniture, with a long table and lots of chairs. Maps and charts hung on the walls. The atmosphere was close and claustrophobic and raised voices filled the stagnant air.

'If you were satisfied that matters vital to the independence of this country were unaffected, would you be prepared to discuss terms?'[12]

"That's Lord Halifax," said Jam-Jar, inclining his head to a very tall, thin man, with a receding hairline and a long serious face.

Halifax's voice was tense and there was a note of impatience in his tone.

"Churchill's having to play it very carefully," observed Jam-Jar, talking quietly to Charles, "If he looks like he won't negotiate with Hitler, he risks looking unreasonable and alienating Conservative politicians loyal to Chamberlain and Halifax. He's got to pretend to be listening to this so-called 'reason', but really, Churchill's just biding his time."

Charles cast his gaze across the room and saw the man himself, Churchill, sitting calmly at the long table, hands resting on the arms of his chair. It amazed Charles how powerful this seeming old man was. His personality filled the room, as did the smoke of his cigar clasped between his old fingers, swirling around him, enveloping him with an air of mystery. Vital energy poured from him like a breaking dam. The lined, old face was strong, courage and determination simmering just beneath the surface of the portly frame; a coiled spring in a 'Jack-in-the-box', as if a much younger warrior was cloaked inside the old man's clothes. Charles could well imagine Churchill taking on a whole army of Nazis single-handedly.

The room fizzed and crackled, the two men hurling words at one another across the table, Halifax throwing his remarks at Churchill like barely concealed knives; Churchill's remarks flung back, as if wielding a sledgehammer wrapped in a blanket.

The civilised air of vaguely concealed anger was palpable. It was a heady mix of power struggle and personality, but Charles was in no doubt as to who was in charge. The energy flowed off Churchill like crackling electricity, prepared as he was, to lay down his own life to protect the land from an advancing evil that must be stopped at all costs.

Charles' great-grandfather felt it too. They both stood and looked on in silence, lest any sound might disturb this moment of history.

And then Churchill spoke. His tone was calm and measured. He chose his words carefully, knowing that what next was said would be of the gravest importance.

'I would be thankful to get out of our present difficulties on such terms, provided we retained the essentials and elements of our vital strength, even at the cost of some territory.'[13]

"He doesn't really mean it," whispered Jam-Jar. "Churchill does rifle-practice as often as he can. If the Nazis landed on these shores, he's already said he would sit with a machine gun in the middle of Whitehall and keep on firing at the enemy until all his ammunition was spent, even if he was the last person left standing. There's no way he's just happily going to give Hitler territory to stop him invading us. He's not even made any plans for his own evacuation if the country's invaded! He's got no intention of leaving us to our fate."

Charles shivered.

Suddenly, their attention was drawn to Churchill, who seemed to have spoken even before the words had left his lips. A whirlwind of energy, like a barrage of gun-fire before an advancing army, filled the room as Churchill sent his whole focus along the table towards the waiting Halifax.

THEN he spoke:

'But the only safe way is to convince Hitler that he cannot beat us and the only way we do that is to fight on.'[14]

Charles shivered as the room went dark and again, voices were heard like drawn swords, only more tense and more urgent this time.

"It's a few days later now, 28th May," said Jam-Jar, softly, in the darkness, "and Halifax is still going on about...?"

"Let me guess," piped up Charles, "Negotiating with Hitler!"

"Exactly! Can you imagine the pressure Churchill must have been under from all sides," Jam-Jar replied, as the light returned to reveal a similar scene and the same strong voice breaking through.

'It is impossible to imagine that Herr Hitler would be so foolish as to let us continue our rearmament. In effect, his terms would put us completely at his mercy. We should get no worse terms if we went on fighting, even if we were beaten...'[15]

"What does he mean, Jam-Jar?" whispered Charles.

"He means, sweetheart, that if we left Hitler to conquer the whole of Europe, there's no way that he would leave us alone and allow us to continue to rearm and build up our army. Hitler's terms may have been reasonable for us, but not for the countries left to the evils of Nazism. Churchill knows that this is about freedom for all, not just for us and that we have a duty to the rest of the world."

Suddenly, they heard Halifax speak,

'We cannot know what Hitler's terms might be unless we ask for them.'[16]

Churchill's reply was immediate,

'Nations which go down fighting rise again, but those which tamely surrender are finished.'[17]

Jam-Jar spoke quietly in Charles' ear, "He's had enough of Halifax now and he's decided to do something very clever. He's going to talk to the full Cabinet, the senior ministers of the government, leaving Chamberlain, Halifax and the rest of the War Cabinet out of the meeting. He's going to try to get the others on his side and prove to Halifax that the rest of them agree with him."

The scene shifted, abruptly. Once more they were in the Houses of Parliament and Churchill was standing in the Cabinet office before a large group of expectant people. Charles and his great-grandfather stood amongst the crowd. An air of excitement rippled through the room.

Suddenly, Churchill's words rang out:

"I have thought carefully in these last days whether it was part of my duty to consider entering into negotiations with That Man. But it was idle to think that, if we tried to make peace now, we should get better terms than if we fought it out. The Germans would demand our fleet – that would be called 'disarmament' – our naval bases, and much else. We should become a slave state...If this long island story of ours is to end at last, let it end only when each one of us lies (dead) upon the ground."[18] Those words floated through the group gathered there and struck a note in the hearts of all. When he had finished speaking, everyone rose to cheer and clap and shake his hand and many gave him hearty slaps on the back.

Charles heard one man say, *'Magnificent, he was quite magnificent. The man, and the only man we have, for this hour.'*[19]

"That's it!" said Jam-Jar, triumphantly. "Churchill's beaten Halifax. The majority of the cabinet support him now and Churchill knows he already has the support of the nation; 'a white glow,' he called it, this knowledge that he and the nation were united as one against Hitler. He said it runs 'through our Island from end to end',"[20] and Charles' great-grandfather spoke with a deep conviction that seemed to come from his very soul.

A shiver ran down Charles' spine, as he looked to where Churchill was standing flanked by his jubilant supporters. The room around them began to fade, leaving only Churchill still visible, standing proud, but it was as if Charles could see through him to the length and breadth of the land, which was glowing white with an energy channelling itself through this man and in that moment, it was as if another figure superimposed himself on the form of Churchill – a great warrior, powerful, tall and strong of resolve, hair flowing in the breeze, which seemed to come from nowhere and everywhere - sunrise on cliffs, cloak flowing, crown of gold glowing bright in the rising sun, eyes warm and shining, reflecting the light of a great sword at his side, sheathed in a magnificent scabbard enwrought with ancient symbols of magic.

"King Arthur!" Charles gasped in awe, transfixed by the scene. His great-grandfather grasped his hand and the two of them stood before the apparition in reverence and gratitude.

The great king unsheathed the sword, which emanated power. Holding it aloft, he faced the sea and the wind, his wise eyes deep pools of memory and knowledge. A beam of light from the rising sun struck the sword, as King Arthur clasped it by the hilt in both hands and plunged it into the clifftop, holding it before him, as he declared,

"Here and no further!" The words swirled in the air, potent and magical, words of challenge, words of command, words of great courage. The cliffs glowed as if in answer, whiter and whiter in the rising sun, lit from within by a great life-force. The land had heard, exhaling and waking like a slumbering giant...

The white light grew in intensity, till all that could be seen was the figure of Arthur himself, as if rooted to the ground, the life force of the sword injecting itself into the earth...and then, the king fixed his gaze on Charles, his mild, gentle eyes seeming to bore themselves into his heart.

"You will be tested and you will not be found wanting," and it was as if Charles felt the sword tip rest lightly on each shoulder and the weight of a sheathed sword appeared at his side, the belt fixed firmly around his hips, as the light grew in intensity, until all that remained was the shining face of Arthur, his companions flanking him in attendance of their lord, cloaks flowing, swords shining, till all was gone and they were no more.

Charles tore his eyes away, as the last point of light faded to nothingness and gazed, wide-eyed at his great-grandfather, who seemed equally amazed and breathless.

"What was that!" Charles exclaimed, emphasising each word slowly.

"A very great blessing!" his great-grandfather replied, and hugged him close, the words of the warrior king still ringing in his ears.

Chapter 7 – The Enigma!

They stood for a moment in the swirling nothingness, still clasping each other as the throbbing energy ebbed away, until they each became aware of a light tapping and clicking and bleeping and the distant sound of women's voices announcing fighter squadron locations and then from somewhere and nowhere the low, deep purr of an engine, a Merlin engine sparking into life. Suddenly, all was action and sound around them; scenes swirling in and out of focus and three words tapped out incessantly, as if on ticker tape: RADAR, ENIGMA, SPITIFIRE – RADAR, ENIGMA, SPITFIRE – RADAR, ENIGMA, SPITFIRE!

"Of course!" Jam-Jar exclaimed. "It's a message – a message to us. You see, Churchill knows this country has three things Germany doesn't have, which give us a great advantage, right now."

"What are they, Jam-Jar?"

"Three words: Radar, Enigma and SPITFIRES!"

"Spitfires! Of course!" exclaimed Charles, "and I think I know what radar is – that's the technology which uses radio waves to detect the speed of moving objects and how far away they are, especially planes and ships and submarines."

"That's right, Charles. Many countries have developed similar systems, but not to the same extent that Britain has and our Royal Air Force will be using it as part of its air defence capability to detect enemy planes during the Battle of Britain. The RAF's Radar system is the world's first early-warning Radar system. It's our secret weapon."

"But what's Enigma?" asked Charles.

"Have you and your friends ever sent secret messages to each other using a code?" asked his great-grandfather.

"Oh yes," said Charles, "already beginning to understand."

"And how do you and your friends understand the code?"

"You use a secret key," answered Charles.

"That's right. The key is a sort of separate code, which 'unlocks' the first one. Well, the Germans would send coded messages to each other using a special machine called an Enigma machine. The machine was used to turn ordinary messages into code and then used by the person receiving the message, to turn the code into an ordinary message again, but a key was needed to read the messages and it was changed regularly. The Polish managed to capture one of these devices and started work on breaking the code. They shared their information with Britain, who continued to work on breaking the code at a place called Bletchley Park, where the first wartime Enigma messages were decoded on 23rd January 1940 and it was here at Bletchley Park that a man called Alan Turing along with a man called Tommy Flowers, later developed the world's first computer, in 1944, to break the codes of the Enigma machine and a much more complicated code called the Lorenz cipher."

"Computer!" exclaimed Charles.

"Yes, computer, but it was huge, filling a whole room and it had teams of people to look after it. It was called 'Colossus'!"

"That's a funny name," thought Charles.

"But before 'Colossus', there were the 'Bombes'!" said Jam-Jar mysteriously.[21]

"And what were those?" asked Charles, expecting an obvious answer.

Suddenly, he was in a large, hot, airless room filled with tall, imposing looking machines, towering over him. On each, dozens of valves, switches, dials, cylinders, and wheels whirred and clattered. Occasionally, bright, angry sparks fizzed and crackled from the hundreds of wires, which snaked down from rows of letters and numbers at the back of the machines. The noise was deafening, and a sharp smell of warm oil filled the room, stinging his nose. Women in uniform were quietly moving around the room, checking the equipment and occasionally feeding the great machines with more oil, which in places, dripped like blood on their shoes, but nobody spoke! Charles went to say something, but realised it was pointless trying to be heard over the cacophony of sound, when one of the machines stopped, unexpectedly and the intensity of noise lessened momentarily.

"This one's found the answer to today's code," said Jam-Jar over his shoulder, "so the German messages intercepted today, can now be decrypted, or decoded and the information sent on. As a consequence, many lives can potentially be saved, especially if the decoded messages are about planned German bombing raids. The code-breaking being carried out here at Bletchley Park will be crucial to us winning the war," said Jam-Jar, as they made their way through the intense heat and noise, "but, like Radar, it's Top-Secret and together with the Spitfire, we now have a chance!"

Turning their backs on the commotion of the room, they opened a door and, without warning, stepped out onto the promenade of Brighton beach! Charles blinked at the sudden brightness and shielded his eyes, shocked to find himself by the sea again, which still sparkled in the sunlight. Glancing back at the open door, Charles could still see the machines whirring away in the dim light of the room within, but when he turned again, the door had disappeared, and old Brighton stretched before him.

Smiling at Charles' surprise, Jam-Jar spoke, "Churchill knows he has a huge team of dedicated and talented people prepared to work hard for him and it's talent and ingenuity that'll win this war, not defeatism, a fact that's going to become blatantly obvious to Churchill in a few days-time."

"Why?" asked Charles.

"Because the crisis of Dunkirk is about to unfold and you're going to see it!"

Chapter 8 - Dunkirk

Charles' great-grandfather led the way across the promenade back to the iron railings and pointed out to sea. As they scanned the dancing waves and the blue horizon, the railings seemed to become long, tall, thin grasses rustling gently in the fresh, salty breeze. The sparkling sea was still calm and blue, but Brighton beach had disappeared. Charles looked around him; he was standing on top of a high sand-dune. Where, seconds earlier, he had seen grey, smooth pebbles, there was now inviting, soft, golden sand! It made Charles think of summer holidays and sandcastles, but then he noticed something unusual. Stretching out into the water were long, dark, straight lines, which to Charles, looked more like piers, lots of them.

"They're not piers," said Jam-Jar, reading his thoughts, "They're men – soldiers, waiting to be collected by those big ships out there at sea," and sure enough, as Charles looked, he saw, appearing on the horizon, several large ships, which were steaming towards the coast and between the ships and the long lines of men, were lots of little boats all bobbing about near the shore.

"What's going on, Jam-Jar?"

"Now Hitler has invaded France, the British army and its French and Belgian allies are in retreat. They've been cornered here at Dunkirk. Dunkirk!" he repeated, impressively, scanning the shoreline, "Northern France, May 1940! The whole of the British Expeditionary Force and its Allies are being evacuated from this beach. Here, we either lose the war entirely, or live to fight another day!"

"The whole of the British army!" exclaimed Charles.

"As much of it as can be saved," replied Jam-Jar, "and it all happens between 26th May and 4th June."

Charles looked in amazement at the thousands of men littering the beach, like jetsam washed up on the sand.

"What's going to happen then, Jam-Jar?"

"You see, the Germans have made a mistake. They've halted their advance and their problem is that they, rather smugly, think that the sea will be our enemy, an impassable barrier, keeping us captive on the beach, but they don't realise that we've always regarded the sea as our friend. We're an island nation," said Jam-Jar gazing out over the gentle waves, sunlight glistening in his eyes. "The sea has protected us in the past, like a moat and it's going to help us again. This time, it's our route to safety and freedom. It's our route home," his voice was deep with emotion.

"So, why have the Germans given the order to halt?"

"Ah! Now, some think it's because Hitler secretly admires the British fighting spirit and wants to show a certain gentlemanly gallantry," said Jam-Jar, slightly sarcastically, "to give us a sporting chance of a peaceful surrender, rather than just *completely* destroying us! He thinks we might then, see our invader in a slightly more *sympathetic* light!" smirked Jam-Jar.

"Well, Hitler's made a mistake then!" Charles said emphatically, looking up at his great-grandfather, who glanced down at him, proudly, a warm smile filling his kind eyes.

"We don't tend to give up easily in a fight," Jam-Jar agreed. "Talk about the Dunkirk Spirit! Well, this is where that expression comes from, but the real reason the German tanks have halted is that, by moving so quickly, they've gone too far ahead of the infantry, which is now a long way behind and can't support them. They've taken France in just one day in their 'Blitzkrieg', or 'Lightning War', but now their communication and supply lines have been stretched too far and they've got to wait for the infantry to catch up."

More British soldiers were arriving as they watched and some, who were obviously wounded, were being supported by their mates. One group of soldiers passed close by.

"Cor, I ain't 'alf glad we're 'ere," said one. "Those bleedin' Gerries ain't far be'ind us though!"

"I fort we'd bought it, for sure," said his mate.

"Come on lads. We're gonna stick togevver ain't we. We've made it this far," said another.

"I fort me ticket was up for sure back then," said the wounded soldier.

"You think we'd leave you b'hind, mate? You must be barmey'!" said his chum. "Don't worry, Ern. You'll live to see anovver day. Your missus'll never let me 'ear the last of it, if I don't get cha back in one piece!"

They all chuckled ruefully and started whistling,

"It's a long way to Tipperary,

It's a long way to go...."

"Look fellas! The beach. Just like being on 'olliday!"

The group soldiered on and disappeared over the sand dunes. Charles could still hear their whistling fading on the breeze, as he turned to look in the direction from which they had just come.

All down the road, there were vehicles on fire, some in ditches, some with bonnets up, but all abandoned. There was carnage everywhere.

"The soldiers have had to disable all the equipment, including military vehicles, artillery and stores, anything they can't take with them and they've put them out of action, so they can't be used by the enemy," said his great-grandfather.

Across the fields, Charles could hear, quite distinctly, the crack and pop of distant gun fire, getting closer by the minute and he started to feel a vague sense of panic.

"So, the plan is to pick up the army from the beach," exclaimed Charles, "like a bus, picking up passengers from a bus stop?"

"That's right," said Jam-Jar, smiling.

At that moment, a plane flew overhead and hundreds of pamphlets started to flutter down from the sky. Charles reached down for one. It had a map of the beach and it read, 'British soldiers!

Look at the map: it gives your true situation! Your troops are entirely surrounded – stop fighting! Put down your arms!'

"They made good toilet paper for the boys on the beach," chuckled Jam-Jar, inclining his head at the pamphlet in Charles' hand.

Suddenly, they heard an awful sound, a wailing and screeching and the rapid pop-pop-pop of gunfire bursts. Charles ran to the top of the sand dune to see two German Stuka dive-bombers screaming down and machine gunning the beach. Men, who had made it this far, dived for cover, but some didn't move from where they had been sunning themselves only seconds before. Charles couldn't look. He buried his head in Jam-Jar's side, who wrapped his arms around him.

"Don't worry, little one. Your Spitfires come to save the day and those Hawker Hurricanes. For the whole time of the evacuation, the German Luftwaffe have been strafing those boys down there on the beach, but our Spitfires prove to the Germans that we're a force to be reckoned with."

And sure enough, diving in from the sun, were Charles' beloved Spitfires, chasing off the Stukas, like dogs chasing birds.

"Those Spitfires are giving our boys a fighting chance to get away."

"How many did get away, Jam-Jar?"

"More than 330,000 Allied Troops, including more than 193,000 British troops, 145,000 French troops and Polish, Belgian, Indian, Moroccan and Canadian troops, who were all able to get back home to Britain and fight another day. A lot of men died so that these men could be saved though. British and French troops had to hold back the advancing German army long enough so that the majority could be evacuated.

"At Calais, the French and British fighting alongside one another, were ordered to hold their position at all costs, to act as a diversion, drawing away Panzer divisions from reaching Dunkirk, which gave more time for the evacuation and elsewhere General de Gaulle with his men, fought bravely to halt the German advance, inspired by the efforts Churchill and the Royal Navy were making.

"The men knew that most of them were facing death or capture, but they sacrificed themselves so that others could be saved and it did make a difference. It meant all these soldiers here could make it back home and fight on."

"How will all these men get off the beach though, Jam-Jar?"

"Look and you'll see. 'Operation Dynamo' it's called."

Down at the shore and out in the shallow water, little boats bobbed in the sea, as soldiers clambered on.

Charles' great-grandfather spoke, his voice resonant with concern "Some of those boys have been standing in line, waist deep in the water for hours, just waiting their turn to get a lift on one of the Little Ships, as they later became called.

"The Royal Navy were ordered to requisition them; ordinary boats, owned by ordinary civilians - small enough to get close to the shore-line and pick up the men from the beaches. The boats were all privately owned and the Royal Navy had been ordered to borrow them from their owners, but here's the amazing thing, Charles.

"When the call went out, many of the private owners of the boats actually volunteered to sail over to Dunkirk themselves, risking their own lives to save the men here. They knew it would be dangerous. Many of the little boats were attacked by the Luftwaffe, but they kept going, doing their bit to help evacuate the soldiers."

"What a brilliant idea," exclaimed Charles.

"It certainly was, sweetheart and can you guess whose clever idea it was?"

"Churchill's?" asked Charles.

"Spot on! It was Churchill's idea alright and together with Vice Admiral Betram Ramsay, who coordinated the operation from naval headquarters at Dover Castle, he saw to it that the Nazis were not going to get the quick win they were expecting."

They both watched in awe, as the little boats chugged out with their load into the deeper water, sometimes with as few as four or five men, as many as could be fitted safely onto the boats without sinking them, which then carried their precious cargo to the larger ships waiting out at sea. When the big ships were full, they turned and steamed away, disappearing over the horizon, heading home to the safety of Britain.

Charles heard his great-grandfather sigh, a great shuddering sigh that came from somewhere deep, somewhere too deep to fathom. Charles glanced up at his face and saw him staring into the distance, a far-away look in his eyes – eyes, which he could tell, had seen too much of life.

"All those young lads!" he said. "Someone's son, all of them, someone's boy," and tearing his gaze from the distant horizon, he cast his eyes down to his great-grandson. "Please God, you never have to face something like this, little one," and he clasped Charles' hand tightly in his, as if he would never let him go and stared deeply into Charles' upturned face. The faraway look in his eyes had returned.

"Your great-grandmother, my wife Gloria, was fostered by an old Brighton fishing family called the Gunns. 'Grandad Gunn', as she used to call him, brought his boat over here too. The war touched everyone Charles."

Charles gazed out to sea, as his great-grandfather spoke again,

"The last of the troops were evacuated on the 4th of June 1940. The sea suddenly turned rough and stormy. It had stayed calm during the whole time of the evacuation. If the weather had closed in sooner, it would have been much more difficult to get all the men off the beach. The sea was definitely on our side and because of Churchill's fighting spirit and because of those wonderful Spitfires you love so much, we lived to fight another day. It was those Spitfire pilots' first taste of combat and the first time the pilots had been able to test the power of this wonderful plane in battle.

"Sadly though, because most of the aerial combat in the skies between the Spitfires and the enemy happened inland, the men on the beaches simply couldn't see the battle going on and thought that the RAF had deserted them, when in fact, the RAF shocked the German pilots with their fierceness and bravery. 132 German aircraft were destroyed at Dunkirk. Here we 'snatched victory from the jaws of defeat'."

"I think I can guess what that means," said Charles.

"Yes," replied his great-grandfather. "It's a famous expression."

"I know. Don't tell me! It's like pulling your favourite toy out of the mouth of a big dog before he can chew it to pieces."

"Exactly, Charles!" his great-grandfather replied and they grinned at each other.

"After Dunkirk, Churchill said, *'Wars are not won by evacuations. But there was a victory inside this deliverance,'* and he wasn't wrong there, was he!" exclaimed his great-grandfather.

"On the day when the last of the troops were evacuated from the beaches of Dunkirk, on the 4th June, Winston Churchill gave his famous speech to the House of Commons."

Suddenly, Charles again, found himself in the large room with the high vaulted ceiling, the room which was lined with long, leather seats - the House of Commons and one man was standing and talking to all assembled there. Charles could hear the deep measured tones of this man's voice, a voice he already knew so well. There, standing before him, was Prime Minister, Winston Churchill and everyone in that room was listening to him in silence and respect:

"...we shall fight on the beaches,
we shall fight on the landing grounds,
we shall fight in the fields and in the streets,
we shall fight in the hills,
we shall never surrender,

and even if, which I do not for a moment believe, this island or a large part of it were subjugated and starving, then our Empire beyond the seas, armed and guarded by the British Fleet, would carry on the struggle, until, in God's good time, the New World, with all its power and might, steps forth to the rescue and liberation of the old."

The jubilant cheers of all present rang in their ears, as the whole of the House of Commons stood in approval.

"Have you watched the comedy, 'Dad's Army', Charles, about the Home Guard?"

Charles blinked, the triumphant noise still ringing in his ears. He looked at his great-grandfather and suddenly he realised they were no longer standing on the windswept, sand dunes of Dunkirk, nor were they in the Houses of Parliament. They were back on the promenade of Brighton beach. He shook his head in disbelief, took a deep breath and gathered his thoughts with all he had just seen.

"Dad's Army – my dad loves watching it," said Charles. "It's about the Home Guard that was formed to help to protect Britain if we'd been invaded."

"That's right," said Jam-Jar. "It was made up of volunteers, men either too old, older than forty-one, or too young to fight, under the age of eighteen and anyone else, who wasn't able to join up, all volunteers determined to do their bit in some way," said Jam-Jar, "Well, you know the song at the beginning," and Jam-Jar started to whistle the tune and then sing the words,

'Who do you think you are kidding, Mr. Hitler
If you think we're on the run.
We are the boys who will stop your little game.
We are the boys who will make you think again.'

"Do you remember the map it shows at the beginning, with the Union Jack arrow and the Nazi arrows fighting it? That's a reference to the German army closing in on the British and their allies at Dunkirk. You see Mr. Hitler thought he had us on the run, but he was wrong."

"He certainly was," agreed Charles. "But what happened to France, Jam-Jar, after the evacuation of Dunkirk?"

"Well, although the French Prime Minister, Reynaud, still wanted to work closely with Winston Churchill, unfortunately several in his cabinet were having none of it and refused. They preferred German influence over British help!" said Jam-Jar, angrily. Reynaud resigned, giving up his job as Prime Minister on the 16th June. Petain, who'd preferred the idea of appeasement all along, became Prime Minister and immediately surrendered France to the Germans and had Reynaud arrested and handed over to the Nazis and so began four long years of Nazi rule in France. General de Gaulle escaped before he could be arrested, never to return until France was liberated."

"Where did he go," asked Charles.

"He came to Britain and set up a French Government in Waiting."

"Waiting for what, Jam-Jar?"

"Waiting for the day when France would be free again, waiting for the day of Deliverance," his great-grandfather spoke impressively. "Whilst he was here, he regularly spoke on BBC radio, broadcasting messages of hope to people back in France, encouraging them to fight on, to resist and not give in."

Suddenly, Charles and his great-grandfather looked on as a man, with care-worn face, seated in a small booth, microphone in front of him, spoke with quiet pride and certainty,

"Now, a great many French people refuse to accept either capitulation or slavery, for reasons which are called: honour, common sense, and the higher interests of the country...

Honour, common sense, and the interests of the country require that all free Frenchmen, wherever they be, should continue the fight as best they may...

I call upon all French servicemen of the land, sea and air forces; I call upon French engineers and skilled armaments workers who are on British soil, or who have the means of getting here, to come and join me...

I call upon all Frenchmen who want to remain free to listen to my voice and follow me.

Long live free France in honour and independence!"

They both listened intently, awe-struck by this man's words.

"Wow", said Charles, wide-eyed with respect and wonder. "I don't understand it all, but I can really feel he means every word he says. What happened to him after the war?"

"After the liberation of France, de Gaulle went back to France and became head of the government."

"and what happened to Petain after the war?"

"Petain was tried for treason, a traitor to his country and spent the rest of his life in prison, whereas Churchill would have rather died, than see this country invaded."

Suddenly, Charles felt the earth move beneath his feet and a shiver went down his spine, as before him again, there appeared the leather benches in the Houses of Parliament. In the Commons, one man was speaking, one man had everyone enthralled, one man was summing up the fight, which lay before them, a fight against seeming impossible odds, but a fight that had to be won, nonetheless.

Charles listened intently to the slow, deep, methodical voice of Churchill.

"'The battle of Britain is about to begin...The whole fury and might of the enemy must very soon be turned on us. Hitler knows that he will have to break us in this island or lose the war. If we can

stand up to him, all Europe may be free and the life of the world may move forward into broad, sunlit uplands. But if we fail, then the whole world, including the United States, including all that we have known and cared for, will sink into the abyss of a new Dark Age made more sinister, and perhaps more protracted, by the lights of a perverted science. Let us therefore brace ourselves to our duties, and so bear ourselves that, if the British Empire and its Commonwealth last for a thousand years, men will still say, 'This was their finest hour.'"

Charles could feel the power of those words echoing around the chamber, as rapturous applause filled the hall - words of defiance and determination - words that spoke of fearlessness and victory. The walls themselves, seemed to swell with pride.

"When people later heard that speech broadcast on the radio, it gave them the strength to fight on. The country's morale was so high with Churchill in charge."

Jam-Jar looked at Charles, "So now," he said significantly, "it's mid-July, 1940. The Battle of France is over and we're next! Hitler thinks he's going to defeat us, by winning the battle for the skies, but he doesn't understand what he's up against - our Spitfires!" Jam-Jar glanced up, "and there they are now!"

Charles blinked at the sudden brightness of the sea.

There in the distance, over the cliffs towards Rottingdean, he could see a dog-fight – a squadron of Spitfires buzzing around a swarm of Messerschmitts. He imagined the Spitfire pilots in their cockpits, their adrenaline rushing, their fear, their exhilaration. He could almost see how the coast and the white cliffs looked from the sky, glowing in the morning sun. Suddenly, it was his hand was on the control stick, his thumb pressing the button to fire off another round, his eyes seeing the enemy plane bearing down on him from out of the sun, tracer bullets arching towards him. Diving, banking, evading the enemy, he rattled off a volley of his own, burning ragged holes along the Messerschmitt's fuselage. The Spitfire moved instinctively, almost reading his thoughts, manoeuvring him out of danger and he knew with every fibre of his being that he and the Spitfire were one.

And over it all, Charles could hear a voice, a voice from somewhere far off, as if coming from an old, crackly radio, a well-spoken voice, giving what sounded like a cricket commentary.

'Now the British fighters are coming up...you can hear our own guns going like anything now. The Germans are haring back towards France now, for all they can go. Here are our Spitfires coming after them. There's going to be a big fight out there, I think. Oh boy! I've never seen anything as good as this. These RAF fighters have really got these boys today.'

Breathing heavily, Charles blinked and looked at his great-grandfather's kind face.[22]

"You see, we were never going to surrender," he said, "at least not without an almighty fight first! Churchill's words on 20th August were so right," and Jam-Jar quoted from memory, a memory deeply ingrained in his heart,

'Never in the field of human conflict was so much owed by so many to so few.'

"We owe those young men of the RAF a huge debt of gratitude," Jam-Jar continued, "but everyone did their bit. Even your great-great grandfather, my wife, Gloria's father, was stationed up on the roof of the Metropole Hotel over there, manning an Ac-Ac gun. He was Head Waiter there by day and did his bit for the war effort by night. Everybody did their bit and it was the sea that kept us safe, protecting us from evil. It's saved us many times. Your great-grandmother, Gloria, wrote a poem about it once," and straight away he started to recite the words, words which Charles knew he would never forget.

"Each little wave which laps the shore on this long Summer's eve,
Tells me how much my island home depends upon the sea.
All through the dreary days of war, on it we did depend.
It gave us strength to see it through and fight right to the end.

> To God alone we must give thanks,
> For he alone did plan,
> That this great almighty home of ours
> Should feel no conqueror's hand.
> Here now my small effort ends,
> Weak though it seems to be.
> It whispers of my feelings,
> Whilst I'm sitting by the sea."

Chapter 9 - Brighton and the Home Front

"Come on, let me show you something," said Jam-Jar, softly, holding out his large hand for Charles, whose little hand was quite lost in his great-grandfather's gentle grasp.

Turning from the Palace Pier, they walked along the Old Steine towards the Royal Pavilion.

"There we are," said Jam-Jar, pointing to it, "King George IV's sea-side palace."

"Oh, I've been there," said Charles. "It's amazing – Indian on the outside and Chinese on the inside."

"It was used as a hospital during the First World War," said Jam-Jar, "for Indian soldiers serving in the British Army. There's a shrine dedicated to them up on the South Downs."

On through the streets they went, not at all looking how Charles remembered. The buildings seemed poorer, more shabby - not brightly coloured, as he knew them, but somehow nicer and more real.

Everywhere, streets were filled with the noise, hustle and bustle of daily life: people chatting, dogs barking, children playing and shop keepers calling out their wares.

"Rag an' bone! Rag an' bone!" called out one man, pushing a hand-cart along the road, his voice echoing above the cheerful busyness of the street. He wore an old, threadbare jacket, a cap and an old piece of cloth tied around his neck.

"Rag an' bone. Rag an' bone!" he called out again.

Seeing the look of curiosity on Charles' face, Jam-Jar explained, "In the days before recycling as you know it, the Rag an' Bone men used to collect any unwanted scraps of metal, old pots and pans, old clothes, anything really for money. They were still around when your mother was a little girl."

Farther up the road, Charles could see a great, big, wooden cart laden with sacks of coal, being pulled by a powerful looking black horse with enormous hooves.

"Coal man's 'ere!" one woman on a doorstep shouted. "Open up the coal 'ole. 'E'll be comin' through the scullery in a minute. Half a mo'! Where's that bleedin' skuttle?"

The coal merchant was dressed all in black: black trousers, black shirt, black waistcoat and a black cap, with a dirty red 'kerchief tied around his neck and every bit of his face, neck and hands covered in coal dust, from the creases around his startlingly blue eyes, to the nails of his strong hands.

"All right, duck? Comin' through. Mind yer backs," he called amiably, as he slung a huge sackful of coal over his shoulder, as if filled with nothing more than feathers, and trundled off down the hallway to the back yard.

Along the street, Charles saw two beautiful Shire horses pulling a cart loaded with beer barrels from the local brewery. Brightly polished brasses hung from their bridles and gleamed against their glossy coats.

"That cart's called a 'dray'," said Jam-Jar, "and it delivers barrels of beer from the local brewery, to all the pubs in the area - a pub on every corner there was and every street had a 'Lady-who-Does'," said Jam-Jar, mysteriously.

Charles looked up at him, confused. "A 'Lady-who-Does'?" he asked quizzically.

"A sort of unofficial community nurse and midwife," Jam-Jar explained, smiling, "working for the neighbourhood to help mothers give birth to their babies, helping to look after the sick and helping with the 'laying out' when people died. Remember, these were the days before the NHS was created and doctors cost money!

"Mind you, everyone was hard up in those days," said Jam-Jar, thoughtfully. "If you didn't have enough money to pay the rent you owed, you'd do a 'moonlit flit', which basically meant running away without paying the rent. You'd pack up all your possessions, which wouldn't be much, to be honest, on a cart or wheelbarrow, including the children and pots and pans and run away in the middle of the night. Your great-grandmother and I had to do a flit once, when times were hard and we couldn't afford the rent money we owed. Hard times," said Jam-Jar wistfully, "but everyone helped each other."

Charles gazed at the bustling life around him: the children playing in the streets, the women talking to each other companionably on their freshly scrubbed doorsteps and marvelled at how normal everything seemed, despite the war.

"Nobody had much," said Jam-Jar, "but everyone was very house-proud. Most houses had a front room, which was kept as the best room, neat and tidy and only used when you had visitors, but mind you," said Jam-Jar, "if you were really hard up, you'd be lucky to live in a single room, the whole family, with barely enough money for a few lumps of coal for the fire. Your great-grandmother, my Gloria, and her sister, Jean, (you remember your great-great aunt Jean, don't you,)" Charles nodded enthusiastically, "Well, one day, they were trying to change Jean's baby's nappy in front of the fire, which they'd just finished struggling to light with the few bits of coal that they could afford, when the baby weed straight into the fire and put it out!"

This made Charles laugh and his great-grandfather suddenly looked at him and smiled gently.

"Cor' Gloria was proud of you, Charles. The day your mother, put you, her great-grandson in her arms, was one of the proudest days of her life. She died when you were nine months old. I wish you could remember her Charles. She was so beautiful the day I married her – gorgeous long, nut brown hair and eyes so blue they were almost violet," and Charles saw tears in his eyes and quietly and respectfully looked away, but as he did so, he saw a long queue forming outside a grocer's shop. It snaked off along the road and more people were patiently joining as he watched.

"What's the Grocer got?" asked one woman, expectantly.

"Dunno love," replied a man, "but whatever it is, I'll 'ave some of it. I've got four young kids at 'ome."

"What *are* they queueing for?" asked a curious Charles.

"It could be anything: butter, eggs, wool, razors! You name it, it was rationed to ensure there was enough for everyone. Rationing started in January 1940. You see for a long time, Britain hadn't been growing enough food to feed everyone, so a lot of food had to be imported from abroad, which meant that our food supply was vulnerable to wars and hostile nations trying to prevent shipping from reaching our shores. So, Germany planned to lay siege to Britain and destroy all the supply ships, because if we'd started to starve, we would've had to surrender to them."

"Like a castle under siege in Medieval times?" asked Charles.

"That's right sweetheart. Well, this 'siege' was called The Battle of the Atlantic, and it lasted for most of the war. German battle ships and submarines called U-boats patrolled the Atlantic, hunting in what were called 'wolf-packs', attacking convoys of ships, which travelled together for safety and trying to pick off straggling ships that weren't keeping up with the rest of the convoy. The convoys were protected by our Royal Navy and the Royal Canadian Navy and later in the war, the United States Navy, but many ships were sunk."

Charles had an impression of swirling seas and billowing mists. He could smell the salty air and hear the crash of waves against the hulls of huge convoys of ships sailing together for safety. A sense of nervousness and anticipation filled his mind, an unsettling feeling of dread, of something lurking beneath the waves, waiting to pounce.

Jam-Jar's words broke into his reverie and echoed in his mind over the rolling water...

"You see, Britain needed vital supplies of food, essential equipment, oil and fuel for things like planes and tanks. Without these, we couldn't have fought the war and when it became more difficult to import from our sources in the Middle East, Britain quickly started to get much needed supplies from the United States of America. This had been arranged before the war, when our own King George VI had travelled to America to personally ask President Roosevelt if he would help Britain in the event of a war with Germany. Luckily, the President had agreed to supply us with what we needed, but couldn't commit to joining a war if it happened, because, at that time, people in America were against the idea. It was only later that public opinion there changed. However, the American supplies meant Britain could continue to fight the war, until the money started to run out!" said Jam-Jar ironically.

"What did Britain do?" asked Charles.

"Churchill persuaded President Roosevelt to lend us the money and Roosevelt convinced his government to allow us to delay paying back the loan until after the war had ended, even though it wasn't certain that we'd win. It was a great act of faith, but such was the trust that Roosevelt had in Churchill and in our determination to fight.

"The Lend-Lease Bill was signed into law on the 11th March 1941 and the British government kept to its end of the bargain and, after the war, paid off every penny it owed to America. The last payment was made in December 2006!"

"Wow!" exclaimed Charles.

"However," continued his great-grandfather, "we still had to have rationing to stop us running out of food and it went on until July 1954, long after the war had ended."

"That was a really long time – fourteen years of rationing!"

"It was, Charles. People didn't starve, but they did have to eat less. Bacon, butter, sugar, other meat, tea, jam, biscuits, breakfast cereals, cheese, eggs, milk, canned and tinned fruit to name just a few things, all were rationed and even soap, paper and material and wool for clothes were rationed. In fact, your mother has still got the ration books that were issued to my Gloria, for the babies' clothes."

Charles remembered seeing them in a well-loved album of old photos at home.

"For every item you bought, you had to use a coupon, so that you couldn't have more than your fair share. No coupon, no food."

"So why the queues?"

"Well often, because of ships being attacked, not all the food made it to Britain, which meant that one month there might be a shortage of something and then the following month a ship would get through and suddenly, whatever it was would be available again. That's why people would queue, even if they didn't know what the queue was for.

"It wasn't easy though, with the German wolf-packs hunting our ships. One German battleship that gave Britain a real headache, called 'The Bismark', was one of two of the largest battleships ever built by Germany and posed a real threat to British shipping. When it sank the British battleship, HMS Hood, which had been nicknamed, 'The Mighty Hood', because it had been the largest warship in the world for twenty years and the pride of the Royal Navy, it was clear that something had to be done. Out of a crew of nearly fifteen hundred, only three men had survived and one of those men, when he was much older, lived not far from where you live!"

Before Charles had time to digest this information, suddenly, the ground under his feet seemed to rise and fall. He looked down and saw that he was standing on the deck of a ship. The shock of cold, salty air and rolling, heavy seas swelling all around him took his breath away. He reached out for his great-grandfather's arm to steady himself, who stood beside him strong and unmovable. The grey, stormy dawn threatened a bitter wind and an eerie sense of imminent battle. Adrenaline throbbed through Charles' expectant mind, as he waited for the danger to be revealed.

As if on cue, the clouds broke to the East, revealing the outline of an enormous battleship, the brightening morning glowing on its prow. It was *The Bismark*!

With an explosive volley, every gun above Charles' head opened fire, the shock of the sudden salvo almost sucking the air out of Charles' lungs. He jumped into his great-grandfather's arms, who held him tightly and The Bismark was no more.

A deep, throbbing silence descended, shrouding the scene and obscuring from view the last, tumultuous moments of the events being played out before them. A warm breeze played on Charles' face, as if gently waking him. He opened one eye and then the other, to find himself back on the busy, bustling street in Brighton, still looking at the queue, which had now grown longer.

Although it was clear that Jam-Jar had seen it all, he carried on talking as if nothing had happened, just holding his great-grandson in his arms and resting his chin on Charles head as he spoke,

"And of course, Charles. We're a resilient lot. We started growing more food for ourselves. Everyone was encouraged to, 'Dig for Victory'," and Charles remembered seeing in a museum, the famous poster of the boot on a shovel, turning the earth.

"Everyone was encouraged to turn over their gardens to grow fruit and vegetables," Jam-Jar went on. "Every spare patch of

land was used and there was the Women's Land Army, too. Women were called up to be Land Girls and work on farms where the men had been called away to fight. So, women did the farm work - heavy work it was too and they did a fantastic job. Most of them loved it, being close to nature, away from the bombing and doing their bit as well. You see, Charles. This one little street, this one little bit of this country, represents in it, everything the war could throw at us and everything we did to stand up to it."

"Wow! There's so much to learn," thought Charles.

Then, they arrived at one street, whose name Charles recognised, Whitecross Street, but it looked very different from how Charles remembered it. Where, in his time, there were nothing but car parks, here, instead, were two neat rows of back-to-back houses.

"Why are there diamond shapes taped on the windows, Jam-Jar?"

"That's to protect people from shattered glass during a bomb blast. The tape holds the glass together."

"Did people have any other protection?"

"People had corrugated Anderson shelters in their gardens and back yards if there was room and then there were the indoor steel Morrison 'table' shelters, which you could use as a table by day and a handy bomb shelter by night!" Jam-Jar said, a note of amusement in his voice. "People also took shelter under their stairs in their houses and then, of course, everyone had gas masks, which they had to carry around with them all the time."

Charles looked around him and sure enough, he could see everyone carrying their gas-masks in bags on their shoulders.

"There were even masks for babies. They had to be put inside the whole thing and then the parent had to pump air into it continuously. Must have been bloomin' frightening for the baby. They weren't easy for the adults to wear either. The rubber they were made of smelt something awful when you put them on!"

Suddenly, Charles heard a loud squawking coming from a nearby house.

"Parrots!" said Jam-Jar, knowingly. "The man who lives there keeps them," and sure enough, as Charles looked through the open door, he saw a long, dark passageway leading to a back yard, which seemed to glow in the sunlight, in stark contrast to the gloom of the hallway inside. In the yard, the source of all the noise and commotion could be seen, an aviary of parrots, whose vivid colours glinted brightly in the warm sun.

"This is the street where I grew up. All life is here," said Jam-Jar, surveying the scene.

The bright sun made the windows gleam and the clean net curtains glowed and gently billowed in the breeze, softly flowing from open windows, as if the houses themselves were breathing peacefully.

And then, a front door opened in one of the houses. A lady came out onto the freshly scrubbed step. Her white starched apron was clean and neatly pressed, her hair was pinned up and she was rolling down her sleeves, as if her morning's work was done. Charles noticed her hands – strong, work-worn hands, but elegant still, with long tapering fingers. She had such a kind face that Charles felt instantly drawn to her.

Suddenly, Jam-Jar stopped. He gripped Charles' hand a little tighter. Charles noticed and looked up at his great-grandfather's face, which was working strangely, as if trying to control a strong emotion. The look of love on his face told Charles all he needed to know.

"That lady's your mother, isn't she!"

"Yes, Charles. She is," said his great-grandfather, "and I loved her dearly." His voice cracked and there were tears in his eyes and for a moment he was silent, lost deep in thought.

As if his mother had felt his presence, she looked up in his direction and gave a startled cry, "Bob! You're home!" Charles' heart skipped a beat. He saw his great-grandfather's chest swell with emotion, taking a sudden intake of breath and then from close behind him, almost over his shoulder, they both heard a call, "Mum!"

They turned their heads to see the warm, smiling young face of a loving son, coming home on leave. He walked past them, so close, Charles could have touched him. He was tall and his tanned face was beaming a lovely smile that seemed to light up the whole street. He looked smart in his Royal Navy Uniform, with his cap sitting jauntily at an angle. He carried the swirling oceans and the freedom of the sea breezes around him.

"Mum!" he said again, as he dropped his kit bag and embraced his mother in a huge bear hug, lifting her quite off her feet.

"Oh! My boy! My boy! You're home!" she exclaimed through tears. "Why didn't you let me know you were coming?"

"Thought I'd surprise you, Mum!"

"Surprise me! You've given me quite a turn, son. I'm all giddy!"

And they both laughed, as Charles' young great-grandfather picked up his kit bag and he and his mother both went inside arm in arm. The door closed softly behind them and Charles could see them no more. He imagined them both walking and chatting down the hallway to the kitchen together – the mother fussing proudly round her son, sitting him in the comfiest chair and busying herself over food and tea for him, whilst they shared stories and jokes, lost, for a while, in their own safe little bubble described by the four old walls of the back parlour and the fire.

Charles turned to see his great-grandfather gazing longingly at the closed door, remembering all the warmth and love filling the house and looking as if the tiniest breeze could have knocked him over.

For a moment, they were silent, until Charles gently squeezed his great-grandfather's hand and smiled up at him sympathetically, bringing him out of his reverie. Still lost in thought, his vision clouded by memories, he slowly stroked Charles' hair, a little breeze playing with one strand. Charles shook his head, bringing his great-grandfather back from far away, who, bending down, as if from a mountain, kissed the top of his great-grandson's head and hugged him tightly.

"I'll always be with you, Charles. Always. I'll never leave you. Even when you can't see me, I'll be with you, just like my old mum. She's always with me, just like your gran-nan, my Gloria, is always with you."

They stood still, together, lost in thought, as the world moved oblivious, around them. Then quietly, Jam-Jar said,

"You know, my Gloria, your gran-nan went to school with my sister, before she was evacuated to Yorkshire, although I didn't know Gloria then. I met her after the war for the first time, when she was nineteen and I was twenty-six. I fell in love with her the moment I saw her."

"Oh. I've heard how the children were evacuated," said Charles.

"Come on. I'll show you."

Off they went, through the town and up Trafalgar Street, to the train station that appeared to jut out over the road, which disappeared through a tunnel underneath. Pausing in the tunnel, Charles' great-grandfather pointed at a dark doorway on their right. "This used to be a doll's hospital when your mother was a little girl," he said, inclining his head towards it.

"A doll's hospital!" said Charles, confused, "What's that?"

"A hospital for sick dolls and teddies, of course!" said Jam-Jar, smiling, "where children took their toys when they were broken. When your mummy was a little girl, she had a doll she loved like a real baby and one day she was running with it and its head fell off!" he said laughing. "She was so upset. So, we brought her doll here, to be made better. The doll had to have an 'operation',"

"What, to reattach her head?"

"That's right," said Jam-Jar, laughing affectionately at the memory. "Every day for a week she phoned for updates on how the sick patient was doing. The toy mender played along with it, like a doctor. Bless her! By then, you see, my Gloria, your great-grandmother, was a district nurse and your mummy was always so interested in her grandma's job. One day, your mum will write a book about all this, I'm sure."

They reached the top of the hill and turned through the gates into the train station. Charles was surprised to notice that the two gate posts appeared to be old cannons.

"From the Napoleonic wars, they are!" said Jam-Jar, seeing that Charles was looking at them quizzically. "They came from Brighton seafront's West Battery, which was a defensive position built to fight Napoleon had he ever managed to reach our shores."[23]

"Napoleon!" said Charles.

"Yes, someone else who thought he'd have a piece of us. No chance there, though, not with the likes of Admiral Nelson and Wellington!"

"I know those names!" said Charles. "I've been to see Admiral Nelson's ship, HMS Victory."

"And a beautiful ship she is too," said his great-grandfather. "Defeated Napoleon's naval fleet at the Battle of Trafalgar! The road we've just walked up is named after that great sea victory."

Charles' great-grandfather thought for a moment, "You know, when I was a little boy, I used to know an old man, who would often say that, when he was a little boy, all round the station here was just fields and countryside. He was probably old enough to remember when those canons were moved here! I hadn't thought of that before and look at it now – all noise and bustle. Here. Hold my hand. Wouldn't want to lose you in the crowd!"

Brighton station was beautiful - great arched ceilings and ornate ironwork. Charles looked down. The platform was made of wooden railway sleepers. He stared, fascinated, as his feet stepped over the planks and gaps. It was like walking on the Palace Pier.

Another pair of feet came into view. A little girl, about his age, stood before him. She looked frightened and bewildered. Around her neck was a label and tightly clutched against her chest was an old, worn, teddy bear. On her shoulder she carried her gasmask and at her feet stood a small leather suitcase, which she bent down to pick up just as Charles and his great-grandfather approached. Straightening up, she seemed to look him straight in the eye.

Charles' stomach flipped somersaults. He felt certain the little girl had actually seen him. There was a sudden shock of recognition, as the girl blinked in surprise and gasped, but suddenly, her father led her away along the crowded platform, which was thronging with children, all with the same anxious and lost expressions on their faces. Some of the younger children, clearly had no idea that they were about to be separated from their parents.

"We must get you a seat on the train, Gloria," said the girl's father and then, with relief in his strained voice, "Oh, there's your friend, Shirley and her brother and ma!"

Charles felt his great-grandfather's hand suddenly grip his more tightly. He turned to look at him.

"That's my Gloria!" he exclaimed almost calling to her, but suddenly stopping himself. "She's just a child. She wouldn't recognise me," he said, sadly.

"I think she saw me!" Charles exclaimed.

"I'm not surprised, sweetheart," said Jam-Jar. "You're connected, connected by blood, connected by love!"

They looked on as the two parents, fighting back tears, hugged their children as if they'd never let them go. The children were bundled onto the train together. Their suitcases were stowed in the racks over their heads and the parents stepped back out onto the platform, leaving their children, there, on the train.

"You look after each other," said the father, anxiously. "I'll write to you, Gloria." The door was closed, separating the parents from their children, nobody knowing when they would see each other again; nobody knowing if the families destined to take them in would be kind to them. All along the train little heads popped out of windows and little hands waved. Fathers were trying to be strong, putting on brave faces, but some of the mothers were beside themselves with grief. All along the platform waving handkerchiefs fluttered and calls of love floated in the air, as the great beast of a train slowly pulled out of the station and was consumed in a cloud of steam.

Quietly, the desolate platform emptied and Charles and Jam-Jar, still holding hands, were left alone to ponder all they had seen.

"It was with a great deal of faith that these parents entrusted their children to complete strangers," said Jam-Jar, his voice thick with emotion. "They were put on trains, with labels round their necks and sent all over the country to get away from the bombing to live with people they didn't know, who took them in and looked after them, most of them, out of the goodness of their own hearts. Some didn't have a very good time of it, though, but many enjoyed the experience. Sadly, some children never saw their parents again; killed in bombing raids, others saw them so infrequently, they became like strangers to each other and some children, who had grown up in the slums of London, were put with families in big country houses and had real difficulty adjusting to life back in the slums after the war. Many received an education they would never have otherwise received, bit like your great-grandmother and many stayed in touch with their host families for years.

"That was where your great-grandmother learnt all that poetry she used to recite off by heart, when she was evacuated to Yorkshire. She had very fond memories of one teacher, Miss Jones. It was Miss Jones, who taught her to love poetry and who inspired your mother to become a teacher too."

"I would hate to be separated from my family," said Charles with feeling and his great-grandfather put a strong arm around his shoulder and held him close.

Chapter 10 – The Blitz

It was starting to grow dark. Starlings and pigeons were flying home to their roosts in the station. The great clock, which hung over the main concourse, ticked towards the hour.

"Come on sweetheart. It'll be dark soon. We must push on. There's so much more to see."

Charles took his great-grandfather's huge hand again and off they went, through the town, which petered out behind them, as the last of the sun's glow poured itself in liquid gold across the distant sea. It glinted jewel-like in the sunset.

The air was getting cooler and they seemed to be going uphill. A fresh breeze quickened in the few scattered trees, as they reached the top of a broad summit. The great, golden sun was settling beyond the horizon, the shadows lengthening across the glorious sweep of fields, sinking into the secrecy of rising mists. The sea had taken on the colour of brushed metal, lit as if from beneath, by a silvery-blue luminescence, which glowed as the darkness descended. The warm scented air from the fields washed over the bare hilltop. Charles took a deep breath, filling his lungs and exhaled slowly, as the last of the sun stretched itself across the quiet water, picking out the distant horizon in a thin line of burnished copper, which dissolved into the depths, swallowed by the darkness of sea and sky, that had now become one.

In front of him, the Sussex countryside lay old and rich and mysterious. Sleepy villages snuggled cosily at the bottom of the long, steep slopes of the Downs. Here, luxurious shadows deepened into rich night, melting over the little villages like warm, dark chocolate.

The long sweeping view back down to the town, which now was just a silhouette in the distance, with the black line of the pier, forming a bridge over the now silver sea, made Charles feel exhilarated. He felt free. He put back his head, closed his eyes, stretched out his arms and gave a great 'whoop' of joy.

As darkness descended like a soft cloak over the land, sound became hushed as silken mists formed in velvet fields, still fragranced with the heat of the day. Wood smoke rose in the warm evening air, mingling with the stars. The last few birds sung their good-night chorus and some nearby animal squeaked and rustled in the bushes. Every living thing was going home to rest.

Charles suddenly felt very sleepy. His eyelids grew heavy and he started to doze, leaning his nodding head against his great-grandfather's strong arm.

"Wake up sleepy head!" said Jam-Jar, gently stroking Charles' hair. "You'll be able to sleep soon."

Charles looked around him. It was quite dark now. It was as if the town had disappeared. Not a single light from street or house could be seen. Even the sun had put itself out and the sea was shrouded in darkest night.

He had seen towns at night-time before; they were usually a blaze of lights. Here, there was nothing.

"Where's the town?" he asked.

"Oh, it's still down there, all right," Jam-Jar replied, "but it's the blackout now. Everyone has to cover their windows and doors with thick black curtains to stop the lights showing outside. You wouldn't want an enemy plane seeing your lights and dropping a bomb straight down your chimney, now would you! And you certainly wouldn't want to light their way for them. Down there, in the town, Air-Raid Wardens, all volunteers, are patrolling every street to make sure nobody is showing a light and if they can see a light, an Air Raid Warden knocks at the door, or worse still, shouts from the street, "Put that ruddy light out!" You can be fined for breaking the blackout rules too. Street lights, office lights, the lot. Even car head lights and traffic lights have to be fitted with slotted covers to minimise the glare and it's the same all over the country."

"Look over there," went on Jam-Jar.

Charles looked along the great sweep of the South Downs, stretching away into the darkness in both directions. He felt their solid mass beneath his feet riding out through the great dark night, a natural barrier against enemies for hundreds of years. The Weald stretched away north in front of him, fields and trees and rivers, waiting in that dark void of softest velvet, old and mysterious as time itself, quietly waiting for their moment to stand against evil and prevent its advance.

Charles shuddered. The smell of wood-smoke wafted up from a house hidden down at the bottom of the hill. All he could think of was home. He suddenly felt very cold. Jam-Jar put his great arm around him.

"Don't worry, Charles. The Downs have always protected us. They're a great defensive position, you know. Even took a few hits for us during the war. See that bomb crater over there? That's where an enemy bomber dropped its last bomb after a raid on London, before it flew back home across the sea. The hill took the damage for us, but it could have been those streets and houses down there, as it so often was. Sadly, a bomb even fell on a cinema in Brighton one Saturday morning when it was packed with children.

My Gloria, your great-grandmother should have been there too, but she'd been naughty and wasn't allowed to go."

"Gosh! That was a narrow escape for her!" Charles exclaimed.

"Yes, it was sweetheart. She was lucky more than once. Life hung on a knife-edge for us all in 1940. It was a very close thing," Jam-Jar replied, "but when Hitler realised he'd lost the Battle of Britain, because he couldn't beat our RAF, he called off Operation Sea Lion and do you know, there's a German invasion map, which actually shows where the German army would have landed if they had invaded. Brighton beach was one of the beaches earmarked as a landing point. They would have swept up through the town, along the Old Steine, past the Royal Pavilion, fanning out on either side, taking control of council buildings, local radio and telephone exchanges and securing the town, before sweeping up the London Road, attacking all who resisted on their path to London and to victory. This was their plan for the whole of the south coast."

Charles shuddered at the thought of his family being in the firing line, among the first to face the wrath of the invading forces. Then he remembered the small concrete buildings dotted around the fields near his home. His father had once told him that they were called 'Pill boxes' and that they would have been used as defensive positions to try to stop the Germans advancing towards London. The thought made him shiver again – the thought that the Nazis could have come so close to his home if they had succeeded in invading, was frightening, even if it was just History for him, it felt very real.

For a moment, they stood quietly, side by side, on the dark hillside, breathing in the rich scents, as the night winds cooled the fields in the valley below. The chalk down-land smelt sweet and warm.

"I love evenings like this," said Jam-Jar, quietly, "when the land exhales and gives up its fragrance."

He took a deep breath and sighed, "Come on, sweetheart. I want to show you London. Let's see what Hitler did next when he couldn't get his own way."

On they went. The great, dark Weald revealed itself to them and then the line of the North Downs came into view, silhouetted against the night's sky. Suddenly, Charles felt a pang of some deep emotion - the pull of home and he knew that it must be close by, nestled beneath those sleeping hills, but the feeling quickly passed as the clouds parted to reveal the full moon, shining brightly and there, sparkling in the pale moonlight, appeared the great River Thames itself, in all its glory. The glinting water snaked through the city and shimmered, as the glare from huge search lights combed the sky for enemy planes.

"A 'bombers' moon', the Luftwaffe pilots used to call it," said Jam-Jar, sadly.

Suddenly, the eerie wail of an air-raid siren started up and rose above the roof-tops. Slowly at first, the sound quickly intensified, growing louder and higher in tone, rising and falling, like the howl of a great dog, its call taken up by many others across the city. It made the hair stand up on the back of Charles' neck.

People were running for cover to the bomb shelters and a terrible feeling of panic and fear gripped Charles' throat. There was a moment's hushed silence and then the hollow thuds began, distant at first, but getting closer with every second. It sounded like a great dragon stomping over the city. The vibrations of the terrifying explosions grew worse, travelling through the ground, ripping through the city and filling Charles with dread to the pit of his stomach. He felt sick with fear, as the hollow booms turned to cracks and crashes like lightning approaching, as if the great angry dragon was tossing buildings aside like trees.

"It wasn't called Blitzkrieg or lightning war for nothing," said Jam-Jar ruefully, the raging fires reflecting in his eyes. "This is the Blitz, Charles. It started in September 1940 and went on till May 1941, although even after that, the bombing still continued at intervals throughout the war. It came straight after we'd won the Battle of Britain. This was Hitler's revenge."

The sky was a fiery orange. Barrage balloons floated calmly above the rooftops. Planes overhead, littered the dark sky - bombers, German bombers, whose undercarriages glowed in the light of the inferno, which raged below them, their dark, sinister hum throbbing in Charles' ears.

All around him was noise and confusion: the whistle of falling bombs, their ear-splitting detonation, which cracked inside his skull, the metallic patter of incendiaries dropping onto rooftops, like hail, far out of reach of any fireman, the white-green blinding flash as they ignited, the searchlights combing the sky, the relentless pounding of the Ac-Ac anti-aircraft guns, the sickening roar of collapsing buildings, the urgent bells of passing emergency vehicles, the air thick with smoke and dust, which stuck in the throat, the rubble and debris everywhere, sparking electricity cables and damaged roads crumpled up like paper! Shock waves rippled through Charles' body with every bomb blast he heard. His ears were ringing, as he shook his head to free himself from the sickening panic which had gripped him. He had no idea how anyone could keep going amidst such devastation.

And then Jam-Jar was there, holding him close.

"Don't be afraid, Charles. This all happened a very long time ago. You'll always be safe with me. There's no need for you to see any more of this, little one."

Jam-Jar took his hand and away they went. Charles looked over his shoulder one last time. Parts of the city were in darkness; parts of the city were ablaze, lit up in a fierce orange glow, which raged like mythical salamanders through the streets and dock yards, reflecting in the river, which looked like liquid gold. Great hot tears, like molten lava, sparked and poured from the burning buildings and dripped and fizzed in the water.

"Not for the first time," thought Charles, thinking of another great fire, which the city had had to endure. He saw an image in his mind, of the brave people desperately working to save lives and buildings from this huge dragon of a fire - small, dark shapes, silhouetted against the inferno with nothing, but buckets of water and a few fire engines; such bravery against such huge odds. He closed his eyes and looked away.

When he opened his eyes again, he found himself in an air-raid shelter. In contrast to the confusion and desperation outside, up at street level, all was very calm and orderly down here. Charles could still hear the thud and boom of bombs and the pounding of anti-aircraft guns, but down here, children were playing, and two babies were trying, rather unsuccessfully to sleep, fussing and fretting in their mother's arms. People were laughing and chatting, whilst others handed out cups of tea. Someone was playing a harmonica, and others were singing along:

'We'll meet again,
Don't know where,
Don't know when
But I know we'll meet again some sunny day.
Keep smiling through,
Just like you always do
Till the blue skies drive the dark clouds far away.'

"Ah! Vera Lynn," said Jam-Jar.

"Who's Vera Lynn?" Charles asked.

"She was a popular singer during the war, Charles. Everyone called her the 'Forces' Sweetheart'. She travelled to many battle zones, including Egypt and Burma, performing concerts for the troops to raise morale. It was quite dangerous for her to go, but she was determined to."

The people continued to sing the song:

'So will you please say "Hello"
To the folks that I know
Tell them I won't be long
They'll be happy to know
That as you saw me go
I was singing this song

We'll meet again,
Don't know where,
Don't know when
But I know we'll meet again some sunny day....'

"It sounds a very sad song," said Charles. "They don't know when they're going to see each other again."

"No, sweetheart and sadly, too many loved ones never did come home."

"Why does no one seem scared, then?" asked Charles, relieved to have escaped the destruction outside.

"Oh, they're scared all right!" Jam-Jar replied, as one particularly loud bomb boomed overhead. Everyone ducked, some dust fell, a few looked up momentarily as if half expecting the roof to cave in, but then, after a slight pause, carried on chatting.

"Cor, lummey," exclaimed one old man, looking up at the ceiling. "Them ruddy Naarzis!" he said with an odd, long 'aar', as he mouthed something else that Charles couldn't quite make out.

People nodded, ruefully, in agreement and then carried on with their song, almost in defiance of their own fear. Charles felt safe amongst this wealth of humanity all crowded together in the confined space of the basement.

"Why is everyone so calm?" asked Charles, puzzled.

"It's us Brits, you see. It's the way we are. Calm in a crisis. Resourceful lot we are, too! Even the underground stations were used as air-raid shelters. Whole families would take their blankets down into the underground and sleep on the station platforms. There'd be people coming home from work, getting off the trains and stepping over people, who'd set up their beds for the night on the platform. All the trains ran on time, even during the worst of the Blitz, the milk was still delivered, the post still found its way to people's houses, businesses still traded. Life just went on," Jam-Jar said with pride.

After what seemed like an age, the bombing stopped. The air raid was over and the 'All Clear' sounded; another ear-piercing wail, which this time, instead of rising and falling like the howling of a dog, rose and held one note. Thinking that it was another air raid, Charles was momentarily filled with dread again.

"It's alright," said Jam-Jar, seeing the alarm on Charles' face. "It's all over for another night. That's the 'All Clear'. There'll be no more bombing for a while."

Everyone emerged from the shelter, yawning and stretching and squinting at the morning sun. Outside, the birds were singing furiously, clearly relieved that the tension had melted away into a new dawn and Charles saw a most amazing thing; people going to work, smartly dressed and going about their daily business, a milkman delivering the milk, a paper boy doing his rounds, whistling. Even amongst the bomb damage, people were carrying on normally, as if nothing had happened. In several places shop signs were planted in the rubble of bombed out buildings, 'Now trading at...' and a nearby street would be named, where the brave shop owner was now trading, having relocated in defiance of the enemy bombers. One business man was even dictating a letter to his secretary amongst the rubble of his bombed-out business - chair, desk, typewriter all there as if surrounded by office walls, instead of sitting outside in the carnage strewn everywhere around him.[24] Some families were picking through the rubble of their bombed homes, salvaging what they could and packing clothes and belongings into suitcases. They looked dazed, but relieved to be alive, stoic in the face of such adversity.

One old lady emerged from her bombed house, clearly in shock, wearing only her nightdress. An air-raid warden went over to help her.

"Come on, luv," he said kindly. "Ain't ya gonna make yer'self a bit decent, like?"

The old lady blinked for a moment, as if trying to clear the fog of dust from her mind.

"Oh yeah," she replied, in a daze, "'arf a mo!" and turning, she stumbled off back into her damaged house, to emerge a few moments later, still only in her nightdress, but with a hat perched precariously on her head.

"That'll do, luv," said the warden, sympathetically and helped her to an ambulance.[25]

Jam-Jar saw Charles looking.

"A brave lot we are. Every act of normality is an act of defiance against the enemy."

They walked on. There, ahead of them, was a clothes' shop with clothes hanging on mannequins in the window, or at least where the window should have been. All the glass had been blown in and lay smashed over the floor. A man was sweeping up the glass, as a smartly-dressed lady customer arrived. She chatted to the shop keeper through the broken window and then he led the way into the shop, but instead of going through the open door, the lady stepped onto the ledge where the window had once been, still chatting normally to the man about the clothes on the mannequin and the two walked inside, quite unconcerned, as if it was the most normal thing in the world to walk into a shop through a broken window![26]

Charles and Jam-Jar smiled.

Suddenly, there was a commotion farther along the road. A group of people seemed to be cheering and waving and flocking around a well-dressed man and woman, who were slowly walking towards Charles and his great-grandfather.

"It's the King and Queen," exclaimed the expectant crowd, who had gathered nearby and Charles felt a thrill of excitement at the thought of being so close to them. "You know, even their home, Buckingham Palace, was bombed on 13th September 1940," said Jam-Jar. "The Queen said that she was glad they'd been bombed so that she could look the East End in the face. 'The most dangerous woman in Europe,' Hitler called her," chuckled Jam-Jar.

"Why?" asked Charles, shocked.

"Because, he knew her strength," his great-grandfather replied simply.

"The East End was bombed so badly, you see," his great-grandfather continued, "and the King and Queen, who had refused to leave London for a place of safety, wanted the people of London to know that they wouldn't desert them in their time of need. They were advised to seek refuge in Canada, but they refused to leave. The Queen said, *'The children will not leave without me, and I will not leave without the King and the King will never leave.'* It raised morale greatly and people never forgot their act of bravery. The Queen even learned how to shoot by doing target practice on rats, in case Nazis had invaded – she was that prepared to fight.

Slowly, the group neared them and stopped close by. The King and Queen spoke to the assembled crowd for a few moments and then suddenly, the King seemed to look straight at Charles and fixed him with his warm, kind gaze, as if he could see through the thin veil of time, which separated them. Then Charles heard these words in his mind, the words of the King,

"Remember all you have seen, Charles and tell your children and your children's children what was done here and the sacrifices that were made." Charles felt the power and authority of the King, emanating from a long line of monarchs leading far back into history. The King nodded to Jam-Jar and the two men shared a look of understanding, a father's understanding. The King and Queen moved on and were encircled once more by the cheering crowds.

Charles and his great-grandfather looked at each other in amazement and the smile they shared was deep and proud.

"I want to show you one more thing before we leave," said Jam-Jar and he took Charles to the roof of a tall building. All beneath them, the city lay in beauty and ruins in equal measure.

"There! Look over there, Charles," said Jam-Jar, his voice deep with emotion. There, ahead of them, through the smoke and devastation, Charles saw a beautiful white dome. The black, filthy fog cleared, as if a curtain had been opened, the sun blazed through the clouds and the glorious domed roof of St. Paul's Cathedral shone in the morning light. It looked magnificent, majestic, as if riding the storm.[27]

"All through the war, all through the bombing, St. Paul's Cathedral stood strong, never destroyed by enemy fire. That was us, Charles, this nation, we never surrendered. At Dunkirk, we turned

defeat into victory; during the Battle of Britain, it was impossible to beat us and even in the worst of the Blitz, we showed the Nazis that we would never give in."

Charles gazed at the city below him and knew that he would never forget.

Then Jam-Jar spoke again.

"Instead, Hitler decided to turn his evil attention to the invasion of Russia. He launched Operation Barbarossa in June 1941 and that's when the Russian convoys began."

"What were the Russian Convoys, Jam-Jar?"

"When Germany invaded Russia, in June 1941," Jam-Jar said, "Russia switched sides and joined the allies, but it needed help to fight the Germans and Churchill was only too glad to give it.

"So, Britain sent ships full of supplies, munitions and equipment via the northern Russian ports of Murmansk and Archangel to support them in their fight and these were the convoys – the ships travelling together for protection from U-boat attacks. Let's go now, sweetheart and I'll show you."

Charles was intrigued. Taking one last look at the dome of St. Paul's Cathedral, bright against the black smoke, he felt the deep strength of the nation and took his great-grandfather's hand, gladly.

Chapter 11 - The Russian Convoys

They were now standing in a cold, crowded train station. The shock of the cold winter's night, after the stifling heat of the burning city, made Charles gasp. His warm breath misted in the freezing air and for a moment, he was bewildered by the sudden crush of people milling about, soldiers, sailors, loved ones, wives, children and sweethearts. Almost everyone was in one uniform or another. Even the train guards looked smart and Charles noticed that everyone wore hats.

There was a great bustle of people and crush of luggage and kit bags, carried on shoulders, or above heads in the crowd. The pungent smell of hot, sweet, over-stewed tea filled Charles' nostrils. It wafted from the Salvation Army stand, where volunteers were handing out tea and buns to the soldiers and sailors, "At least it's warm and wet," said one.

Everyone seemed cheerful. Music spilled out from the station café, where someone had turned on the radio. The tune started with a trumpet call, as if waking the soldiers and calling them to parade and then, like a steam train pulling out from the station, gathering speed and having a party on the way, the music heaved itself into high tempo.

"Ah! That's Glenn Miller playing on the radio, the American band leader. This is his famous, 'In the Mood'," said Jam-Jar. "Always guaranteed to get people up and dancing. You see, the Americans joined the war in the winter of 1941, after Pearl Harbour in Hawaii, which is a group of islands in the Pacific Ocean, was bombed by the Japanese on 7th December. The Americans had stationed a large part of their naval fleet in Hawaii at Pearl Harbour and it was largely destroyed and sadly people died, but luckily, though, most of their more modern ships and their aircraft carriers were docked elsewhere and were untouched. The Americans declared war on Japan the next day, but this is where it gets complicated, because the Japanese had sided with the Germans and Italians, so Germany declared war on America, which led to America joining the war on the side of the Allies."

"Well, that's confusing," Charles exclaimed.

Jam-Jar smiled.

"Ironically though, when America joined the war, it gave us a much greater chance of beating the whole lot of them, because, unlike Britain before the war, who had been slowly disarming and reducing the size of its armed forces and not investing in new equipment," said Jam-Jar with a rueful shake of his head, "America was rich and had been building up its war reserves for years, so they were fully equipped and ready to fight. You see this war really did suck most of the world into its gaping mouth."

Charles imagined the world slowing being swallowed by an ugly monster, greedy for power and conquest, ready to destroy anything in its path and then he saw, standing right in front of it, one tiny patch of green, standing bravely before its spreading claws, standing against the tide of evil, which drooled from its mouth; one brave little island, just managing to keep its head above the wave of war, just about holding on alone, but not for much longer...then he heard that music again, that joyful trumpet-call wafting through the cold, station air, filling his ears. He started tapping his toes.

Then, a wondrous sound rolled into the station, a great beast of a steam engine, its huge wheels turning languorously, beside the platform. The enormous pistons moved the driving rods like arms, which rose and fell, as the heavy wheels turned. Majestically, it pulled to a standstill, like a proud lion, taking full ownership of the space and blew great clouds of smoke and plumes of steam over everyone. The sharp smell of hot cinders hit the back of the throat and made Charles blink hard.

"They should never have got rid of steam trains," said Jam-Jar. "So much character."

Suddenly, the station master blew his whistle and the train answered the call, eager to be away and on the move. In a frenzy of activity, tears, sobs, hugs, 'goodbyes', 'excuse me's,' and 'mind yer backs', there was a surge towards the train and Charles and Jam-Jar found themselves sitting in a crowded carriage, full of chatting people.

Complete strangers talked and laughed and passed the time of day, as if they had known each other for years.

"Cor, luv a duck. It's taters out there," said one chirpy soldier.

"Cor, lummy. It ain't half cold!" replied another.

"What are they saying, Jam-Jar? I don't understand a word!"

"Some of it's Cockney Rhyming slang," replied Jam-Jar. "'Taters' is rhyming slang for 'taters or potatoes in a mould', which rhymes with 'cold'. It's brilliant, isn't it!" he said smiling.

The feelings of camaraderie and companionship were contagious. Charles found himself singing along with everyone in the carriage.

"Roll out the barrel, we'll have a barrel of fun.
Roll out the barrel, we've got the blues on the run.
Zing! Boom! Tarrarel! – ring out a song of good cheer.
Now's the time to roll the barrel – for the gang's all here."

After the song had ended, Charles pondered,

"That's another sad song, really, Jam-Jar, isn't it? It's talking about having the blues on the run, now everyone is together again."

"Yes," Jam-Jar replied. "It was another song that got people through the war. You took your fun times and your good cheer wherever and whenever you could find it, because nobody knew if they would survive another day. Life was so frightening and uncertain. People needed to forget about the war for a little while, when they could."

Charles rested his head on Jam-Jar's shoulder, who put his big, strong arm around him. Dusk was settling. The countryside rolled past, punctuated by great puffs of steam, which plumed from the engine and the shrill, excited whistles of the train, as it entered another tunnel. Its soothing, rocking motion made Charles feel sleepy....

"Wake up sleepy head. We're here," said Jam-Jar softly.

"Where?" asked a dazed Charles.

"The docks," and sure enough, the sounds of whistles and orders to march filled Charles' startled ears. He felt bewildered and disorientated.

In the confusion, sailors jumped up from their seats and gathered their kit bags together. One young sailor called kindly to his mates, "Come on lads. Let's be 'avin yer!" he said, smiling gently.

"Half a mo," shouted one of his chums good-naturedly. "Luv a duck, always in a bleedin' 'urry, that one."

They all crowded off the train together, laughing and joking, as they ran down the platform to report to their commanding officer. A little shock of realisation tingled at the back of Charles' mind. Surely, the young sailor with the kind smile was his great-grandfather again, as Charles had seen him in that street in Brighton - a young lad home on leave.

"Reporting for duty, Sir!" his young great-grandfather said, and stood to attention, tall and smart.

Charles looked at his great-grandfather, standing older beside him. Jam-Jar just winked a knowing smile.

Suddenly, all those laughing, bumbling young lads straightened up, saluted and transformed themselves into every inch the serious, professional young men they were - sailors ready to do a job of war.

"'ten-shun," the column stood tall and stock still.

"By the left, quick march. Left right, left right, left right...." and off those proud men went, marching smartly away to board their ships. Their echoing footsteps faded into the distance and the whole station platform faded with them.

Charles was startled to find they were now on the deck of an enormous ship, which was pitching and rolling in a heavy swell. The night was dark. There was no moon and he could feel, rather than see, the immensity of the ocean around them. The swirling blackness of the great, dark ocean heaved massively beneath them. He could feel its vastness supporting the burden of these great vessels on their dangerous voyage, steaming to save a distant land.

The ship's engines rumbled like a sleeping giant beneath their feet. Snow was falling on the deck, which was covered with a thick layer of ice. Icicles hung everywhere. Ghost-like sailors moved around the deck, wrapped in winter gear.

"It was so cold," said Jam-Jar, "Your hands would freeze to the railings if you were silly enough to touch them. Even your eyebrows and eyelashes would freeze."

"Where are we, Jam-Jar," asked Charles.

"The Arctic Ocean, Charles, on our way to Russia."

"Russia!" exclaimed Charles.

"Yes, sweetheart. Do you remember I mentioned about Operation Barbarossa, which Hitler launched in June 1941? Hitler realised that he couldn't beat us in the Battle of Britain or the Blitz, so he turned his attention on Russia and invaded.

"Churchill quickly arranged for urgent naval convoys of vital war material to be sent to Russia. The Royal Canadian Navy and the United States Navy also helped. He knew that Russia needed assistance in its fight against Germany and he knew how important it was to take decisive and swift action, to send a message, loud and clear, to the Germans that we would stand up to bullies, even when they were bullying our friends. So, throughout the war, Churchill sent ships full of supplies, munitions and equipment, including Hurricanes and Spitfires."

"Spitfires!" exclaimed Charles.

"Yes sweetheart. In fact, there's some on this ship right now, right below us."

Charles looked at the deck and thought about those Spitfires sitting down there in the quiet of the dark hold, waiting for their moment to be off and away up into the freedom of the skies.

Jam-Jar continued, "The ships travelled in convoys for safety, to make it harder for the German submarines, the U-boats, to pick us off. Any ship that broke down, the convoy was ordered to leave behind. They weren't meant to stop for anything. You wouldn't want to be a straggler out here! Here, the winters are kind to no one!"

Charles scanned the dark, invisible horizon, as if an unknown malevolent presence lurked just out of sight beyond the waves. He suddenly felt very lonely and vulnerable, and he became aware of a great weight of fear pressing down on him. He imagined the despair the sailors must have felt watching the rest of the convoy slowly leaving them farther and farther behind.

"There were German battleships out there too," said Jam-Jar inclining his head to the vastness of the seas. "Battleships like the Tirpitz gave our convoys a real headache. The Tirpitz was the heaviest battleship ever built by a European navy at the time and believe you me, you didn't want to see her on the horizon with her guns aimed at you! The convoys had to risk sailing up past occupied Norway to reach the northern Russian ports of Murmansk and Archangel, but we did it to support the Russians in their fight and this," said his great-grandfather, pointing all around him, "is one of those Russian convoys. It's too dark to see them now, but all around us, there are other ships like this one, travelling together."

Charles strained his eyes out into the thick black night. There, in the distance, following on behind and on either side, he could just make out the white breakwater foaming and surging around the bows of dark hulls, the ships' prows slicing through the ocean. The sense that they were not alone was strangely comforting; the knowledge that all these great ships were bound for one destination and with one shared purpose was thrilling.

"It's deepest winter now," said Jam-Jar, ruefully. "The end of February 1942, the coldest and hardest part of winter for all those at war, especially those at sea," he continued and there was a far-away look in his eyes, which seemed to have taken on the colour of the sea, a stormy sea, grey and lonely. "'The worst journey in the world', Churchill called it," he said quietly and a shadow crossed his face. Charles' mother always said that Jam-Jar had never spoken of the bad times during the war, only the funny things that had happened and he wondered what his great-grandfather was remembering and what he had seen and experienced out here.

Presently he continued, "The Russian convoys were also called the Arctic Convoys and the Arctic can be a dangerous place, Charles. I've seen walls of water thirty feet high in the Arctic Ocean, bearing down on us, ready to crush these great ships like they were no more than toys made of matchsticks."

An awful and overwhelming feeling of seasickness began to creep over Charles, as his great-grandfather's voice trailed into the distance.

"We endured temperatures so low, that when water washed on deck, it froze almost instantly and the weight of the ice made the ship top-heavy and in danger of capsizing, if you didn't jolly well get rid of it quickly. Sometimes, the ship would roll so badly, you'd hold your breath and pray that it would decide to right itself again."

Jam-Jar's words faded away, as Charles became increasingly aware of a rope tied around his waist that was tethered to something nearby. He saw men shouting to each other, trying desperately to be heard over the raging wind howling in his ears. Horrified, he saw a mountainous wave bearing down on the ship, the crest of which was out of sight, boiling and swirling like a huge hand poised and ready to crash down onto the deck. The men called desperately to each other, as the ship rolled and rolled and rolled some more, so far over to starboard, that Charles was terrified it would never stop and would plunge them all into the black, open mouth of the dark, freezing waters below. E Stunned, he saw other lifelines stretched taught over the turbulent ocean and from them, like puppets on strings, men dangled helplessly from the listing ship. He felt his own feet start to slip on the icy deck. Time slowed. He heard his own breath coming short and quick, his heart pounding in his chest. He held his breath, expecting any minute to feel deathly cold water closing over his head. The black deeps rose to greet him...and then, as if the ship, too, had seen the danger, it shook itself, as if waking up and righted itself again. Charles felt his stomach churn with the movement and suddenly Jam-Jar's hand was on his arm.

"Charles, Charles," came Jam-Jar's worried voice. "Are you alright, sweetheart? Come back, Charles!"

Charles blinked away the last of the vision and looked around him, relieved to see his great-grandfather standing there, his concerned eyes staring fixedly into Charles' face and one hand on Charles' shoulder, the other holding his arm, as if he'd never let go.

"You gave me a right turn then, you did. You suddenly looked all far away, as if you were disappearing into the mist." His grandfather hugged him, a great big bear hug, as he kissed the top of his great-grandson's head, ruffling his blonde hair and Charles felt infinitely safe in his arms, as if nothing would ever hurt him.

"Don't worry, Charles. We were constantly de-icing with axes and steam hoses and although many ships did sink in this way, this one's safe. Remember, you're with me," and he gave Charles a knowing wink.

Slowly, it started to get light, and the great, strong hulls and proud outlines of the ships began to emerge from the cloak of grey mist, which swirled and floated around them. It was a beautiful and awe-inspiring scene, with the sun just pushing through the white veil of thinning mist. An ethereal glimmer hung in the morning air.

The dark, churning sea was now strangely calm and there was an unusual, viscous quality about the water. It seemed thicker than normal, rather like a half-set jelly, thought Charles, which any minute might set to solid ice...

Jam-Jar saw Charles looking, "You know," he said, "even the Russians awarded us a medal. They were so grateful for what we had done for them. They realised how hard a sacrifice it had been. They still haven't forgotten even now and in 2013 they awarded us the Ushakov medal. That's when we were finally given the Arctic Star medal too."

They both looked at the ocean and at the proud ships gleaming in the morning sun and they thought of the lives lost and the sacrifices made.

Chapter 12 – Malta

"Come on sweetheart. It's time to leave," said Jam-Jar and as they turned to walk away, it was as if Charles stepped into a void of cavernous blackness.

"Where are we going next, Jam-Jar?" asked Charles, his voice echoing in what he could tell was a vast, internal space. He had a sense that they might be below the water-line. He could almost feel the great press of ocean, surging along on the other side of the metal hull. It made him feel slightly panicky.

Beside him, he heard his great-grandfather's voice, echoing in the inky depths.

"To the turning of the tide," his great-grandfather replied, "but first to Malta, because without Malta, there would have been no tide to turn."

Suddenly, a great roar of engines started up all around them. The noise was deafening, but thrilling too and by the somersaults of excitement turning in his stomach, Charles knew, exactly what he was hearing, but how could it be?

SPITFIRES!

The deep, powerful sound seemed to rip through the darkness, letting day-light flood into the hold of the ship and Charles could feel himself strangely floating upwards. He and his great-grandfather seemed to be standing on a large platform, which was gradually rising to the daylight above, that, as it fell across the scene, slowly revealed, to Charles' great delight, a thing of beauty. Overjoyed, he gazed awestruck, for standing right beside him was his beloved Spitfire!

A mark V Spitfire to be precise![28]

There it sat, with its pilot in the cockpit, waiting expectantly, like a dog about to go for a walk, except Charles had the strongest feeling that this great dog was about to slip its lead!

As soon as the platform drew level with the deck above, a signal was given and the Spitfire roared to maximum revs, breaks still on, the pilot's concentrated gaze fixed at a point in the near distance, both pilot and Spitfire straining at the leash, eager to be free.

It was only then that Charles realised they were standing on the deck of an enormous ship, an aircraft carrier and the point on which the pilot was concentrating so closely, was actually the end of the deck and beyond it, nothing but air and sea! Charles couldn't believe that the pilot was about to hurl himself and his precious Spitfire at the great expanse of nothingness beyond the ship! His great-grandfather sensed his thoughts.

"Don't worry," he said. "This is the USS Wasp and it's April 1942. The island of Malta is under siege. The Axis powers, that's Germany and Italy, know this little island in the middle of the Mediterranean is vitally important, because it controls the sea all around and strategically it's crucial to the Allied success in North Africa. Allied air and Naval attacks from Malta have already sunk over half the ships carrying fuel, tanks and personnel sent by Germany to fight in North Africa."

"North Africa! What happens there? It seems like all the world is caught up in this war!" Charles said.

"It's not called a World War for nothing," his great-grandfather replied.

"All that German equipment, which was destined for the German Afrika Korps in North Africa is now at the bottom of the Mediterranean Sea!"

Charles looked confused.

"Don't worry, sweetheart," said Jam-Jar, gently. "We're going to North Africa next, and you'll never forget it, but right now, the Nazis have decided that they must win the battle of Malta, because this little island has made the Nazis' job much harder."

The Spitfire was still roaring at maximum revs, desperate to be free. Suddenly, the signal was given. Like a racing car when the chequered flag drops, the pilot immediately released the breaks. The Spitfire shot along the deck towards the fast-approaching sea. Charles couldn't believe that the pilot would make it into the air. He stared intently as the scene unfolded, the sailors around him surprising him by immediately carrying on with the business of bringing up the next Spitfire from the hold below. Only he and his great-grandfather seemed to be watching the drama unfolding in front of them. The Spitfire raced to the end of the ship's runway, as if unconcerned for its near certain doom and then, for a sickening moment, it disappeared below the level of the deck.

Charles held his breath, unsure of the fate of pilot or plane. Had the sea swallowed them? He couldn't tell and then a great surge of relief washed over him, as the Spitfire appeared again and soared away into the sky, clearly pleased with itself for cheating death so cheekily.

Charles clapped and cheered, as the next Spitfire appeared beside him on the lift and revved up, with the same deafening roar.

"That's what 3,000rpm sounds like!" shouted Jam-Jar over the din.

They watched as Spitfire after Spitfire roared off into the sky, shrinking to dots in the distance. A few, though, did not appear above the level of the deck and Charles was sickened to think of those poor pilots plunging into the expectant sea, swallowing plane and pilot instantly, companions in life and companions in death. Charles was relieved that he couldn't see the tragedy unfolding out of sight. He forced his gaze to those other planes, racing away into the distance.

"They're in a race against time," said Jam-Jar. "They have to make a dash for Malta before the Messerschmitt Bf 109's catch-up with them. It's like a deadly game of 'Cat and Mouse'!" said Jam-Jar wryly. "Malta's been under siege for the last two years and since the fighting started in North Africa in June 1940, the RAF and Royal

Navy have been launching attacks on Axis, German and Italian ships, from the island. Churchill called Malta an 'unsinkable aircraft carrier'.

"Unfortunately, though, because of this, the Luftwaffe and Italian Air Force have been bombing Malta, mercilessly – three thousand bombing raids in two years; houses, towns, churches and airfields alike, all targeted by the Germans. In March and April 1942, alone, more bombs were dropped on Malta than on London during the Blitz and ten thousand homes were destroyed.

"Before 1942, the island's defences were very meagre, a few Hurricanes and some biplanes, which were flown by some very brave pilots, who managed to fend off the first Italian attacks in 1940, but when the Messerschmitt Bf 109Fs came along, there was very little hope. The only plane that was up to the fight was, can you guess, Charles?"

"Spitfires!" Charles joyfully declared.

"That's right. A desperate call was sent to London for Spitfires and the Spitfires came. They were flown from HMS Eagle on 7th March 1942 and when the Luftwaffe pilots realised that the Spitfires had arrived, it initially unnerved them – 'Achtung! Spitfire!', 'Danger! Spitfire!' – was all that could be heard, as they turned tail for home, so afraid they were to take them on, until they saw how few Spitfires there were; just thirty-one, against six-hundred German and Italian fighter planes![29] More were needed and there were no more British aircraft carriers left to transport them!

"So, Churchill acted quickly and wrote a personal letter to President Roosevelt asking if he would be willing to send the

American aircraft carrier, the USS Wasp, to deliver more Spitfires and thankfully President Roosevelt agreed."

Charles looked out to sea, at those little dots in the sky and hoped they would arrive safely. He imagined the pilot he'd seen taking off, flying now, towards a pall of smoke on the island, hoping there would be an airfield for him to land his plane, his head turning and turning, checking in all directions for incoming enemy fighters.

Suddenly, Charles was there! He was the pilot in that Spitfire, the cockpit surrounding him, the sound of his great companion reassuring him with its strength and vitality. It was his eyes fixed on the landing field on the near horizon and it was the hairs that rose on the back of his neck, which instinctively flashed a warning, red-hot and insistent in his mind. He felt, rather than saw the incoming enemy 109 coming at him from out of the sun over his right shoulder, an eerie shadow darkening the cockpit of the plane and he instantly flicked the control stick, sending his Spitfire down into a steep dive.

Just as the Messerschmitt came within firing range, the Spitfire twisted into a sharp turn, evading the tracer bullets, which shot a red-hot line over the top of the plane, just missing it, the Spitfire's speed and superior manoeuvrability enraging the Messerschmitt pilot, who overshot his prey every time.

This was a fight to the death and Charles could feel it. His senses were tuned to this moment. He needed all his wits to survive. There was no past and no present, only now. Nothing else mattered except getting his Spitfire down to that airfield, which he could see being bombed even as he approached it and, in that minute, everything seemed go very quiet; the roaring noise drained away to utter silence; the only sounds he could hear - his own ragged breath coming short and quick and his heart pounding in his chest.

A cold concentration and intensity descended on him. He felt strangely calm and then a voice entered his mind, like a beam of light boring into his brain, "If you've got to die, don't make it easy for them, Charlie!" He knew the voice. It came through strong and clear, from one pilot to another; it was his great-grandfather, Frank – the fighter pilot, whom he'd met from the First World War. Charles knew he was not alone and he knew what he had to do.

129

Suddenly, he put the plane into a steep dive, heading straight towards the air-field. The Messerschmitt was close on his tail, firing at him all the way down. Turning this way and that, Charles saw the tracer bullets missing their mark every time and hurtling past him.

Immediately, he flicked the control stick and flipping out of the way into an extreme roll, he swooped back into attack, letting off a rapid volley of machine gun fire, which found its mark. The Messerschmitt broke off the attack, as oil and smoke trailed out behind and before any more enemy fighters could catch up with him, he aimed again for the airfield. Landing quickly, he pushed back the canopy and jumped out of the cockpit, rushing for the cover of a slit trench, as tracer bullets nipped at his heels, and bombs rained down all around.[30]

As Charles dived for cover, the real pilot of the Spitfire seemed to break free and leap before him, headfirst into the trench, Charles following close behind him like a shadow...

...and landing straight into the outstretched arms of his great-grandfather, Jam-Jar.

"I was so worried about you," he said, very relieved to have his great-grandson safe in his arms.

"I don't know what happened, Jam-Jar," exclaimed Charles, holding onto him tightly. "One minute I was standing beside you on the deck of that ship, watching the Spitfires take off and fly towards Malta and the next minute, I was in one, flying it myself!"

Charles lifted his head and saw before him the sparkling sea, glinting and shimmering in the warm glow of the Mediterranean sun. A fresh, breeze blew gently on his face, refreshing him, as his heartbeat calmed.

"Well, did you enjoy it, Charles?" his great-grandfather asked, still holding him tightly and stroking the top of his head.

"I was scared, very scared," and then he thought, "but yes, I enjoyed it!"

"You've had the very great privilege, sweetheart, of finding out first-hand, what it was like for these young men. You couldn't have been hurt yourself, but you had the chance to walk in that lad's shoes, or, to fly in them at least," and Jam-Jar inclined his head towards the young pilot, who was still recovering his breath beside them. He seemed to sense their presence, because he looked over to where Charles and his great-grandfather were crouched beside him.

Had the young pilot looked straight into Charles' eyes? Charles wasn't sure, but he inclined his head, almost in acknowledgment, as the pilot turned away.

Charles turned to his great-grandfather.

"It's possible, sweetheart," said Jam-Jar, reading Charles' thoughts. "You've just experienced the most intense and dangerous few minutes of this young pilot's life. It's not surprising that he might have felt you with him. That poor boy has no idea what is waiting for him here. The battle was fiercer here and more intense than anything seen during the Battle of Britain and these pilots, who worked so hard to save this island, starved with the islanders, whose rations they shared. Ships sending much needed supplies and rations were regularly bombed and very little food got through, but the islanders' loyalty to Britain and to the cause of freedom was unshakeable and King George VI awarded Malta the George Cross in recognition of the islanders' great sacrifice and heroism."

"Did they win, Jam-Jar? Did the islanders survive the siege?"

"They did, sweetheart. The siege of Malta was won by the allies, which meant that the next stop, North Africa, was much harder for the Germans, who found it much more difficult to get supplies to their troops in North Africa. If the Allies had lost Malta, they may well have lost North Africa and possibly the war and it was those Spitfires again, which saved the day."

Charles still felt the thrill and exhilaration of all that he had just experienced, as his gaze settled on the sea, so calm and so serene. The battle still raged in the skies overhead. The bombs still fell. The guns still pounded, but the sparkling water called to him.

Chapter 13 - El Alamein

The swell of the bright, sparkling Mediterranean Sea stilled to rolling sand dunes and a vast desert spread itself before Charles' eyes. The golden horizon glowed and shimmered with the heat of a setting desert sun.

"Egypt, North Africa," Charles heard Jam-Jar say, "The Western Desert, on the edge of the Sahara!"

As the last rays of a stunning sunset poured themselves in liquid beauty over the rose-tinted desert, Charles gasped in awe at the majesty of the scene. It was vast and breathtaking.

"Why are we here, Jam-Jar?"

"This marked the turning point in the war for us," Jam-Jar replied. "We had to win here to protect the Suez Canal and the Persian Gulf oil fields. Without that oil, it would have been very difficult for us to win the war. Before this battle, it seemed impossible for us to defeat the Germans, but here, was the first time the allies actually won a decisive victory. After this, the tide of the war started to turn in our favour and it was all down to one man,

Field Marshal Montgomery, Monty for short, one of the first generals in whom Churchill really had faith."

"Oh! He's the man, who was in charge of South East High Command, where I live" exclaimed Charles. "I've heard about him."

"Well," said Jam-Jar, "He was a brilliant general - he didn't believe in retreat; a perfect match for the German general, Field Marshal Rommel, whose brilliant battle tactics had so far, outwitted the Allies. Rommel was known for being a man of honour - fair to his enemies as well, especially when captured, insisting that prisoners were treated with respect. It was as if these two men were plucked from a bygone age of Knights and Chivalry to fight it out here. Strange, isn't it, how fate turns up pairs like this, Churchill and Hitler, Monty and Rommel and right now these two great generals are pitting their wits against each other out there in this vast desert."

Charles and his great-grandfather settled themselves into a dugout, protected by a wall of sand.

"It's like we're about to watch a film," said Charles, nervously.

"Got any popcorn?" Jam-Jar chuckled, but Charles could see that he was nervous too. "Nineteen days this lasted, Charles. Nineteen days of non-stop fighting, a lot of it hand to hand, from the 23rd October 1942 to the 11th November, when Rommel finally, had to admit defeat and retreat. Hitler didn't like that one little bit."

Charles felt his heart beginning to pound with anticipation.

"Full moon, Charles. Clear sky. We'll be able to see the lot."

Jam-Jar gestured to the desert, "On one side you have the Germans and Italians and, on our side, we have forces from the United Kingdom, India, Palestine, Australia, New Zealand, South Africa, Free French."

"Free French?"

"Yeah, the ones who'd got away with us at Dunkirk, also we have the Free Greeks and the United States providing air support, along with our very own Hurricanes and Spitfires, all fighting together in what was called the Western Desert Air Force.

"Right now," continued Jam-Jar, warming to his subject, "195,000 men, 1,029 tanks and 1,451 anti-tank guns are lined up along 40 miles of front line and in a minute, at precisely 21.40,

Operation Lightfoot is going to commence with a 1,000-gun barrage and 882 rounds that are going to land right along that 40-mile front, all at exactly the same time and 116,000 Germans and Italians, with their 547 tanks and their 496 anti-tank guns, are not going to know what's hit them." He spoke slowly and decisively, fully aware of the importance of this momentous occasion.

Suddenly, there was the sound of distant, heavy gun fire, which shattered the peace of the desert. It lasted for a few minutes and then, like a passing summer storm, it stopped, echoing in the distance as it rolled away. The desert air pulsed and throbbed in Charles' ears and then was still again.

"Was that it, Jam-Jar?" asked Charles, hopefully.

"No. 'fraid not, sweetheart. That was the 24th Australian Brigade creating a diversion, subjecting the German 15th Panzer Division to heavy fire to put them off their guard. Yep, that should do it. Put the wind up them a bit!" smiled Jam-Jar.

Then, all was silent again, waiting.

From nearby, they could hear noises in the dark; quiet, muffled, whispered commands, stifled coughs, the click of rifles being loaded. Something was stirring. The desert was coming alive. A great battle was nearing, fate rolling in on the dust that suddenly stirred in the desert breeze, blowing gently across the scene.

"Three, two, one."

A huge explosion, like thousands of balloons all bursting at exactly the same time, boomed and pounded in Charles' stomach and chest. It felt like he'd been hit in the head with a huge, comic boxing glove that came at him from somewhere out of the darkness of the desert. For a minute, he almost forgot to breathe, stunned by the sheer force of that sound still thundering out there across the sand dunes, which were silhouetted against a huge, pale full moon, impassively surveying the scene, whilst the fierce wild glare of heavy gun fire bloomed in the night sky like wild, desert flowers.

Instinctively, Charles dived down, burying his head between his knees, covering his ears as best he could, but still that booming raged above him. It seemed to be coming at him from all sides. The intensity was overwhelming. He felt himself almost slipping away and then his great-grandfather was there, crouching beside him, whispering in his ear and somehow, above that furious cacophony of sound, Charles could hear him, quietly talking, a small voice of calm beneath the firestorm.

Suddenly, a different sound piped up from somewhere nearby, a sound Charles knew, a sound he knew from somewhere deep down and from somewhere far back, an urgent, deep, throaty piping, which started as one note and then another, rising to many notes in a tumultuous sound of bravery and triumph.

"Ah! It's the pipes, Charles, the pipes. The 51st Highland Division are on the move. Listen! Listen to that sound."

Across the desert, a beautiful wail of bagpipes pierced through the raging noise of battle, brave sounds of courage and hope rising above the dust and in the darkness, men identified their regiments by the piping of their company marches, calling the soldiers to arms and the soldiers answered that call.

"A fine, brave lot those Scots you know!" said Jam-Jar and Charles looked at his great-grandfather - Scottish by decent and Charles knew why he had also felt that call of the bagpipes in his own heart, too.

Before them, the storm raged. Fierce crashes tore the air with their intensity. The thunder of explosions and the huge lightning burst of bullets and heavy machine gun fire ripped through the night sky like fireworks. The whole of the horizon, as far as the eye could see in either direction, was lit up with the constant, angry flare of the bombardment.

Rumbles were heard in the distance. The earth shifted and moved, as tanks rolled into war. The ground shook with indignation. The storm raged on.

"Look at this, Charles," said Jam-Jar, standing up to peer over the safety of the sand bank. "It's magnificent, magnificent and terrible."

Gingerly, feeling for his great-grandfather's strong hand, Charles stood beside him and shivered at the magnitude of the scene.

In the flickering glare of the night, amid the awful noise and fury, the desert earth moved and from hidden dugouts all around, there suddenly arose from the dust, soldiers as far as the eye could see, all in their kilts, bravely marching into battle.

"Good on you, boys!" Jam-Jar chuckled. "They were ordered not to wear their kilts, but their Major, General Wimberley, 'Tartan Tam' they call him, has ensured that they do. They've had their kilts with them in their backpacks and they're wearing them tonight, regardless of orders! This lot were at Dunkirk, too, and later, in the thick of it at D-Day."

Away the men went into the heat and smoke of battle, kilts flowing, bagpipes calling; the desert dust closing in behind them, till Charles could see them no more.

Tearing his gaze away, he glanced at the shining face of his great-grandfather and the fierce flashes of battle dancing in his gentle eyes.

"We've got them now," his great-grandfather said, almost to himself. He looked tall and strong, standing fearlessly, illuminated by the glowing, night sky and the light of the moon. He seemed distant and far away, as if the power of the moment was urging him to join.

"*The turning of the Hinge of Fate*", he said, almost to himself. "Those were Churchill's words, '*before El Alamein never a victory; after Alamein never a defeat*'." He spoke wistfully, lost in his memories and closing his eyes, he bowed his head

Charles was suddenly overwhelmed with pity for his great-grandfather and for all his generation, who had had to endure such times and grasped his hand more tightly, drawing him back to the moment. He looked down at Charles, smiling gently and squeezed his hand.

For a while, they stood together in silence, awed by the battle that raged before them.

"Have you heard of the Desert Rats," Jam-Jar asked, suddenly breaking their silence.

The name was familiar to Charles, but for a moment, he couldn't think why and then it came to him.

"I know! There's a pub back home near where we live, which used to be called, 'The Desert Rat'. Dad told me that Monty used to go there with his officers. I think it annoyed my father that the name had been changed."

"It would have done, Charles, because in that one name is summed up an awful lot of history, history that happened right here in this desert."

"What's a rat got to do with the war, Jam-Jar?" asked Charles, almost shouting to be heard over the noise of battle.[31]

His great-grandfather smiled. "There's a rat that lives here in the desert, called a Jerboa and the 7th Armoured Division chose to wear an image of it on their uniform badges. They were crucial in the main attack that broke through the enemy lines here at El Alamein and they became known as the Desert Rats, because they fought so hard, like all the men here and never gave up. They played an important role in all the key battles against Rommel, who, funnily enough, was nicknamed The Desert Fox and the Desert Rats helped Monty's Eighth Army drive the Germans and Italians out of Africa and protect the Suez Canal. They drove the Germans out of Libya, too and recaptured the port of Tobruk; they fought the Japanese in India, they fought in Burma, Syria and took part in the D-Day landings and fought all the way to Berlin, just like the 51st Highland Division. All brave, brave men and that one pub your father mentioned to you, encapsulated all that history, until some bright spark decided to change its name."

Suddenly, Charles thought of home, his home and his little bed and his bedroom and his Mum and Dad and in that moment, he heard a beautiful sound, a silver peel of bells, faint at first and coming from somewhere far, far away and from somewhere deep inside him. A feeling of sheer relief and pure joy rose up and enveloped him, like climbing into a warm bath after a long, tiring day.

"I can hear church bells, Jam-Jar. Where're they coming from?"

"From home," Jam-Jar said. "They're coming from home!"

It seemed so real, almost as if he was back in England and in that moment, he pictured himself standing in front of the Houses of Parliament, looking up at the clock tower, as the deep, serious tones of Big Ben rang out over the great city of London and over the great River Thames, which danced and glistened with the flowing chimes.

It seemed to Charles that he could almost see a white silken ribbon of sparkling sound flowing across the city, across the countryside, across the fields, down the lanes and along the streets of every town of Britain. Between each sonorous peel, there was silence, full and expectant, growing and building, as if a great up-swelling of energy was taking breath, before bursting forth over countryside and town alike. It was like an eclipse of the sun passing overhead. Everything was still. Even the birds had stopped singing, as if listening to the message carried on the wind.

Old church towers awoke from their slumber, as the chimes washed over them. Their bells, long silent and waiting, took up the call, ringing out over the land, calling to one another in joyful celebration. A crescendo of exultation threaded itself through city, town and village alike, cleansing the earth of tension, dispelling fear and darkness, invigorating people with a new-found hope of victory. He felt the power of those sparkling chimes flow over him like a great wave of relief, bathing him in sound.

Birds started to sing. Their sweet tunes mingled with the chiming chorus, still ringing faintly in the breeze that slowly ebbed away. Charles caught the faintest whiff of rich Autumn fields and mossy earth, of strong English oak trees and fallen leaves the colour of jewels and for a brief moment, the promise of hope lifted the dark clouds of war from the land.

Suddenly, he heard in the air Churchill's voice, clear and strong.

"...this is not the end.
It is not even the beginning of the end.

But it is, perhaps,
the end of the beginning."

Then his great-grandfather spoke quietly beside him.

"All the church bells in Britain were silenced during the war. They'd only been rung once before, during the Dunkirk evacuations. When success at El Alamein was declared, that the British 8th Army had broken through the German front lines, Churchill ordered all the church bells to break their silence and be rung again to celebrate this enormous victory. The British 8th Army, under Montgomery, destroyed a third of the fighting strength of Rommel's Africa Korps and saved the Middle East from a long Nazi occupation."

Charles thought about all the soldiers out there in the darkness of the desert. It lay deep and mysterious before him. The battle had moved on, but the boom and crack of explosions, told him where the soldiers must be – in the middle of the action.

"All this," said Jam-Jar, casting his eyes across the scene, "all this marked a turning point in the war. After this everything changed. Four days after victory at El Alamein, the United States invaded North Africa in Operation Torch. They passed through Gibraltar at night, took Morocco and landed in Algeria, where they fought Vichy French troops, who were loyal to the Nazis."

"French loyal to the Nazis!" exclaimed Charles.

"Sadly, yes, sweetheart. Not the brave lot, who fought with the Allies, but the lot, who were ruled from a part of France called Vichy by the French collaborator of Hitler, called Petain."

"Petain! I know about him. He became France's Prime Minister in 1940 and immediately gave into Germany."

"That's right," said Jam-Jar, "but, once the Vichy French were defeated in Algeria and Rommel and the Nazis were pushed out of North Africa, British supply routes to and from India and the Middle East, particularly supplies of oil via the Suez Canal, were protected and our chances of winning the war were greatly improved."

"What happened to Rommel?" asked Charles.

"He continued with the war, overseeing the building of defensive positions along the Normandy coast. Towards the end of the war, though, he finally saw how mad Hitler was, but it was too late. He was implicated in the Stauffenberg plot to kill Hitler, but it didn't work. Rommel was found out and arrested and that was the end of him, sadly."

"And what happened to Monty?"

"He survived and lived a long life. Do you know, Rommel's son and Monty's son became good friends after the war? Ironic, isn't it! Monty and Rommel probably could have been good friends too, under different circumstances."[32]

"It's sad how war can make enemies of people, who might have been friends in peacetime," said Charles, thoughtfully.

"but, one thing that you should know, Charles, is that the people of Egypt were so grateful for the liberation of their country, that in 1945 they raised over £500,000, to thank Britain for its part in liberating Egypt from Axis forces and a lot of that money went to a rehabilitation centre for injured servicemen in a little, sleepy, Hampshire village, called Enham, where many of the injured from the Battle of El Alamein were sent. As a thank-you for the gift, the village changed its name to 'Enham Alamein'."[33]

Charles imagined a map of the world with hands reaching out from Egypt and Britain, meeting in the middle to shake in friendship.

Charles' great-grandfather looked at him and smiled. "Yes, Charles. There's more that unites than divides the peoples of this lovely planet of ours. I've been all over the world; customs may be different, but manners and courtesy, kindness and consideration are the same wherever you go."

Chapter 14 – The Resistance

The booms and bangs of battle raging all around them seemed less frightening now and somehow fainter, as if disappearing into the distance, muffled by the desert sands.

History was moving on and Charles could feel the wheel of time revolving.

The angry incessant rat-a-tat-tats of infantry fire started to take on a strangely hollow tone like someone tapping out the rhythm on a wooden table. It seemed to rise up from the pit of Charles' stomach. It was an urgent beat, a beat of alarm or warning, which rose to his chest and then to his throat. It mingled with the sounds of the desert and the receding gun fire.

He was still intently watching the scene before him, safe in his great-grandfather's warm embrace, but at this new sound he looked round. Gone were the rolling sand dunes and the glare of gun fire against the dark sky and in their place, were round wooden café tables, covered in red and white checked tablecloths. Behind them, quite distinctly, but quickly fading, was the desert and for a moment Charles found the sight of neat little café tables and chairs sitting happily in the middle of a battle zone, faintly amusing, but when he blinked the vast expanse of desert was gone, replaced by the wood panelled walls of a pleasant looking café.

Polished wooden floorboards now covered the ground and nearby, someone was playing an accordion. A woman was singing. Her voice was deep and rich, filled with sadness and yearning, but Charles could hear a fierce strength, too.

And there was that tapping again, that urgent rat-a-tat-tat, but now it was clearer and Charles could see the source of the sound, for outside the café, leaning against the window frame, was a man, wearing a beret, casually reading a newspaper, seemingly nonchalant, but behind his back, one hand was beating out that warning rhythm on the wooden window frame – rat-a-tat-tat, rat-a-tat-tat.

Immediately, the sound was taken up by people in the café, people, who only a moment ago had been sitting and chatting happily, appearing relaxed, enjoying their coffee and wine. Now they looked more alert, still chatting, but tense. One, or two flung nervous glances at the door and every one of them was now tapping out that rhythm. Charles could feel the anxiety in the room. It coiled tightly like a spring around them all.

At that minute, the bell over the café door rang sharply. The tapping stopped instantly, as in walked two very smart German officers, who promptly sat down at a table and ordered coffee.

"Deux cafes s'il vous plait," said one, curtly.

"Oui, monsieur," replied the efficient waiter, who proceeded to busy himself with their order, but all around, Charles could see people casting furtive glances in the direction of the German officers, who seemed quite oblivious, arrogant almost, in their confidence; so self-assured they appeared to be.

"It's as if they think they own the place," observed Charles.

"In a way, they do," replied his great-grandfather, ruefully. This is France, Charles, 5th June 1944. It's been under Nazi rule for four years now, like the rest of Europe, all under the control of one man, Adolf Hitler."

Charles looked around him again, at these people, sitting apparently calmly at their tables, drinking their coffee, putting on a very good show of normality, but the set jaw of one man, the angry gaze of another and the tense, rigid fingers of a woman clutching the stem of her glass, her knuckles white, told Charles all he needed to know. There was a barely suppressed rage seething in the breast of every one of them and it was directed at the two German soldiers chatting and laughing and ordering more coffees.

"These people," went on his great-grandfather, "have had to endure four years of occupation, four years of seeing their country ruled by Nazis and their vile creed. For four years now, the black and red flags and banners of the Nazi swastika have hung from buildings and monuments in the streets of Paris and all over Europe, forcing people to feel the weight of Nazi terror and making them believe that there was no escape, but the tide is turning, Charles. Look!"

At one table sat a woman, who seemed to be gazing at it, intently. Her chin was resting on her hand. With her other hand she was writing something on the table in some salt that had spilt across it. Over and over again, she was drawing the sign of a letter 'V', with one finger, slowly and methodically.

"You see that woman, Charles," went on his great-grandfather, that 'V' stands for 'Victory', victory over the Germans. It's a symbol of hope, Charles and defiance against the Nazis, a symbol of resistance.

"A Belgian radio producer, Victor de Laveleye, who worked for BBC radio in London, came up with the idea. In his country, the words for 'freedom' and 'victory', both began with the letter 'V'. On the BBC radio, he broadcast a message to the Belgian people. He told them his idea of painting the letter 'V' on everything they could, just to annoy the Nazis, who occupied their country and to show them that they were still defiant, that they were still resisting this occupation. The Nazi soldiers very quickly started finding this symbol scratched on everything and anything, including the mudguards of Nazi cars and by golly, it annoyed them!" said his great-grandfather.

"Churchill heard of this idea quite early on in the war and in June 1941 he broadcast a message on BBC radio, asking the British people to make the 'V' for 'Victory' sign with their fingers.

"Churchill said, *'The V sign is the symbol of the unconquerable will of the people of the occupied territories and of Britain; of the fate awaiting Nazi tyranny.'* Powerful stuff, eh, Charles?"

Charles nodded, looking at this woman, so calmly and quietly defiant and felt how important this symbol must have been for the people of Europe. How, when they had nothing else with which to fight, their spirit and will to remain free, were the only weapons they had and Charles could see how this one letter had summed up so much for them.

"Resistance groups all over Europe worked to fight the Nazis in whichever way they could," said Jam-Jar, "through sabotage and by sending vital messages back to Britain. They also helped escaped Allied Prisoners of War and Allied fighter pilots, who had crashed in enemy territory, to get back to Britain, where the SOE, or Special Operations Executive, the forerunner of MI6, helped to co-ordinate these efforts. It was known as 'Churchill's Secret Army', or the 'Ministry of Ungentlemanly Warfare!'" said Charles' great-grandfather, smiling.

"Trained agents, men and women, like Odette Sansom[34], Noor Inayat Khan[35] and Violette Szabo[36] were sent from Britain into enemy territory to co-ordinate and carry out attacks alongside local resistance groups, sending back to Britain vital information. They had to keep their nerve in very dangerous situations, because they knew, full well, that if they were ever caught by the Nazis, they would be interrogated and the Nazis could be very cruel."

Charles and his great-grandfather looked on again.

Eventually, the German officers paid their bill and left the café. Everyone visibly relaxed and conversation began to flow more easily, whilst on the accordion, the musician quietly played the Marseillaise. Slowly, people began to join in, humming at first and then singing, tentatively, nervous that the German officers might burst through the door again. Gradually, though, their singing grew in confidence, filling their words with deep feeling and pride.

"The French National Anthem," said Jam-Jar, respectfully.

Suddenly, an unusual crackling sound, punctuated by intermittent whistles and squeals, came from the back of the café. It was seeping through a doorway that was covered with a heavy curtain. A wiry, tinny sound was emerging like some strange animal just waking up. Only Charles and his great-grandfather seemed to have heard it, though. No one else seemed to pay it any attention and they both now found themselves on the other side of the curtain, standing in a small, dimly-lit room, where a group of people were crowded round an old radio that had just been retrieved from its hiding place.

Through the peculiar crackling noise, which Charles could now see was coming from the old radio, he heard another sound - that unmistakable staccato rhythm again. It was the sound he had heard before, tapped on the window frame of the café and on the tables, but this time the rhythm had a stronger booming quality, as if beaten out on two big drums, one slightly deeper in tone than the other.

Boo, boo, boo, boom.

"What *is* that sound, Jam-Jar? I keep hearing it. Why was everyone tapping out that same rhythm earlier on? What's so important about it?"

"It's Morse code, Charles. Dot, dot, dot, dash, is Morse code for the letter 'V' – 'V' for Victory."

Charles remembered learning about Morse code when he had visited a museum with his Mum and Dad. They'd had fun sending messages to one another using Morse code on a special machine that was on display in the museum.

Jam-Jar went on, "You've heard the beginning of Beethoven's Fifth Symphony, haven't you Charles? It's the one that everyone knows, or at least, the first four notes," and Jam-Jar hummed the tune,

"Da da da daah. Da da da daah."

"It sounds powerful and heroic, doesn't it? Well, the dot, dot, dot, dash of the letter V in Morse code, matches the rhythm of Beethoven's 'da, da, da, daah', and the BBC used these first four notes at the start of every radio broadcast to Europe. They broadcast the news across the world in thirty-four languages and to listen to it in German-occupied countries was a real act of defiance and courage. If the Germans caught you listening to the BBC news, you could be shot, but it was our way of letting the people of Europe know that they hadn't been forgotten and that there was hope.

"The funny thing was, Charles, that Hitler loved Beethoven's music, too. He thought it represented the German spirit and here we were using it for our own ends to put two fingers up to the Germans."

"Two fingers?"

"Yes, Charles. Churchill was always fond of doing the 'V' for 'Victory' sign, except that he used to turn his fingers round the

145

wrong way!" and Jam-Jar chuckled. Charles looked at his great-grandfather sideways, not too sure what the joke was, but half suspecting that he knew the answer and then he remembered a postcard of Churchill, that his mother had hung on the fridge at home, with Churchill, wearing his funny hat and cigar in his mouth, holding up two fingers defiantly, to the camera.

"Bo, bo, bo, boom." There were those two kettle drums again, closely followed by a faint voice,

"Ici Londres. Ici Londres. Les Francais parlent aux Francais."

The sound was faint, but the voice was clear.

"That's BBC Radio London," Jam-Jar whispered.

The reception was weak, but the voice was strong. The booming beat could clearly be heard through the radio static, which crackled loudly, as someone turned the dial to tune in.

"Radio London - The French speaking to the French," said Jam-Jar respectfully. "It was run by French people, who'd escaped Nazi occupation and had made it to Britain. It broadcast messages of hope and also secret coded messages to resistance fighters in France. Even with the Germans trying to jam the airwaves making it harder to tune into the station, the 'Bo,bo,bo,boom' of Beethoven's Fifth was loud enough and strong enough to be heard like a beacon of hope, guiding people to the correct channel."

The crackles and whistles of radio static faded, as the dial on the tuner found the signal that was calling from across the waves, both radio waves and real waves alike. It called to them from London, calling from the free in Britain.

'Here are some personal messages...', the people huddled closer to the radio, drawing nearer in anticipation.

"Some of the messages," said Jam-Jar, "were from French refugees, who had managed to escape to Britain, sending messages back to loved ones left in France. Some were speeches from General de Gaulle, but others were coded messages to Resistance Fighters, telling different Resistance groups what action to take against the German troops."

"The postman has fallen asleep. The postman has fallen asleep."

Charles looked at his great-grandfather quizzically, who smiled at him, but the group gathered around the radio did not laugh. They listened intently.

"Grandma is eating our sweets. Grandma is eating our sweets."

Charles stifled a laugh.

"What could those mean," asked Charles?

"Maybe, the first one means that some German troops have moved away from a certain area and there's less chance of them seeing supplies being dropped to resistance fighters," Jam-Jar said, thinking hard.

"Or possibly," said Charles, "it means that a supply drop has been delayed and maybe, the second one means that the Germans have found where a resistance group is hiding their supplies. So, the message is warning them not to go back there in case the Germans catch them."

Suddenly, in the close atmosphere of that darkened room, one short sentence flashed through the radio static like lightning on a dark night and straight as an arrow, pierced the hearts of everyone there.

"Jean a une longe moustache! Jean has a long moustache!"

The listeners crowding round the radio suddenly looked stunned. Overjoyed and evidently excited, they hugged each other. One immediately grabbed his coat, kissed his wife and went out into the night.

Then another message came over the radio.

"Blesse mon coeur d'une langueur monotone."

"Wounds my heart with a monotonous langour."

"C'est ici," said an elderly lady, calmly and deliberately, as she sat down, heavily in the nearest chair. "C'est le début de la fin!"

Charles instinctively knew what she had said, "It is here," he repeated, quietly, almost to himself, "The beginning of the end!" and he shivered with expectation.

Two young women, evidently sisters, wrapped scarves around their heads, kissed their grandmother and left.

"Dieu t'accompagne, mes enfants!"

"God go with you, my children," she said, as the door closed behind her granddaughters, her voice choked with fear for them and her eyes shining with pride.

Charles looked at his great-grandfather, "Does this mean what I think it means, Jam-Jar?"

"Yes. It's the beginning of the end," said Jam-Jar. "The Allied invasion is about to begin. Those messages are to let resistance groups know that now is the time to start their sabotage plans to distract the Germans and keep them busy."

Charles felt the same thrill of excitement that was animating the faces of the other listeners. Desperately, he scanned the room for some clue, as his eyes fell on a newspaper that was sitting on a table; the date on the newspaper - 5th June 1944.

"It's the eve of D-Day!" he exclaimed.

Chapter 15 – D-Day

Suddenly, Charles lifted his head and found himself in a large, flat-bottomed boat with very high sides. It felt like being inside an enormous wheelbarrow, pitching and rolling violently on the choppy sea and it was full of soldiers, all sitting quietly, cross-legged on the floor. Everyone seemed pensive, anxious and some of the younger ones looked petrified. The older men just sat grimly determined, jaws set.

Occasionally, freezing cold spray would break over the sides of the boat and a few of the soldiers were being violently sick, some of them using their helmets as bowls and all the men, from time to time, would flick nervous glances at the strangely flat-ended bow of the boat, which seemed to slope forwards slightly. It looked as if it might lower to form a ramp, but Charles had no idea why, or why the men were looking at it so fearfully. They clearly knew their destination and not one of them wanted to arrive, but the craft moved on, inexorably, towards the danger which awaited them, somewhere out there beyond the craft's blank wall of steel and the rolling waves. Charles could feel the tension in the air - men powerfully aware of the importance of their role and that the fate of the whole free world, the fate of their families and their children sleeping peacefully in their beds at home, hung on what they would achieve that day.

The awful reality of this deadly war was no more powerful to Charles than at this moment. For a second, he was filled with an unwelcome sense of panic. Sickening fear gripped him, fear chilled him, fear that he, too, might be called upon to run at this unseen enemy. He felt trapped, imprisoned by the dark, metal walls.

Desperately he looked around him. Jam-Jar wasn't beside him! He was nowhere to be seen. Cold panic gripped Charles' throat. His tummy started turning somersaults. His mouth went dry. Adrenaline pumped. His heart raced. His breath came short and fast, and he knew exactly how these men were feeling.

Then, with a wave of pure relief flooding his veins, he saw his great-grandfather talking to another man and in that moment, they both glanced over to Charles and smiled!

Slowly and carefully, they started to pick their way through the huddles of seated soldiers, who were so deep in thought that they seemed not to notice them at all. The two smiling men appeared quite untroubled by the violent motion of the landing craft, unlike Charles, who was being thrown about dreadfully. He was beginning to feel terribly sea-sick and gratefully, he stood up to greet them.

They both grinned at Charles like two Cheshire cats, Jam-Jar with his hands resting in the small of his back, clearly accustomed, old seadog as he was, to the pitch and roll of the deck, when a particularly violent jolt and judder nearly threw Charles quite off his feet. Instinctively, both men quickly reached out and caught him. At their steadying touch, Charles instantly felt secure, as if surrounded by a protective bubble, keeping all three of them safe from harm. The pounding engine and the roaring seas, suddenly all seemed strangely muffled and far away. A peace and silence descended on them and Charles looked up at both men, the one he knew and loved already and the one, whose kindly, but care-worn face looked at him benignly with mild, gentle eyes and in that moment, Charles saw the face of his father, deep within the face of this man, and Charles knew that he was looking at his father's father, Maurice.

"You're my grandpa!" exclaimed Charles, without needing to be told. "My Dad often talks of you. You were a Royal Marine Commando, the elite squad and you were here, weren't you! I know where we are now! It's D-Day isn't it! 6th June 1944! And we're heading towards the beaches of Northern France!" Charles was breathless with anticipation.

"Well done, Charles. You're right. My son's taught you well. He's a bright one, that son of mine. You make sure you always listen to him, because he really knows his stuff. I'm very proud of him and I can see you love him very much, like I do. I would have loved to have met you and been a proper grandpa to you. I'm sorry I had to go before you were born, but I'm here now and I'm going to enjoy getting to know my little grandson," and Maurice gave Charles a pat on the head and ruffled his fair hair.

"Over there," said Maurice, inclining his head towards the direction of the boat's destination, "is the coast of Normandy,

France, Nazi-occupied France and very close now, is Gold beach. Shortly, all these men," continued Maurice, gesturing with his hand and looking sympathetically at the waiting soldiers, "will take their part in the largest naval, air and land operation in history. This day marks the start of the long campaign to liberate north-western Europe from Nazi tyranny. It's codename? 'Operation Overlord'!" all three of them chimed together.

"Get ready, because in a minute, you'll see the largest seaborn invasion in history!"

Maurice took an old black and white photo out of his pocket and showed it to Charles. A group of Commandos were lined up, dressed in combat fatigues, berets at jaunty angles, smiles shining out of faces camouflaged with black paint – men looking calm and relaxed, but clearly all having just returned from some daring raid. He could almost see the adrenaline ebbing away from them, as they stood there, but all of them looked as if they could have snapped a tree in half like it was a twig, "Goodness, they look tough!" thought Charles and there amongst the group, was his grandpa, Maurice, looking just as tough and just as wiry as all the other men, "Like coiled wires," he thought, "ready to spring into action!"

Charles turned his head and gazed in amazement at this tall, thin, quite bony man, at the lines on his face, the distinctive wide eyebrows, the sense of humour buried deep within those dark eyes and he couldn't believe that this man was capable of the power and strength such as was clearly in evidence in this photograph.

Maurice knew what he was thinking. "Amazing what inner strength you can find to protect your family and the country you love. Still, the basic training helped, live ammo and all that. Keeps one alert, somewhat! I joined up before I was drafted so I could choose where I went - Royal Marines – best uniform of the lot. Really smart. It impressed the ladies!" he said, with a twinkle in his eye and Jam-Jar chuckled too, "although, I soon found out it wasn't all about the uniform."

Nearby, a soldier was violently sick into his helmet. Maurice cast a sympathetic glance.

"Of course, us Commandos didn't have helmets to be sick into and we would never have been sick in our berets!" said Maurice smiling, "but there again, none of us would have dared show that we were scared, either!"

Suddenly, shells started to fall in the sea close to the landing craft, making it rock violently and sending huge plumes of water cascading into the boat. The soldiers looked at each other anxiously, one cracked a grim joke.

"Blow this for a game of soldiers," he said. His mate nearby merely smiled, ruefully.

"I was actually glad to get off this blasted thing," Maurice chuckled, looking around him. "I'd never felt so sick in all my life!"

Suddenly, the men stiffened in anticipation, as the sergeant called to them, "Right lads. Let's be 'avin' yer! Look lively now!"

The men readied themselves, shouldered their rifles and heaved their equipment onto their backs. Nervously, they swallowed hard. Every man's gaze was fixed on the prow of the boat.

Some of the soldiers glanced up at the sky one last time. Others took a last look at treasured photos and then buried them deep in their uniforms close to their hearts.

Some men exchanged one final look.

And then it began.

Charles heard the scrape of shingle on the underside of the landing craft. There was a shudder and a jolt and the sloping end of the landing craft suddenly fell open onto the beach and became a ramp, like a tongue unrolling from a huge, awful mouth, out of which the men poured, disgorged onto the beach like too much undigested food.

Some immediately fell wounded. Others managed to find shelter from the hail of bullets, which rained down on them. Shells and gunfire cracked and fell all around, but still the soldiers came in their thousands.

Charles stood aghast, shocked by the fierceness of the battle and the destruction all around. It took his breath away and suddenly he felt an intense danger, which seemed to flash an angry, red warning in his mind. His head started to swim, making him feel dizzy. His vision blurred and shifted, as it focused on something miles and miles away. He knew he was seeing something that wasn't real; he knew it was just his over-anxious imagination, but fear still gripped his throat, none-the-less.

The very real sounds of the actual battle faded into the distance, as his sight seemed to stretch and race across the land and across whole countries, towards an image, which grew larger and larger by the second, until, as his sight cleared, he saw, to his alarm, an enormous wasps' nest sitting right over the heart of Berlin. He'd seen that wasps' nest in his mind before.

Horrified, he looked on, as the nest seemed to divide and open like a dark curtain, which writhed with thousands of crawling wasps and behind the curtain was revealed a small, windowless, claustrophobic room with bare, grey concrete walls, lit only by the cold glare of one overhead lamp. It cast a pyramid of hard light over a large table, on one side of which were gathered a group of men wearing smart suits. They could have been ordinary businessmen, but for the warning in Charles' heart. Instantly, he knew where he was, deep within the evil lair of Hitler's underground bunker, at the Reich Chancellery in Berlin, Germany!

Charles was in shock. His heart raced. His mouth went dry. Frantically, he swung his head to left and right, but Jam-Jar and Maurice were nowhere to be seen. He was alone. Cold fear gripped him. Instinctively, he clenched his fists tightly as if ready to fight. His head pounded again, just as it had done on Brighton beach, what felt like an age ago and with growing dread, he knew who those men were and who was standing in the middle of that group right in front of him. There, surrounded by his henchmen - Goring, Himmler and

Goebbels standing closest to him, pouring over the maps of Northern France and Britain spread across the table, was 'that man', HITLER himself!

With a sudden intake of breath, Charles stared at the scene in disbelief, unable to move, or to make a sound. None of the men had seen him and Charles didn't want them to. He was fascinated and appalled in equal measure.

Hitler leaned and rested his hands on the map, which Charles could now see was swarming with ants, wasps, cockroaches and all manner of vile, unspeakable creatures. Hitler only looked on and smiled, an evil, malevolent smile.

Suddenly, a white line of brilliant light seemed to cut through the map, like a shining sword piercing the table from beneath, as if emerging from the sea itself. It cleaved through the map all along the line of the Normandy coast, sending rays of blinding light into the foetid atmosphere of the room. The vile insects, which had threatened to cross the coast and cover the paper sea with their foulness, were momentarily checked in their advance.

Surprised, Hitler and his henchmen looked on, as the light grew in intensity and began filling the room. Then an awful transformation took place. Hitler's face, which had seemed almost normal and civilised a moment before, crumpled before Charles' eyes, like paper being screwed up and formed itself into one of complete rage and hatred. Instinctively, Charles knew he was seeing the **TRUE FACE OF HITLER!** .

A second later, his henchmen's faces did the same – all now revealing themselves in their true form. Horrified, Charles stepped backwards, deeper into the shadows, but his back and heels hit the wall behind him. At the sound, the group around the table looked up and seemed to stare straight at him. Their evil gaze bored into Charles' soul, like shards of ice, chilling him to the core. He put his hands over his mouth and held his breath, afraid even to blink. His heartbeat pounded in his chest, so loud, he was sure it could be heard. For an awful moment, Hitler's gaze seemed to hold his own. Charles felt the evil seeping out of every pore of this man's skin, reaching across the floor to him like poison ivy, almost infecting him. Dark, malevolent whispers filled his ears.

His mind swirled in panic. His thoughts screamed, 'This isn't real! This isn't real!' Frantic with fear, he scanned the room for a means of escape. 'Is this the end? Is this really it?'

When suddenly, the sword of light, which had risen from the paper sea of the map, shone before his face, blinding his vision. Silhouetted behind the gleaming battle light, he saw the outline of a huge warrior, hair flowing, cloak billowing, gauntleted fists clenching the sword's hilt. He stood between Charles and the evil group behind and these words filled Charles' mind,

"Only the King can see you!"

The shining light filled the room, encircling them both and instantly, Charles knew he was safe, as the warrior swung round and drew the sword in a great arc of light above his body and sliced through the map of Normandy that was strewn across the table.

Hitler and his men looked up in rage. Their clothing changed before Charles' eyes and became as if from a different age. Dark frock coats flapped around their knees, motioned by a strange, warm, infernal wind, which swept upwards from angry, steaming vents that now appeared issuing from cracks in the floor, which glowed an ominous red. A foul, sulphurous stench, like the smell of things rotting, spewed from the vents, filling the room and making Charles gag and retch.

Stunned, Charles watched on, as the insects on the map swarmed over Hitler's hands and up his arms, but instead of being scared, Hitler seemed to revel in this. The insects moved to his command, strangely melting to a thick, black tar that clung to Hitler's hands, as he pulled them, heavily, away from the table. Long, black, dripping tails of thick, sticky, ooze like sludge from the bottom of a filthy puddle, stretched from his fingers, elongating them, turning them to claws, which he now drew above his head and flung with all his evil might, straight at the blinding light, which still shone powerfully in the room. In that instant, Charles could see that he was no longer in the deep, cavernous bunker in Berlin...

...but back amongst the shrill calls of battle and the sound of violent waves crashing on a Normandy beach, his grandfather and great-grandfather, at his side again. Relief flooded his veins, until his eyes were drawn up to the headland rising above the beach, to where Hitler and his henchmen, appeared on the cliff-top, surveying the scene, now wearing long, dark robes and cloaks, which flowed in the breeze. Apparition though it was, the scene had a powerful effect on Charles, who shivered from head to toe.

"This isn't real! This isn't real! I know this isn't real!" Charles kept saying to himself, but still, he was scared.

In the middle, stood Hitler, like a dark wizard, surrounded by his acolytes - an evil necromancer, around whom the insects and black tar and flowing robes swirled and twirled like black dust. Hitler's hands worked strangely, like a conductor, commanding his dark orchestra, which waltzed around him menacingly and all the while the dark wizard's hands gestured dramatically around his head and body, as if choreographing the dance - 'a dance of death', thought Charles.

Charles knew that his grandfather and great-grandfather had also seen this ghostly apparition. They flanked him on either side and stood tall, chests broad, shoulders squared against the evil pretender. They breathed rapidly, nostrils flared, poised for the last great fight and with that, a huge upswelling of power surged from the foaming seas behind them - a shining force from across the waves, from across the lands of the world which still believed in the light of truth and the light of goodness and ahead of all, the great warrior king, leading the way into battle.

Then, Charles saw, standing on the coast of England, on the white cliffs of Dover, another king, King George VI, a line of powerful white light beneath him, with Churchill, his friend, at his side and all the kings and queens, presidents and prime-ministers of this age and ages past, stretching back into history, surrounding them, all who believed in freedom and justice. Standing shoulder to shoulder with them, were men, women and children, civilians and soldiers, pilots and sailors, nurses and doctors, air-raid wardens, dock-workers and factory-workers, all who had made the ultimate sacrifice for resisting such evil; Sikh, Hindu, Buddhist, Muslim, Christian, Jew, Communist and Capitalist, Democrat and Republican, Conservative, Labour and Liberal from countries that spanned the globe, all united against their common enemy – tyranny; while behind the crowd massed on the shining white cliffs, a large cinema screen flashed scenes from the films that Charles knew his mother and father loved so much and their words screamed out into the violent air – *'That Hamilton Woman'* – "….He means to be master of the world…You cannot make peace with dictators. You have to destroy them – wipe them out…", the actor playing Admiral Nelson in the film, made during the war, said, referring to Hitler; then *'The Way to the Stars'* – "Do not despair for Jonny head-in-air. He sleeps as sound as Jonny underground…Better by far for Jonny the bright star, to keep your head and see his children fed…".

Charles heard those words ring true and clear and they went straight to his heart – glimpses of films that had reached the hearts of so many people during the war, giving them courage and raising morale: *'The First of the Few'*, *'Pimpernel Smith'*, *'Went the Day Well'*, *'One of our Aircraft is Missing'*, *'49ᵗʰ Parallel'*, *'In Which We Serve'*. They all flickered and sparkled behind the crowd assembled around Churchill and the King.

Charles knew none of this was real, but it was impressive never-the-less. There was Elizabeth I, with her commander of the English Fleet, Lord Howard of Effingham. Charles recognised him from a painting he had seen hanging on a wall in his school.

"There's Wellington and Admiral Lord Nelson, who defended Britain against Napoleon! - another man who wanted to invade Britain," said Jam-Jar amazed.

At the name of Nelson, Charles pricked his ears. He had visited Nelson's beautiful flag ship, HMS Victory at Portsmouth. He had been on board and smelt the smoke of battle imprinted in the English Oak that made her. He had imagined the struggle and bravery of the men, who had sailed her and seen the place where Nelson fell wounded, in his finest hour, dying to save his country from another threat to its freedom, dying at the moment of victory at the Battle of Trafalgar in 1805 and he knew why Nelson and his ship, so aptly named, the Victory, was here at this hour, even if it was only in his imagination.

"There're all here today, Charles!" said Jam-Jar deeply moved. "They weren't going to miss this! They know they're needed again, even if only in spirit!"

"There's no 'only' about it!" said Maurice, laughing. "After all, isn't that what we are? Spirits! Even King Arthur is here too!"

"King Arthur!" exclaimed Charles. 'That's who I saw!'

"Yes, sweetheart! Another King who swore to return in time of need, if Britain was ever in danger."

"Do you think Churchill can feel them all with him?" asked Charles, knowing what the answer would be.

"Oh yes! Most definitely!" said Maurice.

Suddenly, Charles heard a drumming beat, like the heartbeat of the land, throbbing through his chest.

"I've heard that sound before," thought Charles, "on Brighton Beach with Jam-Jar, when we went to Dunkirk and at the Houses of Parliament" and he looked in amazement at his great-grandfather, who in that minute turned to him, the same thought on his mind.

"That's Drake's Drum," Jam-Jar exclaimed.

"What's that?" Charles shouted above the cacophony of noise. He knew it must be important.

"Drake's Drum," Jam-Jar exclaimed again, smiling. "The drum owned by Sir Francis Drake."

Charles looked over to where the ghostly figure of Sir Francis Drake was standing on the cliffs of Dover with his queen, Elizabeth I, smiling. Beside him, the drum was sounding.

Jam-Jar pointed and shouted over the noise, "When he was dying, Drake ordered that his drum should be returned to Britain and if Britain was ever in danger, it should be beaten to call him from Heaven and rescue the country. That was the sound you heard Charles, before Dunkirk. That sound! It was Drake's Drum!"[37]

Charles shivered with emotion as, suddenly, an energy shone from all who were gathered on the cliffs of that little island, encircling them like a ball of light, a light of goodness, which the King and Churchill, Queen Elizabeth, Drake and Nelson and everyone there present, now took and balled up in their hands, simultaneously flinging it with all their might at the dark, evil group standing on the headland on the coast of Normandy.

Suddenly, the sword of shining light, which Charles now knew must be Excalibur, the same sword he had seen slicing through the map in the bunker in Berlin, flashed around the dark, swirling mass like a glorious ray of brilliant light, which silvered the edges of the now diminishing storm cloud.

Charles saw a great force rise up out of the sea behind him, the immense scale of it was breathtaking. It appeared powerful, majestic and strong. All along the coast of Normandy he saw a huge fleet, with HMS Victory leading the way, in full sail and streaming above the racing wind was Nelson's famous message to his fleet before the Battle of Trafalgar:

"England expects that every man will do his duty."

Grandpa Maurice stared hard, reading the message out loud, which seemed to float in the sky above the scene for all to see and the three of them cheered and clapped and jumped up and down, hugging each other in excitement.

"England expects that every man will do his duty."

Charles remembered those words from somewhere and then it hit him, Churchill had said something similar in his radio broadcast to the nation during the Blitz on 11th September 1940:

"Every man and woman will therefore prepare himself to do his duty," and now he knew why Churchill had said it. Charles shivered with pride.[38]

When suddenly, all that massed power of light surged towards the coast, heading straight for Hitler, flinging itself at the beaches, as thousands and thousands of warriors flowed from the sea, like a shining mist, flowing across the land beyond, flooding the country and cleansing it of evil. It surrounded the dark group, which struggled in the grip of the much stronger power, the power of goodness, the power of liberty, that carried it away in the full-force of the surging tide.

Charles blinked away the vision, as his eyes adjusted to the morning sun. Fearfully, he glanced up at the cliff, where moments before, that tumultuous scene had played itself out and was relieved to see it no longer there – the waking nightmare of his imagination had passed. Thankfully, he turned and looked back to the sea...

...to thousands of real ships and real landing craft, which were emerging from the early morning mist. More lined the coast as far as the eye could see and there, amongst the warships bombarding the coast, Charles saw the familiar signal of HMS Victory again, only this time, hoisted from a warship called HMS Erebus, "England expects that every man will do his duty." Jam-Jar and Grandpa Maurice saw it too and were stunned.[39]

A hail of bullets rained down continually. The noise was deafening.

"This is the largest invasion force in history," said Grandpa Maurice, "and by the end of this day," said Maurice, "the Allies will have established a foothold along this coast to begin their advance into France. This day is the day we begin to wash the dirt and filth of Nazi rule from the world."

All three cast their gaze across the beach, at the devastation and the bravery, at the injured men calling for help and the thousands of soldiers, still pouring from landing craft all along the shoreline, fighting on with grim determination, making headway and establishing positions.

The sky was dark with hundreds of planes, gliders, bombers and Spitfires, newly painted with white stripes, to mark them out as allied planes, providing support to the troops below. Allied bombs fell on enemy lines, as the enemy returned with heavy mortar and shellfire, which landed on the beaches. The sky boiled with activity.

"Terror Flyers, the Nazis called our Spitfires," Grandpa Maurice said, looking up at the sky. "The Nazis knew they had nothing to match them."[40]

"So, what happened here, Grandpa?"

"First," replied Grandpa Maurice, "there were the Special Paratrooper forces, who were dropped in, just after midnight on D-Day to make pathways for the troops on the beach so that they could move further inland. They were called Pathfinders. They had to knock out enemy positions and secure them for the beach landings and those beach landings happened right here," and he gestured with a long sweep of his hand, along the length of the shoreline as far as the eye could see.

"I bet those Germans got a nasty shock up there, when they saw this lot appearing from the mist this morning," laughed Jam-Jar, ruefully as they all looked up at the huge, imposing concrete German gun-emplacements on the hill, with the thin slits cut into their walls like nasty eyes. Bursts of metallic machine-gun fire were erupting from them, like angry dragons spitting fire. The rapid, violent flashes of bullets looked like sparks flying.

"Out here," said Grandpa Maurice, "are five beaches, earmarked for the assault and each one has a codename – Utah and

Omaha beaches, where the Americans landed, then Gold, Juno and Sword beaches where the British and Canadians landed. I was on Juno beach with the Canadians and here we are on Juno beach now."

Charles stared around him. The noise of gunfire and shell-bursts had increased in intensity. Putting his hands over his ears did nothing to lessen the fierceness of the noise. He felt like his brain was in a blender – all sound collided into one awful din.

Bodies lay strewn on the beach, like discarded toys. Injured men called for help, but horrifyingly, oblivious tanks were almost rolling over them, unable to see the injured men in the sand. Charles saw one furious Officer, a Commando, pull the pin of a grenade and hurl it near the tank, in a desperate attempt to alert it to the helpless men lying on the beach in its path.[41]

Many soldiers floated face down in the sea. They had drowned.

Charles was stunned.

Grandpa Maurice looked at him with sad eyes.

"They're fellow Commandos, Charles. Their landing craft was disabled by those metal spikes there."

Charles saw them sticking out of the sea – long, angry spikes.

"German sea-defences," said Maurice quietly, beside him, "with mines attached to them. Crude, but effective," he said ironically. "Quite a few of our landing craft were destroyed by them. Some Commandos tried to wade ashore, but were swept away by the rising tide and drowned, weighed down by the weight of their equipment."

Charles did not want to see anymore and his grandpa and great-grandfather sensed this.

"You've seen more than you were meant to see, little one," said Jam-Jar, cupping Charles' head in his big hand and wrapping his huge arm around Charles' shoulders. He pulled his great-grandson close into his protective embrace and Charles buried his face in his great-grandfather's side.

Grandpa Maurice was deeply moved. He gazed sympathetically at his grandson and the two men shared a look of understanding.

Charles turned to his grandfather. "You could have been killed here, Grandpa!"

"It's just as well that I wasn't then," Grandpa Maurice replied smiling, "otherwise, you would never have been born!" and he affectionately squeezed Charles' chin.

All three of them grinned.

"Besides, it wasn't all bad, little one," Maurice continued. "By the end of the first day, us Commandos and all the allies, had secured a foothold along the coast to begin our advance into France. Despite heavy losses we did indeed make our way inland.

"We had to capture the bridges to be able to get our troops and equipment across into enemy territory and one bridge that was crucial to this, was Pegasus bridge. My unit had to relieve the troops already holding Pegasus bridge, the troops you've already come across, the 51st Division, who were at El Alamein, with Lord Lovat. Look! There he is now, down there on Sword Beach, with his Commandos, on their way to Pegasus bridge, to relieve the paratroopers, who have been holding it since just after midnight."

Suddenly, Charles could hear bagpipes, that familiar sound again, that made the hair stand up on the back of his neck. He looked at Jam-Jar, who glanced at him and they both shared the memory of that tumultuous night at El Alamein, when those men of the 51st Division, had stood so proud in the flickering firestorm, bagpipes calling through the smoke of battle.

Charles blinked and squinted hard and there, sure enough, through the chaos and noise and the heat of war, a familiar shape started to emerge, a shape of a lone piper, walking slowly up the beach, piping with all his might, rallying the troops and the men of the 51st, with Lord Lovat standing tall, confidently leading his men.

"The man playing the bagpipes, is Bill Millin, Lord Lovat's personal piper," continued Maurice. "They're off to Pegasus bridge now."

Charles watched them go, watched them making sense of all the carnage, bravely fighting their way through the devastation, which was strewn across the beach all around. Bill Millin kept on piping for all he was worth. The smoke closed in behind them and Charles could see them no more, but the bagpipes still floated on the breeze, like a fragrance of long ago and far away, which spoke of heather and cool hillsides and home.

Charles and his grandfather and great-grandfather were now at the top of the beach. They looked back and cast their eyes over all the devastation littered across the sands below them, never-ending as far as the eye could see in every direction, but through it all, and despite the heavy enemy fire, Charles could see that there were men getting through; soldiers were making headway to the relative safety at the top of the beaches. Little groups of men were gathering around their officers, taking cover and rallying, before pushing up the beach together. Slowly, amid all the chaos, progress was being made.

Relentless and determined, the soldiers pushed on. Some ran for all they were worth until they found cover, advancing slowly from one tiny bit of shelter to the next, until they made it to the top of the beach, others fell as soon as their feet touched the ground and did not move again.

Charles watched, his heart in his throat, as one young soldier fell to his knees, frantically digging a hole in the wet sand with his helmet, in the desperate hope that the hole might provide him with a bit of shelter from the hail of bullets that just kept raining down all around. Another soldier thundered past him, intent on making it alive to his rallying point, then seeming to stop in his tracks. Quickly, he turned and ran back to the poor young soldier, yanking him up and virtually dragging him across the sand to find cover.

Charles looked at Maurice, who was watching this small drama unfolding down below, this one point of humanity, amidst so much death and destruction.

"That's one very brave man," he said, clearly moved. "He could have died trying to save that young soldier. They weren't meant to stop for anyone."

Grandpa Maurice looked at Charles and smiled. "Come on, Charles. There's more to see." The Royal Marine commando he once had been, was awakening again. Charles could see the adrenaline rising in him, the spark and fury of battle taking hold in his eyes. He looked at his grandson, eyes shining and held out his hand and Charles grasped it, proudly.

Chapter 16 – Pegasus Bridge

The machine gun fire and noise of fierce battle on the beaches faded into the distance and suddenly, they were standing at the side of a road, before a large metal bridge and another battle was raging all around.

"Pegasus Bridge!" exclaimed Grandpa Maurice, staring intently at the road, as if waiting for something, "and that's the River Orne. You see, Charles, it was of vital importance to capture this bridge, and the other bridges and waterways in the area of Caen, otherwise the German Panzers could have come across and easily destroyed the Allied troops landing on the beaches back there. In total 29,000 paratroopers were dropped in the early hours of 6th June, made up of US, Canadian, British, Free French and Polish troops. Can you imagine how those Free French, who landed on that morning felt, knowing they were here to help liberate their own country!"

Charles looked. "Just an ordinary street and just an ordinary road," he thought to himself and he shivered.

His great-grandfather noticed, "Are you alright, sweetheart. Is there anything wrong?" Jam-Jar asked, kindly and Grandpa Maurice, quickly turned his gaze to his little grandson, suddenly concerned for him.

"It's nothing, Jam-Jar. I can't believe I'm actually watching History happening here in front of me, that's all," said Charles and he suddenly felt very small and very insignificant in the midst of such momentous events and Charles' grandfather and great-grandfather shared a look, a look of understanding, a look that said so much, that spoke of each man's memories of the war and of its grim realities, which they both knew all too well; a look, which spoke of the love they both felt for their charge and the care and responsibility they felt for him. Instinctively, they moved closer to him as if to protect him and Maurice put an arm around his little grandson's shoulders.

Both men knew what the other was thinking and praying – that this little boy might never have to face such danger.

Maurice turned his head away and coughed a little, as if to clear his throat and continued, "The bridge was first taken and defended by men of the 2nd Battalion the Ox and Bucks Light Infantry

(6th Airborne Division), who landed in gliders, in the early hours of D-Day, sixteen minutes past midnight, to be precise and took the bridge, which was held by about fifty German soldiers. Their orders were to hold the bridge until reinforcements arrived," he explained, still looking down the road, "and hold it they did, for all they were worth."

Charles gazed at the scene. "What's a Glider?" he asked.

"It's a plane without an engine," Maurice replied, "and it's 'towed', if you like, through the sky, by an ordinary plane, attached to it by a long cable. At the right moment, the cord is detached and the glider 'glides' to the ground. The pilot in the glider controls its rate of descent and where it lands and the advantage is that, as it has no engine, it's completely silent, which is a great advantage in enemy territory, especially as these gliders were full of soldiers, ready to attack the Germans and take the bridge."

Maurice pointed to a nearby field. "There's one glider just over there."

Charles stood on tiptoes and peered down a small embankment into a narrow, small field. There was the glider, sitting discarded, it's soldiers long since departed.

"How many were still alive?" thought Charles.

"The pilot of that particular glider was so good that he landed it in the dark, exactly on target, where it was meant to land, on a narrow strip of land," said his grandfather and Charles imagined those men, faces painted with camouflage paint, sharing final looks, as the glider came into land. He heard the pilot warning them to brace themselves. He saw the soldiers jolt as the glider silently skimmed along the field and came to a sudden halt, just in front of the embankment to the bridge. The door opened and out poured twenty- nine men, including the pilot himself and with weapons in hand, they disappeared into the field under the cover of night, the element of surprise all theirs.

Charles imagined the shocked expressions on the faces of the German soldiers, as the battle-hardened men descended on them from out of the darkness. Grandpa Maurice's words gently edged into his mind.

"They took the bridge in just five minutes under the command of Major John Howard, exactly according to plan and over there is the first house in France to be liberated," said Maurice pointing to a lone, tall building, "the Café Gondre and the little girl, who lived there, still runs it as a café with her family, in honour of the Allies, who helped to free her country. It was used by the Allies as a makeshift hospital to treat the wounded, because there was a fierce counter-attack by the Germans afterwards, but all Major Howard and his men could do, was follow orders and hold the bridge until reinforcements arrived, no matter what. The first lot of reinforcements were the 7th Parachute Battalion, led by an officer named Pine Coffin, wearing cowboy boots, who arrived at three in the morning." Charles smiled at the name.

"And who do you think were the next lot of reinforcements?" asked Grandpa Maurice.

Charles thought. He had no idea, but suddenly the sound of bagpipes could be heard coming from down the road. It was getting closer. Maurice and Jam-Jar were staring fixedly in that direction, grinning, as the call of the bagpipes drew closer.

"I know," Charles exclaimed, "Lord Lovat!"

"That's right," said Grandpa Maurice. "Ah! And here he is now with his Commandos."

Lord Lovat and his men were making their way along the road towards the bridge and there was Bill Millin, Lord Lovat's piper walking proudly ahead of the men.

Charles and Jam-Jar and Maurice watched them pass and take their first steps onto the bridge, but instead of running across,

Charles saw a curious thing. Lord Lovat and his men walked across in an orderly fashion! Tough they looked and strong, poised for action, like tigers ready to pounce, dignified and disciplined and unafraid, the piper piping them all the way.

Bullets ricocheted all around them, pattering and singing off the metal of the bridge, but still they walked on. Charles watched as the last of those berets they wore so proudly, disappeared over the other side.

He was awestruck. "Why did they do that, Grandpa? Why didn't they run?"

"To show that they weren't afraid," said Maurice, "which is why Lord Lovat ordered his piper, Bill Millin, to walk ahead of the men playing the bagpipes. Crossing this bridge was of great significance to the allies. It meant the beginning of the end of Nazi occupation and Lord Lovat wanted to show the Nazis that they were dealing with a serious and determined force. Do you know Charles, after the war the German snipers explained to Bill Millin through an interpreter that they hadn't shot at him because they'd thought he'd gone mad," and all three of them laughed.

Suddenly, Charles and Jam-Jar and Grandpa Maurice found themselves on the other side of the bridge. They could hear the call of the bagpipes swirling in the air and Charles looked over to Major Howard, commanding officer of the 6th Airborne Division, who with his men and the men of the 7th Parachute Battalion, had bravely held Pegasus bridge all this time since they'd landed in their gliders in the early hours of the morning. It must have felt like an age away to those weary paratroopers.

Bill Millin appeared, his bagpipe sending a note of hope to those embattled soldiers, closely followed by Lord Lovat and his commandos.

Major Howard looked up, "It's Lovat," Charles heard him exclaim, relief and amusement both playing on his face.

Lord Lovat approached him, "Sorry I'm late!" he said, with understated humour. Quickly, he gave orders and his men fanned out on either side and reinforced the defensive positions.

Charles looked at Grandpa Maurice and his Jam-Jar. Both men's gaze was fixed on this drama and their chests swelled with pride.

Grandpa Maurice took a deep, shuddering breath, "He was only two minutes late! But, you know, the next lot, who relieved Lovat's men, came over at a run!" said Maurice, smiling wryly and Jam-Jar and Charles chuckled.

"How do you know that, Grandpa?" asked Charles, intrigued.

"Because I was one of them!" said Maurice, quietly.

The hair stood up on the back of Charles's neck and he stared in wonder at this man, whose eyes were now fixed on the far side of the bridge.

Charles followed his gaze.

Fighting could be heard on the other side – the rapid fire of guns and the burst of shells.

Suddenly, Maurice spoke, "It was the 11th June, when we arrived to reinforce the troops holding Pegasus Bridge. We'd taken the village of Saint Aubin after three hours of fighting, which wasn't helped by the fact that our Naval Ships off the coast, were accidentally shelling us. They were giving covering fire, but hadn't realised we'd moved as quickly as we had. They were given orders to stop firing so we could then move east to our next objective and attack the town of Langrune-sur-Mer. It was close combat, fighting house to house. Nasty business, but it was a job that had to be done and we knew it and our next objective was to proceed to Pegasus Bridge."

Suddenly, the Royal Marines were there, the 48 Commando charging over the bridge towards them. Charles thought he caught a glimpse of his grandfather among the men as they ran past, so close he could smell the smoke of battle on their uniforms after five days of hard fighting.

Shivers ran down his spine. His skin tingled with adrenaline. He grasped his grandfather's hand, who held his tightly.

"Grandpa, where did you go after D-Day?"

"We went up into Belgium, stopping off in Brussels on the way, but not before we'd accidentally liberated a French village," said Maurice.

"Accidentally!" exclaimed Charles.

"Yes," chuckled Maurice. "We didn't know we'd gone beyond the Allied front lines and unknown to us, we'd gone into German occupied territory in our lorry. So, we entered a French

169

village, thinking it was now in Allied hands, and suddenly all these young French women came out of their houses to greet us, waving armfuls of flowers. You see, they thought we'd come to liberate them; just one lorry of commandos!

"So, naturally, being young lads, as we were then," said Maurice, eyes twinkling, "we started handing out bars of chocolate to them, when suddenly a German heavy machine gun opened up on us. Shocked, we looked down the road to the other end of the village. I was in the front seat next to the driver, so I got the full view and to our great surprise, there was a German armoured car, with guns pointing straight at us! You see the village was still occupied by the Germans!

"The young women scattered and disappeared back into their houses; a lot of choice words were said by us and you never saw a lorry reverse so quickly in all your life. We shot out of there backwards like a bat out of hell!"

And Charles and Maurice and Jam-Jar all laughed at the memory.

Chapter 17 – The End of it All

"What happened in the end, Grandpa, at the end of it all?" asked Charles, suddenly exceedingly tired.

Maurice looked kindly at his sleepy grandson and smiled.

"Well, there was another year of fighting - another year of war and bloodshed before the end and there was Operation Market Garden - an Allied campaign, which happened in the Netherlands. The Allied aim was to create a bulge, otherwise known as a salient, into enemy territory, to create a quick invasion route into Northern Germany. Nine bridges had to be captured by the Allies and the campaign looked as if it would be successful. The Nazis were in retreat, Dutch cities were liberated, V-2 rocket sites were destroyed, sites which had launched rockets that bombed British cities and German forces were depleted, forces that would have been used to strengthen the German counter-attack, which came later, but it's this bridge, the one the Allies failed to capture, this is the one we will never forget, the bridge at Arnhem."

For a moment Charles was there, standing by a bridge, surrounded by the carnage and the destruction of bombed out buildings, rubble strewn across the roads, bullets whistling overhead and a Panzer Battalion sitting there!

"They'd been sent here to rest and regroup," said Maurice, stepping up beside him. "In fact, the northern Netherlands was so littered with Panzer tank divisions and SS units, it's remarkable just how much of a success Operation Market Garden actually was, although it was ultimately seen as a failure. Just seven-hundred and forty brave men held this blasted bridge for four days, twice as long as expected."

Immediately, as if on cue, shell bursts peppered the air just above their heads. They all ducked, instinctively and Charles looked up at the pockmarked sky, as Allied planes flew over dropping supplies to the soldiers trapped below.

"But, they're dropping the supplies in the wrong place!" Charles exclaimed.

"It's the right place alright," said Maurice, sadly, "just the wrong army! Our boys were meant to be there by now, but they're pinned down by this ruddy Panzer division and their radios aren't

171

working. They can't tell anyone that they're not where they should be. They have no way of letting anyone know the supplies are dropping straight into enemy hands."

They all looked on, as the supplies continued to fall. Charles could almost feel the desperation of the tired soldiers scattered all around in the bombed-out buildings.

Suddenly, a plane was hit by enemy fire. Men bailed out, their parachutes opening, almost gracefully, as they floated to the ground. Jam-Jar counted the men.

"All out, bar one," he said. "Come on, come on lad. Bail out!"

Enemy fire arched across the sky, reaching out towards the plane, like long, malevolent fingers, seeming to tap one wing, as smoke poured from the plane's engines.

"It's going down," said Maurice, fatalistically.

"Hold on!" exclaimed Jam-Jar. "It's turning! It's aiming straight down the tracer fire. It must be the pilot left of board. He's deliberately aiming at the enemy guns. He's going to crash straight into them."

"He is!" Maurice said quietly, staring fixedly at the rapidly descending plane. "He's going to put those blasted guns out of action."

"A brave, brave lad!" said Jam-Jar, as he and Maurice shared a look only fathers would understand.

The scene shifted and faded away, the yells of the men left behind, still ringing in their ears.

"Then what, Grandad? What happened next? I want to know it all," said Charles, determined never to forget the bravery of the pilot, who had given his life to save others.

"There was the Battle of the Bulge," said Jam-Jar, slowly, "when the enemy Axis powers launched a counter offensive in December 1944 and can you guess where it was fought, Charles? Do you remember where the German army first entered France in 1940?"

Charles thought of everything he had seen and experienced. Then he remembered -a forest with one long, narrow road.

"The Forest of the Ardennes!" he said in surprise.

"That's right and they nearly succeeded in using this road again in 1944." said Jam-Jar, "but the Germans failed in the end, thank goodness! Sadly though, this ruddy war still raged on against the Nazis and the Japanese for another year."

"The Japanese!" exclaimed Charles.

"Yes, sweetheart. Do you remember they attacked the American fleet in Pearl Harbour on 7th December 1941. That's why the Americans joined the war and the men who fought the Japanese were called the Forgotten Army."

"The Forgotten Army?" asked Charles, puzzled.

"After everyone back home had celebrated VE Day, Victory in Europe day, they got on with their lives and sort of forgot about the war that the Allies were still fighting against Japan. Victory against Japan came later, so by the time those soldiers came home from Burma, people weren't so interested and the men, who had been captured and held in Japanese Prisoner of War camps, the ones who had survived, came home looking like skeletons, just skin and bone. Those poor men had suffered a great deal at the hands of their captors. The conditions in the Japanese Prisoner of War camps were appalling, with slave labour, starvation and disease."

"Gosh, that's awful," exclaimed Charles.

"And it took two bombs to make the Japanese surrender – two bombs the likes of which the world had never been seen before," said Maurice, ominously. "Atomic bombs – dropped on the cities of Hiroshima and Nagasaki."

Charles didn't need to be told what those bombs meant. In his mind he saw a frightening image – a blinding, searing flash of light, a burst of terrible heat and a shock wave, which radiated out across the city, suddenly draining it of colour, as a dark cloud of enormous proportions, blooming and growing just like a mushroom, suddenly filled the sky, while all around people turned to shadows on the walls...

That was all Charles needed to see. He closed his eyes and blinked away the scene.

"And back home there were the V1 and V2 rockets to contend with," said Maurice, gently

"What were those!" Charles asked, alarmed.

"Rocket bombs, fired at us all the way from main-land Europe and they took this war to another frightening level," said Maurice, sadly.

"You had a chance with the V1 rockets. People used to call them 'Doodle Bugs'," said Jam-Jar. "You could hear them coming. They used to sound like really sleepy bees and as one got closer, it would slow down, as if it was about to land and then the engine would cut out. You knew you were in for it then and it was time to take cover, but there was a way of knocking them off course and making them ditch into the sea, before they reached land. Can you guess what was used to do this, Charles? Something you love very much."

Charles didn't need long to think about it. "You don't mean Spitfires, do you?" he asked, surprised.

"Yes, that's right," his great-grandfather replied. "The Spitfire pilots would fly really close to the rocket, in the same direction that it was going and angle the Spitfire's wings just under the wings of the rocket and literally tip it off course."

"Wow! That's so clever and so brave!" said Charles, stunned.

"But," said Maurice, "if you were on the ground and heard that engine cut out, you jolly-well made sure that you got out of the way! In fact, my wife, Mary, your grandmother, your father's mother, had a very close shave with a Doodle-Bug in 1944. She was only seventeen and she'd just started her first job, working in an office in London, when suddenly everyone heard that familiar sound. They all waited for it to pass over, but then the engine cut out. When Mary looked round, all the people in the office had disappeared – they'd already taken cover, you see, and the only place left to hide was the bottom shelf of a tea-trolly!" Maurice laughed gently. "Luckily, nobody was hurt that time."

Charles pictured his grandmother, as a young woman, trying to squeeze into a tea trolly. It made him smile.

"Luckily, she wasn't very tall," said Maurice, smiling. "She just fitted."

"And then there were the V2 rockets," Jam-Jar joined in, "and unfortunately, you didn't stand a chance with those."

"V2! What did that mean?" Charles asked.

"The 'V' stood for *'Vergeltungswaffen'* or 'Retaliatory weapon', otherwise known as 'Vengeance weapons'," Jam-Jar replied. "They were very different from the V1 Doodle bugs, because they were so fast, you couldn't hear them coming. The V2 rockets only took *five minutes* from being launched from Nazi occupied Holland, to reaching their target of London and other cities in England. The rockets were fired straight up into the stratosphere – that's the part of the Earth's atmosphere, just before space. When they reached the stratosphere, they would come straight back down again right on top of their target, without any warning. There would just be this sudden, 'whoosh' and then a huge explosion.

"When they were first used in September 1944 to attack London, people thought it was a gas main exploding, not a bomb at all. It was feared that there would be mass panic when people found out that it was really a new type of bomb, but there wasn't any panic. People just coped.

"After the war, the German engineer, who invented the V2 rocket, Wernher von Braun, surrendered himself to the Americans and went on to invent the rocket technology that launched the Space Age, which saw the Americans be the first to land a manned spaceship on the moon in 1969," Jam-Jar added.

Charles was stunned. "So, the man who'd invented this horrible weapon, actually got a job with the Americans after the war, a country that Germany had been fighting!"

"I know," said Jam-Jar. "Crazy, isn't it - but it's true!"

"What else happened, then, in that last year of the war?" asked Charles. He almost didn't want to know.

His great-grandfather was the one to answer. "The Italian Fascist dictator, Mussolini, met a sticky end and after many long, tiring months of the Germans fighting almost to the last man, when there were only children left to fight against the Allies in Berlin, Hitler, himself died on the 30th April 1945 and finally, the evil died too."

Chapter 18 - VE Day - Victory in Europe

"And then there was VE day?" Charles guessed.

"Yes," said Jam-Jar. "On the 7th May 1945, Nazi Germany surrendered to the Allies, unconditionally and the 8th May, VE Day, was declared a National Holiday. Churchill and the King both made radio broadcasts to the nation and shared the joy and relief that the nation felt."

As his great-grandfather spoke, Charles was sure he could almost hear floating on the air, the faint cheer of jubilant crowds and Churchill's words, *'Advance Britannia! God save the King!'*

"The Royal Family made eight appearances on the balcony of Buckingham Palace," Jam-Jar continued, "Churchill joined the King and Queen and the young princesses. The crowds cheered and partied all night long, even the young princesses, Elizabeth, who was just nineteen and Margaret, sneaked out to join in the fun."

"Really!" Charles exclaimed.

"They did indeed," Jam-Jar replied. "The King and Queen let them go. Sixteen friends went with them, and they all just blended into the crowd and partied the night away."

"But most of us," Jam-Jar continued, inclining his head towards Maurice, "missed out on all the fun, because we were still on active service, but at least they all had a jolly good party back home. Street parties sprang up everywhere, people danced the conga, complete strangers shared a drink,"

"Or a kiss!" chuckled Maurice.

Jam-Jar smiled, rolling his eyes.

As they were talking, Charles became aware of a sound in the distance that was getting closer. He tried to ignore it, as he listened to his grandfather and great-grandfather talking, but the noise was drawing nearer. Charles couldn't ignore it anymore and confused, turned to look...

...and to his amazement, a SPITFIRE was coming in to land close by. Charles blinked and stared around him. The fighting and bombing, the soldiers and Pegasus Bridge itself had all disappeared and he saw that the three of them were standing in a perfectly ordinary, rather lovely field by the banks of a sparkling river. Birds were singing, the air was fresh and clear and the smell and heat of battle had been replaced by the drowsy hum of bees and the purr of an idling Spitfire engine!

He peered again at the Spitfire, which had now taxied to a halt, but he was even more amazed when he saw who it was jumping out - his great-grandfather, the one who had been a fighter pilot in the First World War - his father's grandfather - his great-grandfather, Frank, with whom Charles had flown in the cartoon world, whilst fighting the Red Baron!

Frank walked up to the group and smiled. "Hello, Charlie!" he said. "Remember me?" he asked, with a cheeky smile.

Charles' face broke out into a broad grin.

"How is this possible?" he said, overjoyed to see him. "I heard you! I knew I'd heard you in my mind at Malta. You were with me somehow in that cockpit but how is this possible. You're here. You're actually here!"

"Anything's possible, Charlie, if you believe," said Frank, "and you think I was going to miss this! All this!" he said gesturing around him. The distant sound of gunfire could just be heard. "So different from my war, the First World War!"

And in that minute Charles saw that war – dead fields scarred by potholes and bomb craters, merciless razor wire – no living thing in sight, no birds, no trees, just stumps where they once had been and miles of desolate land carved up by trenches, which zigzagged as far as the eye could see and that noise, that incessant pounding of heavy guns, the barrage of death on an industrial scale, like some out-of-control machine.

Charles blinked and glanced at Frank, who was looking him straight in the eye and they shared a knowledge in that moment, of that tumultuous time that Charles knew he would never forget.

"There were no winners then," Frank said, simply. "No decisive victory. On the 11th November 1918, at 11 o'clock in the morning, the whistles blew and the guns fell silent. No more noise, no more fighting, just silence. Not another bomb or bullet was fired. Just peace. Like flicking the switch and turning off the machine. The bloodshed stopped, four years too late," and there was emotion in his voice, as he looked away.

For a moment they all stood quiet, thinking about all they had seen and then Frank spoke again,

"And you think I was going to miss the chance to see you, Charlie, or the chance to fly - that," and he pointed to the Spitfire, sitting patiently in the field beside them.

"I've heard so much about these beautiful things and I wasn't going to pass up the opportunity to fly one, when it came my way!"

"But how did it come your way," Charles asked excitedly. Frank just tapped the side of his nose with his finger and winked at him.

"Where there's a will there's a way, Charlie!" and he beamed at his great-grandson, the cheekiest smile Charles had ever seen and the smile that Charles returned was exactly the same.

"Like two peas in a pod, you two!" exclaimed Jam-Jar.

"Oh, I think we can all take a bit of credit for this little one," chimed in Maurice, wisely, and it was true; in Charles' face there was clearly discerned the imprint of all these men; three lives, three histories, three families, whose lifeblood had come to rest in Charles' veins and the sacrifices they had made and the bravery and the love.

"So, do you want a lift home, Charlie?" said Frank, holding out his hand.

"You mean with you, in that Spitfire?" said Charles, excitedly.

"Naturally!" said his great-grandfather, simply, as if it was the most obvious thing in the world!

Charles' stomach leapt with joy and excitement at the prospect, but then he thought and turned to Grandpa Maurice and Jam-Jar.

"But how will you two get home?" asked Charles, dismayed.

"Don't worry about us, sweetheart," Jam-Jar replied, smiling gently. "We'll meet you back home. We'll be waiting for you when you land."

"You go on," said Grandpa Maurice, "and have fun."

The two men stood side by side looking proudly at Charles, who saw them as if for the first time. Part of him still could not believe all that had happened and all that he had seen, or that these men were really here with him. He hugged his great-grandfather and grandpa, tightly, as if he'd never let them go and they in turn, wrapped their strong arms around him and held him close.

Then Charles turned to walk with Frank, but as he did so, Jam-Jar called after him,

"Remember we love you, Charles. Always remember that," and Charles ran back and hugged them again and then it was time to go.

"Ready?" said Great-Grandfather Frank. Charles nodded, speechless with anticipation. The moment had arrived! Great-Grandfather, Frank, made sure Charles was safely strapped into his seat and casting one final sparkling smile at his great-grandson, flung himself into the pilot's cockpit.

The Merlin engine roared into life. Charles waved to Jam-Jar and Maurice, who both waved back a little anxiously.

"Hold on tight!" Frank bellowed over the purr of the engine and then they were off, trundling at speed across the open ground. Charles' stomach turned somersaults. Tingles ran up his spine. He felt like screaming with glee, but no sound came.

The Spitfire gained speed, gave a little leap and suddenly it was free of the earth, free of gravity itself. It did one circuit in the brilliant blue sky above the field, where Grandpa Maurice and Jam-Jar watched a little worriedly, necks craned upwards, hands shielding eyes and then raced away, above the clouds towards the setting sun, Charles and Frank laughing gleefully all the way.

Over London they went. The peeling chimes of Big Ben rang out joyfully. Cheering crowds thronged the streets. VE day was in full swing. Low over Trafalgar Square they flew with people splashing in the fountain and then up the Mall towards Buckingham Palace, where the greatest mass of jubilant people Charles had ever seen, were dancing, singing, cheering and running congas, which snaked through the excited crowd.

There, on the balcony of Buckingham Palace were the King and Queen with their daughters and Churchill, all waving and smiling to the crowd, sharing their exhilaration and pleasure.

Charles waved at the people and at the King, knowing full well, that all below were oblivious to the presence of this Spitfire, but suddenly the King looked up and fixed his gaze directly at the little plane, which was skimming over the crowds and Charles knew that the King had seen them.

He felt goosebumps all over and again, in his head, he heard those words, "Remember all that you have seen here, Charles and tell your children and your children's children of the sacrifices that were made." Charles gazed in awe at the upturned face of the King and waved one hand in salute. The King nodded in acknowledgment and then turned his attention to the cheering crowds once more. Charles gazed in wonder, with the chimes of Big Ben still ringing in his ears...

Chapter 19 – Home

...and on they flew, into the setting sun, whose golden light filled the cockpit of the little Spitfire with a glorious glow, as Charles and his great grandfather, Frank, sung and laughed together and beamed with the sheer joy of being free up there in the clouds.

Suddenly, a brilliant white light filled Charles' eyes and when he could see clearly again the Spitfire had landed. After the roar and hum of the Merlin engine, the sudden silence pulsated in Charles' ears.

A few summer bees were taking advantage of the last of the day's warmth and Charles could hear their contented hum of quiet industry. Ducks quacked gently on the still lake, water dripping from their bills, as their beaks dipped and rose. A weeping willow leant to the water's edge, its boughs bending gracefully in a cascade of green. A slight breeze whispered through the reed beds, their feathery flags rustling softly. All was hushed and peaceful.

Blinking in surprise, Charles realised that his feet were sinking into damp grass and looking around him, he saw, with a shock, that he was nearly home, in the park, where it had all begun...

...and he was standing beside his Spitfire and there were Jam-Jar and Grandpa Maurice waiting for him, beaming with pride.

Frank hopped out of the cockpit and leapt to the ground, clearly exhilarated.

"What a flight! What a machine, eh Charlie?" said Frank and Charles ran to his outstretched arms and clasped him tight.

"Thank-you, Great-Grandad, thank-you!"

"Well, well," he spluttered, in pretend surprise, "What a polite boy you are, Charlie! It was fun. I enjoyed it. Thank-you, Charlie, for sharing it with me and thank-you, Spitfire!" he exclaimed, patting the side of the plane, as if it were a horse.

"Yes," said Charles, "Thank-you, Spitfire!" and Charles imagined he almost saw that wonderful Spitfire smile.

"Well, my darling," said Jam-Jar, approaching. "It's time to take you home."

"But I don't want to leave you, Jam-Jar. I want to stay with all of you," exclaimed Charles.

"Now, now sweetheart!" smiled Jam-Jar, gently. "Your Mummy and Daddy will want to hear all your wonderful adventures," and with a pang, Charles realised how much he was missing them.

So, the little group walked Charles home slowly through the woods, chatting all the way, until they reached the door of his house and there, they said their goodbyes.

"Cheerio, Charlie," said Frank, cheerfully, but Charles could hear the catch in his voice and there was a lump in Charles' throat, too. They shook hands and laughed and Frank rubbed the top of his great-grandson's head, smiling that cheeky smile again.

Then Charles turned to Grandpa Maurice, who smiled at him and said, "Bye-bye, little one. I'm so pleased I met you at last. Say 'Hello' to that son of mine and remember, Charles, I'll always be here if you need me."

And then finally, Charles turned to his great-grandfather, his Jam-Jar, hoping with all his heart to delay their moment of parting.

"Remember, sweetheart," said Jam-Jar, "we'll always be with you. Like I said before, my mother has never left me and we'll never leave you," and Charles flung his arms around his great-grandfather and his great-grandfather held him tight, as if he would never let go. "Say 'Hello' to your mother from me," said Jam-Jar. "I miss her dearly. We were the best of friends, you know, two buddies together on our adventures and this name she gave me, I never shook it off!" and he smiled at the thought of his little, blonde haired grand-daughter running in and demanding to be put on his shoulders. Charles felt the warmth of his memory and the love he felt for her and for him.

And then he took one last look at these three men, his Great-Grandfather Bob, whom his mother had called Jam-Jar and who would always be Jam-Jar to him; his Grandpa Maurice, his father's father and finally, his Great-Grandfather Frank – three men, who had seen so much of life, who had been part of so many momentous events, who had seen so much of the hardship and the pain and suffering that life could throw at them, but all still able to love and laugh and to show the loving kindness, which he himself had felt and he was filled with love for them and pride for the sacrifices which they had made.

As he walked away, he stood on the step of his house and turned one last time to look at the three men, whom he had never thought to meet. The light was fading fast and the three men seemed to be fading with it. Everything in Charles wanted to run back to them, but then he glanced up at the window of his parent's bedroom and thought of them sleeping, safe in the knowledge that he was tucked up in his little bed and he felt a pang of longing for them.

A soft drowsiness descended on him, as he threw one last dart of love towards those three men standing proudly in the silent road. They smiled back at him and faded with the light, as Charles turned his head to soft pillow and warm duvet and slept deeply.

Chapter 20 – The Lake

It was a beautiful autumn day. The morning mists had cleared and a balmy, south wind ruffled the leaves, sending showers of gold confetti fluttering through the air. In the park, dog walkers were enjoying the last warm days of the year, their dogs sniffing the rich scents carried on the breeze. Sounds floated dreamily on the wind and drifted over the lake, sending ripples flowing across its surface and stirring the reflections of the old willow tree. Its long, leaning limbs, dripped liquid gold, which mingled with the yellow leaves, that drifted across the pool of molten light.

Charles and his parents were walking together by the lake, along the path that wound around the water's edge. They watched the swans, gliding lazily, leading the last of the Spring's signets, who were now almost full-grown and slowly paddling amongst the swirling leaves.

Charles went a little way ahead to the water's edge to feed the ducks, whilst his parents looked on.

The early afternoon sun shone brightly on the lake's golden surface, which flung glistening sparkles through the Autumn air and suddenly, they saw Charles standing with three figures, who were silhouetted against the glinting water. The gleaming light seemed to emanate from them, creating a luminescent halo around the whole group. For a moment Charles' parents wondered who they were, when suddenly the sun disappeared behind a cloud and the three figures could be clearly seen.

Both caught their breath. Charles' father moved as if to run towards them, but his wife reached for his hand and they stood still, transfixed, as the three figures standing with Charles glanced up and held their gaze. The look they shared was golden in the sun, which in that minute appeared from behind the cloud, as the three figures were lost again in the glistening water.

Charles ran up to his mother and father.

"You see! I told you they were real," he said.

His parents looked at him with tears in their eyes and smiled.

When the day was over, they walked home. The long rich Autumn was coming to an end. The leaves had lingered, crispening to copper and gold and the landscape glowed bronze in the Autumn light.

It was dusk and wood smoke hung heavy on the evening air and a sweet smell of blackberry wood burning on bonfires floated over the water, lingering on the gentle wind like a memory of longer days and warmer nights. Across the lane, mists rose slowly from peaceful fields, as the land exhaled with a scent of rich earth and evening settled softly over the resting countryside with a fragrance, like sweet incense carried on the breeze.

The seasons, again had turned. The night's breath was cooling, the days were shortening and Autumn Equinox approached gently, like an old, familiar friend...

Chapter 21 – Father Christmas

It was nearly Christmas and one afternoon, just as it was getting dark, Charles went with his parents to a big department store to visit Father Christmas.

All the shop windows were decorated for Christmas and the streets were criss-crossed with hundreds of sparkling lights. Even the trees bloomed with twinkling stars.

The department store was old and creaky, with dark, oak-panelled walls and creaky floorboards covered with thick, plush carpet. Charles looked down and was struck by how his feet sunk into its deep pile.

They walked through the different departments, each one festooned with red and gold and silver decorations, which glinted in the warm light, past counters selling everything and anything: leather gloves, handkerchiefs, scarfs, belts and bags; counters selling canisters of shortbread and tea – Charles looked at the names, Lapsang Souchong, Earl Grey, Keemun, Goomtee First Flush Darjeeling – Charles' tongue almost tied itself in knots trying to pronounce the names.

Another counter sold hats of strange shapes and sizes – Charles giggled at the sight of one particularly large hat with a particularly large feather and imagined who might wear it. His mother put it on and pulled a funny face at him and they all laughed.

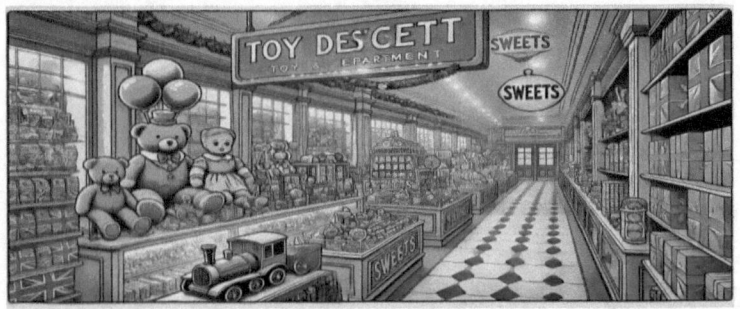

Next was the toy department! Charles' eyes almost popped out of his head at the sight. Shelves were filled with all manner of wonderful toys; cars, train sets, action figures, dolls, plushies, planes and box games. Mechanical toys swirled around on tables, beeping and talking with their robot voices. Remote controlled cars whizzed around people's feet. Toy planes, suspended from the ceiling by thin wires, were flying in circles above people's heads and toy steam trains whistled past along the tops of the shelves. Charles was thrilled by the noise and fun of the room.

"We're definitely coming back here after we've seen the Big Man," said his gleeful father. "I rather like the look of those steam trains," he said.

"And I like the look of those cars," said his mother.

"I like the look of it all," said Charles, excitedly.

Rather reluctantly, they left behind the room of toys and on they went to the perfume department. The rich scents floated towards them enticingly and greeted them before they entered the hall. Like a hand beckoning them, the intoxicating fragrances drew them in. Charles felt as if he was floating on an invisible cloud.

Sounds were quieter here, more muffled. In the centre of the room was a counter bathed in a soft, mysterious light, upon which sat a large container made of black glass, which gleamed with a deep, purply wine-dark glow. It looked like an elegant old-fashioned vase and was almost as tall as Charles. Around the narrowest point of its neck, near the rim, were little brass taps. From each tap a different perfume dripped large sticky drops of gold and amber liquid, like the sap from a tree. The effect was heady and magical and Charles felt himself almost drifting into a dream.

On again they went, past a sign saying 'Haberdashery'. Charles' father kept saying the word over and over again in more and more silly ways. Past rooms filled with great rolls of beautiful, exotic material they went, material of gold threads, strange patterns and unusual designs; past paper packs of dress patterns, shiny buttons of all colours and sizes, past knitting needles and pins and then down a long, narrow corridor, lined on either side with dark wooden shelves full of balls of different wools of every shade, each arranged by their bright colours in their own wooden compartments.

Sounds were softened here and, as they walked, Charles ran his hand along the rows of bulging wool - their rounded ends felt like rabbits' tails. He closed his eyes, sleepily and felt the wool brush softly past his face, as his mother gently guided him by the hand. She looked back at him, smiling.

"We're here," she whispered.

Charles opened his eyes.

Before him, two narrow wooden doors slid open to reveal an old, wood panelled lift and what seemed like an even older man dressed in a grey suit with gold braid and a smart peaked cap, which was also trimmed with braid. His smile was infectious.

"Climb aboard, climb aboard, Young Charles," he said. "Today, we are going on an adventure. Today, we fly to the North Pole in my hot air balloon!"

Charles and his parents squeezed, giggling into the small lift with him. It felt more like a cupboard than a lift. On one side was a padded seat, lined with red velvet, on which they now sat and on the opposite wall was a little revolving screen on two rollers, painted with a picture of clouds and birds.

The lift doors closed.

"Hold tight for lift off!" said the man, who looked as creaky as the lift itself, which shuddered into motion. The revolving screen began to scroll downwards, as the lift moved upwards, rather shakily at first and then more smoothly. It felt as if the hot-air balloon had taken flight and was floating up into the sky, gliding up, up, up through the canopy of white fleecy cloud and away to the North Pole!

"Now we're off," he said, "to see Father Christmas!" The man was old, but his voice was surprisingly young and full of good humour. He seemed as excited as Charles to be going!

There was a slight bump, as if they had landed. The lift doors slid open soundlessly and a draught of cold air swept in around their feet and faces.

Charles stared in wonder. Ahead of him was a long tunnel. Curtains of shiny silver and white and ice-blue material were draped across, through which Charles and his parents walked, slowly pushing them aside, guiding themselves towards the source of a magical sound that wafted up the tunnel with the cool breeze.

Charles looked back at the wooden lift with its red seat and the old man in his grey suit and peaked cap, who was standing in the open door, smiling and slowly waving, the warm light from the lift spilling out onto the cool snow, turning it pink.

Charles pulled his gaze away and holding his parents' hands, they walked on together. The chimes of sleigh bells were tinkling all around them and the soft hum of winged creatures would occasionally come close to their ears and then move ahead of them and if guiding them on. A strange music floated on the air – the music of ice crystals and frozen water and snowflakes falling.

Charles sensed a change in the atmosphere, as if the space ahead was opening out. Nosing their way through the last few silver drapes, they were confronted with a wonderous scene.

There He was – Father Christmas, sitting on a huge chair of ice and warm furs. All around was snow and crystals. Icicles grew on the roof of the great hall and drops of silver water caught the light and sparkled everywhere.

Father Christmas smiled and held out his arms.

"Hello, Charles! Welcome!"

Charles was a little nervous and his parents gave him a gentle nudge.

"Go on, sweetheart. We're here with you," said his mother, quietly.

He moved nearer to Father Christmas, whose kind face glowed with warmth. Little creases of mirth played around his eyes, as he spoke, "Now, Charles – a little elf has told me that you have an interest in Spitfires!"

"That's right," said Charles, surprised that Father Christmas should know this.

"I've flown in one," he exclaimed, "with my Great-Grandfather Frank. He called me Charlie!" and then he stopped himself and looked at his mother; a little, quizzical smile passed across her face.

"Although, I think it must all have just been a dream," he said, quickly.

"Well," Father Christmas replied, "I think you have been a very lucky little boy!"

"I was," said Charles, proudly.

"So, what would you like for Christmas," Father Christmas asked.

Charles thought for a moment. He thought of his Great-Grandfather Frank, the pilot, who had flown him home in the Spitfire; he thought of his Grandpa Maurice, the Royal Marine, who had landed on D-Day and he thought of his Great-Grandad Bob, whom his mother had always called, Jam-Jar; he thought of all their wonderful and thrilling adventures together; he thought of everything he had seen and everything he had heard; of everything he had experienced, both the frightening and the fun and he thought of the love that he knew for these men and the love that he knew they felt for him and he wished with all his heart that he could see them again, just one more time.

"I know what I would like," said Charles, quietly, "but I don't think it can be possible," he said, a little sadly.

Father Christmas looked at him and smiled. He took a deep breath, put his finger to the side of his nose and winked.

"Chin up, Charlie," he said. "If you wish hard enough, it might just come true!"

Charles was surprised and with a little intake of breath, looking deep into his kind eyes, he saw a kaleidoscope of time revolve and spin, like a crystal-clear waterfall, through thousands of years, tumbling starlight, colliding and spinning and in that moment, Charles believed that Father Christmas knew his deepest wish.

Picking up his great sack of presents and opening it, Father Christmas leant down to Charles, saying,

"Remember, if you wish hard enough, it might come true!"

Carefully, Charles reached into the sack and pulled out a box, wrapped in silver paper.

Father Christmas inclined his head.

"Go on, Charlie. You can open it," he said, encouragingly.

Charles looked at Father Christmas and then at his parents and then at the present and slowly, heart racing, opened it and pulled out the box it contained.

Inside, there was...can you guess? There was a model SPITFIRE, but not just any old Spitfire! This one was remote controlled and could actually fly!

Charles gave Father Christmas a huge hug, for he knew what this must mean.

"Thank-you, Father Christmas. Oh, thank-you!" he cried.

Father Christmas just chuckled and smiled a knowing smile...

Then, Charles and his parents thanked Father Christmas and said their goodbyes, as they left behind the great hall of crystal light and ice, the magical sounds still lingering in the air, fading like a mist as they came blinking out into...

...into, a GREAT ROOM OF SWEETS! SWEETS as far as the eye could see – SWEETS of every flavour – SWEETS of every type, every type of sweet that there has ever been, all stacked in big glass jars on shelves behind the counters, where staff were measuring them out into enormous scales and pouring them into paper bags, which they deftly twisted with a flourish and gave to expectant children.

Charles was awestruck and speechless with amazement. There were jelly sweets, boiled sweets, sour apple sweets, gobstoppers, laces and bubble-gum. There were great big lollies on enormous sticks, sherbet space-ships and marshmallows. Candyfloss ballooned as if by magic from great warm tubs and mounds of ice-cream were piled high. There were frothy ice-cream milkshakes and knickerbocker glories. There was every topping and sauce to choose from: multicoloured sprinkles, chocolate sprinkles, mini-marshmallows, little silver balls, toffee sauce, butterscotch sauce, bubble-gum sauce and strawberry, chocolate sauce, raspberry sauce, maple-syrup and honey.

There was even a stall selling pancakes and waffles, with lashings of cream and ice-cream, with strawberries and bananas and rivers of warm runny chocolate.

Charles just stood with his mouth open and stared.

"Right!" said Dad, rubbing his hands together, gleefully, "What shall we have?"

Chapter 22 – Christmas Eve

It was Christmas Eve and it had started to snow. Little flakes fell softly through the cold night air and brushed against the window pane, gathering on the window sill, as if envious of the warm, cosy fire inside, around which Charles and his mother and father were sitting, eating hot mince pies.

Little candles flickered on the mantlepiece and coffee table, their mellow, buttery light playing prettily on the walls and ceiling and melting in a golden, honey glow across the table-top. The only other light came from the warm gleam of the fire and from the glinting lights of the Christmas tree, which twinkled and sparkled, as the sweetness of tree sap and pine needles scented the air. The crackle of flames and the occasional spit of sap from the rich-smelling logs, filled the room. Charles' little black cat slept on the hearth-rug peacefully.

Outside, a beautiful, ethereal light hung over the frosty garden, which was slowly being covered in a thick blanket of fresh snow.

Charles was so excited. Christmas and snowing! How lucky!

It was peaceful by the fire, as they snuggled up together on the sofa, listening to Christmas Carols on the radio and watching the dancing flames. It felt so warm and cosy under the ample blanket, which covered their laps and Charles started to feel rather drowsy.

"Come on, sleepy head. Bed-time," said his mother, gently.

Upstairs, she tucked him into his warm, comfy bed and kissed him goodnight, as he wriggled down under his duvet. Surely, he was too excited to sleep though!

The Christmas nightlight beside his bed, moved gently - a little Father Christmas glitter ball, with Father Christmas in the snow juggling multi-coloured snowflakes, that twinkled and glittered all around his head. Charles' eyes started to close...

"Come on, Bob. Put yer back into it."

"All right, Maurice. I don't see you doin' much, though!"

"Well, someone's got to give the orders, aven't they?"

Charles snapped his eyes open and crawled to the end of his bed, pulling back the corner of the curtain, to look down at the commotion below.

It had stopped snowing now. The sky had cleared to reveal the pale face of the full moon. The cold world was white and strange outside, beautiful in the soft, bluish light, which seemed to hover over the ground in the frosty air.

Charles heard the crunch of crisp snow and muffled chuckling and sniggers in the quiet garden.

"Oh! I'm covered in snow now!"

More chuckling and the hiss of barely suppressed mirth.

"That's it! Don't forget the scarf!"

"Hat! Hat! Where's me bleedin' 'at."

"Ah! Now, that's just the ticket!"

And there below him, looking up at his window, stood two figures, proudly and expectantly trying unsuccessfully to conceal their efforts, so as not to spoil the surprise. There, stood Charles' Grandfather Maurice and his Great-Grandfather Bob – his Jam-Jar!

With a leap of joy, Charles tapped on the window, smiling and waving excitedly at the two figures waiting down below.

They stood side by side, shoulder to shoulder, their chests puffed up with pride, as if on parade. Then, bowing theatrically, they moved to one side to reveal their efforts. There, beside them, stood a rather wonky and comical snowman! He was wearing an air-raid warden's tin helmet, RAF pilot's goggles and scarf, which seemed to be flying out behind him, as if in a wind and from his shoulder was perched a gas-mask bag.

They all waved at each other, Jam-Jar pretending to wave the snowman's stick arm at him, as they beckoned to Charles to come down to play.

With a great 'whoop' of joy, Charles was out of the bed, down the stairs, throwing on coat, hat, scarf and boots over his pyjamas and shouting to his Mum and Dad to come with him, as he ran outside.

His mother and father had just settled down in front of the fire with a not so little glass of something, when they heard what sounded like a whole herd of stampeding animals thundering down the stairs. The little black cat woke with a start, arched his back, stretched and yawned, as their excited son shouted to them to come outside.

In a flash they were up, grabbing coats and boots and following Charles out into the frosty garden where they stopped in their tracks.

Standing beside a snowman, looking just how Mum remembered him, was her grandfather Bob, her Jam-Jar. Her heart leapt with joy.

"Jam-Jar!" she cried, running into his outstretched arms. "I've missed you so much."

Tears of joy glistened in Jam-Jar's kindly eyes, as he wrapped her in his warm embrace. "Katy! My little Kate!" was all he could say.

"It's been so long!" she exclaimed. "Still the same brown cardigan," she said, as she rested her head on his shoulder, her tears beading on his arm.

"Still the same long hair," he replied, as they looked into each other's beaming faces, discerning the years that had passed, before hugging each other again.

Beside them stood Maurice, tall and proud, staring straight at his son. Wrinkles of humour played around his serious face, but the emotion deep in his eyes was clear to see. Slowly, his son walked the few paces across the snow-covered lawn and stood before his father, trying to take it all in.

"Hello, Dad!"

"Hello, son!" said Maurice, simply, as they shook hands.

Dazed, Charles' father gazed at Maurice's hand that still clasped his own, unable to believe what he was seeing.

"Dad!" was all he could say again.

Maurice's smile was warm and proud, as he placed his other hand on his son's shoulder. "You've done well, my boy!" and the two men shared a look of understanding that spoke a thousand words.

"But how is this all possible?" said Charles' mother, overjoyed.

"It's Christmas Eve," Jam-Jar replied. "Everything's possible!"

And then they were all hugging each other, as a warm, rich love encircled the whole group, with Charles at the centre of it all.

Suddenly, they heard a familiar sound, a low, warm, friendly hum in the cold, night sky and it was getting closer. It made them all shiver with a thrill of delight. They looked round and Charles realised that his Great-Grandfather Frank, was not with them.

"Eh up! Here he is!" said Jam-Jar.

"Wondered where he'd got to," chuckled Maurice.

And there, in the field beyond the garden, just rolling to a standstill was Charles' Great-Grandfather Frank, in the cockpit of his wonderful, Spitfire. He waved and jumped out, striding over the crunching snow towards them.

"Where have you been, Frank?" said Maurice, knowing full well that he had been up in that plane, just flying around in the night sky to his heart's content.

"I can't get enough of that wonderful machine," said Frank. "It flies so beautifully. It's alive – I know it is! It seems to know what I want to do even before I know it myself!" and he looked at the group smiling at him, when his eyes fell on Charles' father, his namesake, Frank, his grandson.

"Hello, Frank, my lad!"

"Hello Grandpa," replied his grandson, stunned at being face to face with a man, whom he had only ever seen in photos.

"Nice to meet you!" he replied. "I've heard lots about you. Your son, Charlie, he's a smashing boy."

Charles' father stared, speechless, at this very young version of his grandpa, still not much more than a boy himself, not old in years, but old in wisdom.

Everyone looked from one to the other.

Suddenly, young pilot Frank spoke,

"Come on. Who's coming with me for a ride?" he said, looking straight at Charles, a cheeky smile playing on his excited face.

And, as if a spell had been broken, Charles' father blinked and nudged his wife with his elbow.

"Go on," he said, beaming. "You've always wanted to."

Mum's eyes brightened with joy. She held out her hand to her son.

"Come on, Charles. You can sit on my lap."

And because it was Christmas Eve and because everything is possible at Christmas time, Charles, his mother and his Great-Grandfather Frank flew up into the frosty, moonlit sky and flew straight towards the great city of London, flying over Trafalgar Square, laughing and smiling in their Spitfire!

"There! Look down there!" called Frank. "That's what I wanted to show you. The Norway Spruce! The Christmas Tree sent as a gift from Norway, sent every year at Christmas, as a sign of the bond of friendship between us - a gift of gratitude from the people of Norway - another proud seafaring nation - given in thanks for our efforts to save their country and their monarchy during the war.

"That tree down there," he continued, "symbolises all that can be done when people help each other, when people act with generosity of spirit and selflessness. My generation, and your Jam-Jar's and Maurice's generation, understood that idea of duty and service, of doing the right thing, of helping others despite the cost to yourself. That tree is a sign of the bond of trust between our two great seafaring nations and may it never be broken," he said, almost to himself.

They flew over the lights of Trafalgar Square and the lights of that beautiful Christmas tree, twinkling in the evening breeze and Charles looked in wonder at his mother and her expression matched his own...

...And then it was time to go home for one last, final goodbye.

Slowly they walked from the plane back towards the house and looking at each other, they all shared one last, long hug with the people they had never expected to see again when...

...suddenly, young Frank piped up, "Cheer up you lot! There's always next Christmas!" and he threw the biggest snowball at Charles, who immediately joined in the fun and returned the volley, as they all descended into laughter and joy, in the biggest snowball fight ever, whilst Christmas carols played indoors on the radio, the fire flickered warmly in the grate, the little cat slept on and the Christmas Tree lights twinkled in the glow of a magical Christmas Eve.

The End....

Patriotic Quotes

On 9th August 1588, at Tilbury Docks, before a further expected invasion attempt by King Philip's Spanish Armada, from Dunkirk, led by the Duke of Palma,
Queen Elizabeth I, arrived on horseback in silver cer⋯ armour, as if ready to lead her troops into battle and gave this famous speech.

'My loving people.

We have been persuaded by some that are careful of our safety, to take heed how we commit ourselves to armed multitudes, for fear of treachery; but I assure you I do not desire to live to distrust my faithful and loving people. Let tyrants fear. I have always so behaved myself that, under God, I have placed my chiefest strength and safeguard in the loyal hearts and good-will of my subjects; and therefore, I am come amongst you, as you see, at this time, not for my recreation and disport, but being resolved, in the midst and heat of the battle, to live and die amongst you all; to lay down for my God, and for my kingdom, and my people, my honour and my blood, even in the dust.

I know I have the body but of a weak, feeble woman; but I have the heart and stomach of a king, and of a king of England too, and think foul scorn that Parma or Spain, or any prince of Europe, should dare to invade the borders of my realm; to which rather than any dishonour shall grow by me, I myself will take up arms, I myself will be your general, judge, and rewarder of every one of your virtues in the field.

I know already, for your forwardness you have deserved rewards and crowns; and We do assure you on a word of a prince, they shall be duly paid. In the meantime, my lieutenant general shall be in my stead, than whom never prince commanded a more noble or worthy subject; not doubting but by your obedience to my general, by your concord in the camp, and your valour in the field, we shall shortly have a famous victory over these enemies of my God, of my kingdom, and of my people.'

The Spanish fleet was almost completely destroyed. King Philip's invasion attempt had failed and for Britain it was a great victory.

The last ever entry in the diary of Admiral Lord Horatio Nelson on the morning of the Battle of Trafalgar, the great British victory over Napoleon's battle fleet, which ended Napoleon's dream of invading Britain

Monday, 21st October 1805.

At daylight saw the Enemy's Combined Fleet from East to E.S.E. bore away; made the signal for Order of Sailing, and to Prepare for Battle; the Enemy with their heads to the Southward: at seven the Enemy wearing in succession. May the Great God, whom I worship, grant to my Country, and for the benefit of Europe in general, a great and glorious Victory; and may no misconduct in any one tarnish it; and may humanity after Victory be the predominant feature in the British Fleet. For myself, individually, I commit my life to Him who made me, and may his blessing light upon my endeavours for serving my Country faithfully. To Him I resign myself and the just cause which is entrusted to me to defend. Amen. Amen. Amen.

[Autograph, or facsimile Copy, in the possession of Philip Toker, Esq.]

William Pitt the Younger, Prime Minister

In October 1805, after the Battle of Trafalgar, which had ensured British naval supremacy for the rest of the war against Napoleon, Prime Minister William Pitt the Younger at the annual Lord Mayor's banquet in London, was hailed as "the Saviour of Europe".

Pitt responded in a few words that became the most famous speech of his life:

> 'I return you many thanks for the honour you have done me; but Europe is not to be saved by any single man. England has saved herself by her exertions, and will, as I trust, save Europe by her example.'

"I feel very privileged to have been in a position to have defended this country in a Spitfire in the Battle of Britain."
Geoffrey Wellum – Spitfire Pilot

'The day of giants is gone forever.'
Sir Arthur Bryant, tribute on Churchill's death, *Illustrated London News*

From King George VI's VE Day radio broadcast to his people 9pm 8th May 1945

"...as your King I thank with a full heart those who bore arms so valiantly on land and sea, or in the air; and all civilians who, shouldering their many burdens, have carried them unflinchingly without complaint.

With those memories in our minds, let us think what it was that has upheld us through nearly six years of suffering and peril. The knowledge that everything was at stake: our freedom, our independence, our very existence as a people; but the knowledge also that in defending ourselves we were defending the liberties of the whole world; that our cause was the cause not of this nation only, not of this Empire and Commonwealth only, but of every land where freedom is cherished and law and liberty go hand in hand. In the darkest hours we knew that the enslaved and isolated peoples of Europe looked to us; their hopes were our hopes; their confidence confirmed our faith. We knew that, if we failed, the last remaining barrier against a world-wide tyranny would have fallen in ruins. But we did not fail. We kept our faith with ourselves and with one another; we kept faith and unity with our great allies. That faith and unity have carried us to victory through dangers which at times seemed overwhelming...

There is great comfort in the thought that the years of darkness and danger in which the children of our country have grown up are over and, please God, for ever. We shall have failed, and the blood of our dearest will have flowed in vain, if the victory which they died to win does not lead to a lasting peace, founded on justice and established in good will. To that, then, let us turn our thoughts on this day of just triumph and proud sorrow; and then take up our work again, resolved as a people to do nothing unworthy of those who died for us and to make the world such a world as they would have desired, for their children and for ours. This is the task to which now honour binds us. In the hour of danger, we humbly committed our cause into the Hand of God, and He has been our Strength and Shield. Let us thank Him for His mercies, and in this hour of Victory commit ourselves and our new task to the guidance of that same strong Hand."   www.royal.uk

Recommended Museums

Amberley Transport Museum – excellent exhibition on the History of telecommunications, including Morse code, also has an excellent, hands-on exhibition on the History of electricity.

Biggin Hill

Bovington Tank Museum – here is an excellent recreation of the trenches of the First World War, including the journey the soldiers took to get there and even including recreations of German trenches, via a German machine gun emplacement, (watch out for that), to a German soldier's eye-view of a British tank trundling over German trenches!

Brooklands – you just have to go here!

Cabinet War Rooms

RAF Imperial War Museum Duxford – The Operations Room is a must see.

The Imperial War Museum, London – includes a very harrowing exhibition on the Nazi holocaust.

Royal Air Force Museum, Hendon – on my list of places to go – apparently you can 'fly' in a Spitfire simulator!

RAF Uxbridge museum – also on my list!

And of course, take every opportunity you can, to see and actually hear for yourself, Spitfires

Recommended Documentaries

in flight. It is a joy and a thrill you will never forget!

The World at War narrated by Laurence Olivier (David Elstein 1973) – a 26-episode documentary series chronicling the events of the Second World War.

Spitfire (Anthony Palmer and David Fairhead 2018)

D-Day-The Last Heroes Dan Snow documentary for BBC One

Battle of Britain – Ewan and Colin McGregor Timeline (World History Documentaries 2011 Director: Ashley Gething)

Recommended Films

Some of these films will not be for younger viewers

London Can Take It (Humphrey Jennings and Harry Watt – GPO Film Unit 1940)

49th Parallel (Powell and Pressburger 1941)

That Hamilton Woman (Alexander Korda 1941)

Pimpernel Smith (Leslie Howard 1941)

The First of the Few (Leslie Howard 1942)

Went the Day Well (Alberto Cavalcanti 1942)

In Which We Serve (Noel Coward and David Lean 1942)

The Foreman Went to France (Charles Frend 1942) – released in the USA as **Somewhere in France** – story by J.B. Priestley

This Happy Breed (David Lean 1944)

The Way to the Stars (Antony Asquith 1945)

A Matter of Life and Death (Powell and Pressburger 1946)

Theirs is the Glory (Brian Desmond Hurst 1946) - In my opinion, the best war film ever made. Using the original locations of the battle and featuring over 200 veterans, who were participants in the real battle, it used original footage and re-enactments shot on location at Oosterbeek and Arnhem. The film was made only a year after the real battle and featured the local people, who had been there at the time and who re-enacted their roles for the film. It has a poignancy and authenticity unmatched by any other war film I have ever seen.

Odette (Herbert Wilcox 1950)

The Cruel Sea (Charles Frend 1953)

Malta Story (Brian Desmond Hurst 1953)

The Dam Busters (Michael Anderson 1955)

Reach for the Sky (Lewis Gilbert 1956)

Carve Her Name with Pride (Lewis Gilbert 1958)

The Longest Day (Darryl F. Zanuck 1962)

Battle of Britain (Guy Hamilton 1969)

Darkest Hour (Joe Wright 2017)

Dunkirk (Christopher Nolan 2017)

Operation Mincemeat (John Madden 2022)

Bibliography

Shrabani Basu – *Spy Princess: the life of Noor Inayat Khan* – (The History Press 2008)

Candace Fleming – *The Enigma Girls* – (Scholastic Focus 2024)

The Earl of Halifax – *Fulness of Days* (Collins 1957)

Larry Loftis – *Code Name Lise The True Story of Odette (Mirror Books 2020)*

R. J. Minney – *Carve Her Name With Pride'* (Pen and Sword Military Reprint edition 2012)

Gordon Mitchell – *R.J. Mitchell Schooldays to Spitfire* (The History Press 2006)

Field-Marshall the Viscount Montgomery – *The Memoirs of Field-Marshal Montgomery* (Collins 1958 The Companion Book Club 1960)

Field-Marshal the Viscount Montgomery – *Memoirs* (Odhams Press Ltd. 1958)

John Nichol – *Spitfire A Very British Love Story* (Simon and Schuster 2018)

Andrew Roberts – *Churchill Walking with Destiny* (Penguin 2018)

Andrew Roberts – *The Holy Fox The Life of Lord Halifax* (Phoenix 1991)

Desmond Young – *Rommel* (Collins/Book Club Associates 1973)

References

[1] Ralph Waldo Emerson (1803-1882) The Complete Works 1904 Vol V English Traits XIX Speech at Manchester November 1847 (source ref: bartleby.com)

[2] *Field-Marshall The Viscount Montgomery Memoirs Montgomery of Alamein* 1958 p60-61

[3] Andrew Roberts *Churchill Walking with Destiny* 2018 p2

[4] Poem by Edwin James Milliken entitled *Death and his Brother Sleep* – Milliken, an editor for *Punch* magazine, wrote the poem for the magazine in October 1890, after a train crash that was blamed on a sleeping train driver.

[5] nationalchurchillmuseum.org

[6] From an account given by the pilot himself, Sergeant Ray Holmes, in *Sky Spy: From Six Miles High to Hitler's Bunker,* retold in John Nichol *Spitfire: A Very British Love Story* Ch 3 p86

[7] John Nichol *Spitfire: A Very British Love Story Ch 3* p87

[8] From an account given by the uncle of a family friend – Cecil Millard

[9] royal.uk - Wartime broadcast, 13th October 1940

[10] **Baron Von Richthofen,** known as The Red Baron, German Air Force flying ace of the World War 1, leader of the *Jagdgeschwader*, also known as the 'Flying Circus' owing to the squadron's brightly coloured planes, or just the Richthofen Squadron. He was known for his bravery and chivalry, originally a cavalryman, but transferred to the Air Service in 1915. Shot down in his plane and killed in April 1918 and given a hero's funeral by the Allies. Hermann Göring, later member of Hitler's Nazi party, was the last commander of the Richthofen Squadron.

[11] John Nichol *Spitfire - A Very British Love Story* p124

[12] Andrew Roberts – *Churchill* p542

[13] ibid

[14] ibid

[15] op cit p545

[16] ibid

[17] ibid

[18] op cit p547

[19] ibid

[20] op cit p548

[21] Candace Fleming – *The Enigma Girls* – Ch 19

[22] This broadcast was made on the 14th July 1940 on the coast of Dover, at what was called 'Hellfire Corner', for the BBC Home Service, by a journalist called Charles Gardner. Three Hurricane planes, not Spitfires, were attempting to deal with over forty German aircraft.

[23] mybrightonandhove.org.uk Entrance and Exit | Brighton Station | My Brighton and Hove The canon were moved to the station from the West Battery when it was demolished in 1859 to build the Grand Hotel, where on 12th October 1984, the IRA exploded a bomb targeting Prime Minister Margaret Thatcher and the Conservative party, who were holding their annual conference in Brighton.

[24] From the wonderful series, 'The World at War', narrated by Lawrence Olivier - 'The Home Front'

[25] ibid

[26] Ibid

[27] A famous photograph taken in the early hours of 30 December 1940, by photographer Herbert Mason from the office roof of the Daily Mail newspaper, off Fleet Street.

[28] John Nichol – *Spitfire* – p137

[29] John Nichol – *Spitfire* – p140

[30] A dramatization based on an account as detailed in John Nichol – *Spitfire*

[31]   www.desertrats.org.uk   *The Telegraph* Tom Whitehead 6th March 2013

[32] Ibid

[33] https://www.culture24.org.uk /history-and-heritage/military-history/art310997

[34] **Odette Sansom** grew up in France, but moved to Britain with her English husband, where she was recruited by SOE (Special Operations Executive), which was the British Secret Service, to return to France undercover in order to support the French resistance. She was eventually captured and tortured by the Nazis, but refused to tell the Nazis anything and was sent to Ravensbrück concentration camp. She was one of only few agents who survived the war and became the first woman ever to receive the George Cross in 1946 and the only woman to be awarded it whilst still alive. A film was made about her experiences during the war, which is detailed below in the list of suggested films. *Odette, WWII's Most Highly Decorated Spy Code Name Lise (Mirror Books) 2020*

[35] **Noor Inayat Khan**, also known as Nora Baker, was a British spy, who worked for SOE. She was the first female wireless operator to be sent from the UK into occupied France to support the French Resistance. She had an amazingly rich parentage. Born in Moscow to an Indian Muslim father, who was a Sufi mystic (and whose son, Vilayat, Noor's brother, later became head of the 'Sufi Order of the West') and an American mother, they moved to Britain and lived in London, until moving to France, near Paris in 1920. Extremely intelligent and coming from a long line of talented musicians, she studied music at the Paris Conservatory and child psychology at the Sorbonne and later became a children's author, writing a fascinating collection of stories for children based on the Buddhist stories of the life of Gautama Buddha. After the German invasion of France, Noor, her mother and siblings, escaped to Britain, where she was eventually enlisted by SOE and sent to France and where she successfully continued to send messages back to Britain even as the Gestapo destroyed other Resistance cells around her, as she dodged them by escaping from one safe house to another. She was eventually betrayed, captured and tortured. She tried to escape several times, but never gave up her secrets to the Nazis, who eventually executed her at Dachau concentration camp. After her death she was awarded the George Cross. In 2012 a bust of her was installed in Gordon Square Gardens close to the Bloomsbury house where she lived as a child and where she returned while training for the SOE during World War II. www.independent.co.uk/arts-entertainment/books/features/noor-anayat-khan-princess-who-became-spy-6108704.html Shrabani Basu – *Spy Princess: the life of Noor Inayat Khan* – (The History Press 2008) https://www.bbc.com/news/world-asia-20241322

[36] **Violette Szabo** – Born of a French mother and British father – lived between France and London, Britain. She joined the Women's Land Army and then in 1940 married an officer, named Etienne, who was a member of the French Foreign Legion, whom she had met during a Bastille Day parade in London in 1940. They had one daughter, Tania. Etienne died, fighting

the Germans at El Alamein, 1942, having never seen his daughter. Violette was later recruited by SOE as an agent and was sent to France twice, the second time, after volunteering for a particularly dangerous mission, when her daughter was just two years old. Violette never saw her daughter again. She was captured, interrogated by the SS Security Service for four days and then sent to Paris, where was interrogated and tortured by the Gestapo. Not breaking under torture, she gave nothing away and the German's gained no information of any value from her. She was sent to Ravensbrück concentration camp where she was executed in February 1945 at the age of just twenty-three. After her death, Violette was awarded the George Cross, only the second woman to be awarded this honour. It was presented to her five-year-old daughter, Tania, who received the medal, on her mother's behalf, from King George VI. Violette was also posthumously, awarded the French Resistance Medal and Croix de Guerre, an honour also posthumously awarded to Violette's husband, Etienne. Tania

had lost both her parents during the war, fighting for freedom against the Nazis. The 1958 film, 'Carve Her Name With Pride', from the book of the same name, is detailed below. R. J. Minney – *Carve Her Name With Pride'* (Pen and Sword Military Reprint edition) 2012

[37] **It is said that Drake's drum really was heard at Dunkirk.** Strangely, the author did not know this until after this piece had been written!

[38] Andrew Roberts – *Churchill* – p595 The author, strangely, also did not know of this speech, or Churchill's reference to Drake and Nelson, until after they had been included!

[39] **A true account of HMS Erebus**, which the author only discovered subsequent to writing the events previously written. Strange coincidences indeed!

[40] Although, the Me109s were faster, they were not as manoeuvrable. In fact, a German *Luftwaffe* general, Adolf Galland, cheekily once asked Hermann Goring, Hitler's military leader, for Spitfires. He was joking, of course, but the Nazis knew that the Spitfire was special.

[41] 48royalmarinecommando.com

For Charles

with all my love

Thanks

To my mother, who was always asking if it was 'bloomin' written
yet?' You know how I feel about you.
To dad – I'm glad I found you.
To my husband for always being there.
To our boy – I love you. This book's for you.
To my Nanny and Jam-Jar – you both gave me so much.
To Adrianna, Connor, Eddie, Jacob and Thomas – thank-you for
your enthusiasm for my book and for being such brilliant students,
and to Felia, Flynn, Elizabeth, Bella, Cami, and Milo, always believe
in yourselves.

To Nanny and Jam-Jar.
Sunday lunches together, afternoon black and white war films,
cheese-on-toast teas and all the old stories in front of the fire.
It's all in here.

And to the park and the lake and the woods and the fields.
You gave me so much inspiration.

THE BRUGES GROUP

The Bruges Group is an independent all-party think tank. Set up in 1989, its founding purpose was to resist the encroachments of the European Union on our democratic self-government. The Bruges Group spearheaded the intellectual battle to win a vote to leave the European Union and against the emergence of a centralised EU state. With personal freedom at its core, its formation was inspired by the speech of Margaret Thatcher in Bruges in September 1988 where the Prime Minister stated, "We have not successfully rolled back the frontiers of the State in Britain only to see them re-imposed at a European level."

We now face a more insidious and profound challenge to our liberties – the rising tide of intolerance. The Bruges Group challenges false and damaging orthodoxies that suppress debate and incite enmity. It will continue to direct Britain's role in the world, act as a voice for the Union, and promote our historic liberty, democracy, transparency, and rights. It spearheads the resistance to attacks on free speech and provides a voice for those who value our freedoms and way of life.

WHO WE ARE

Founder President:
The Rt Hon. The Baroness Thatcher
of Kesteven LG, OM, FRS

Chairman:
Barry Legg

Director:
Robert Oulds MA, FRSA

Washington D.C. Representative:
John O'Sullivan CBE

Founder Chairman:
Lord Harris of High Cross

Former Chairmen:
Dr Brian Hindley, Dr Martin Holmes
& Professor Kenneth Minogue

Academic Advisory Council:
Professor Tim Congdon
Dr Richard Howarth
Professor Patrick Minford
Andrew Roberts
Martin Howe, KC
John O'Sullivan, CBE

Sponsors and Patrons:
E P Gardner Dryden
Gilling-Smith
Lord Kalms
David Caldow
Andrew Cook
Lord Howard
Brian Kingham
Lord Pearson of Rannoch
Eddie Addison
Ian Butler
Thomas Griffin
Lord Young of Graffham
Michael Fisher
Oliver Marriott
Hon. Sir Rocco Forte
Michael Freeman
Richard E.L. Smith

MEETINGS

The Bruges Group holds regular high–profile public meetings, seminars, debates, and conferences. These enable influential speakers to contribute to the European debate. Speakers are selected purely by the contribution they can make to enhance the debate.

For further information about the Bruges Group, to attend our meetings, or join and receive our publications, please see the membership form at the end of this paper. Alternatively, you can visit our website www.brugesgroup.com or contact us at info@brugesgroup.com.

Contact us
For more information about the Bruges Group please contact:
Robert Oulds, Director
The Bruges Group, 246 Linen Hall, 162-168 Regent Street, London W1B 5TB
Tel: +44 (0)20 7287 4414 Email: info@brugesgroup.com

www.brugesgroup.com

www.ingramcontent.com/pod-product-compliance
Lightning Source LLC
Chambersburg PA
CBHW032000180726
48283CB00008B/2505